IN HER SUITE AT CLARIDGE'S, MIRANDA GLENN LUXURIATED IN A LONG, LANGUID SOAK

in her overlarge bathtub. She brushed hot water against herself, and rubbed her most sensitive parts slowly, with a soft washcloth. She stretched her long legs and stroked herself, flowing with the water. Paul Christopher came into her thoughts uninvited, pressing his lips roughly to her breasts, and then pressing himself more fully into her than any man ever had. . . . After a moment, a low cry escaped her lips. Miranda climbed from the tub and rubbed herself harshly with a thick towel. She felt achingly unfulfilled. She would show Paul tomorrow. He would know that he was under pressure from the best in the business. She turned to a fresh page in her notebook. At the top of the page she wrote a single question. *Who is Paul Christopher?* Miranda Glenn did not intend to leave the question unanswered for long. . . .

Books in the HAROLD ROBBINS PRESENTS™ Series

Blue Sky
  by Sam Stewart

At the Top
  by Michael Donovan

Published by POCKET BOOKS

Harold Robbins Presents:

At The Top

A Novel by
Michael Donovan

PUBLISHED BY POCKET BOOKS NEW YORK

Another *Original* publication of POCKET BOOKS

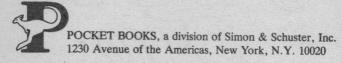

POCKET BOOKS, a division of Simon & Schuster, Inc.
1230 Avenue of the Americas, New York, N.Y. 10020

ISBN: 0-671-52680-4

First Pocket Books printing March, 1986

10 9 8 7 6 5 4 3 2 1

POCKET and colophon are registered trademarks
of Simon & Schuster, Inc.

HAROLD ROBBINS PRESENTS is a trademark
of Harold Robbins.

Printed in the U.S.A.

For Donnie and Sarah—
Lawyers in Love

At The Top

1

AFTER ALL THE years the coin still gleamed, and after all the years its luster still left Paul Christopher cold.

He stood before a wide window in his office overlooking Wall Street, but Christopher's complete attention was focused upon the coin that rested in the palm of his right hand. He hefted it, feeling once more the weight of ancient Byzantine gold. Christopher stared at the coin's crude decoration: an image of winged Victory trampling a serpent. That image, Christopher recalled from the lessons of his youth, represented the triumph of law over barbarism, of order over chaos. It was a conceit that amused Paul Christopher—there was no more order in the world today than when the coin was minted in Constantinople more than fifteen centuries ago. *But then,* he thought, *it has been fifteen years since I last saw this coin, and in that time I have at least created some order for my clients. And a fortune and a business for myself.* Paul Christopher frowned, sudden sharp lines forming at the corners of his gray eyes. Fifteen centuries, fifteen years—both pasts had been equally dead. *But now this piece of my past has come back to me,* he thought. Christopher closed his fingers over the Byzantine solidus, making a fist as though to crush it. He closed his eyes and thought back.

After a moment a soft metallic chime from his communications console interrupted Christopher's reverie. He opened his eyes, and without looking at it again slipped the coin into the pocket of his dark vest. He took a breath, turned, and walked quickly back to his long desk. Standing, Christopher touched a stud. "Yes."

"Barbara Webster from Buenos Aires," his secretary said. "Scrambled."

"Of course." Christopher checked the time. It was 2:30. "Hold anything after this, Diana. *Anything.* Even priority access. Understood?" It was a command he'd never before given.

"Yes, Mr. Christopher," Diana Lowen said evenly. Her voice registered no surprise. Christopher doubted if a squad of heavily armed terrorists bursting into the office would be capable of surprising Diana Lowen. It was one of the qualities Christopher valued most about his secretary. She was unflappable.

He seated himself behind his desk, the firm molded contours of the Brayton International chair pressing against his tight muscles. "Thank you, Diana," he said. "Put Barbara on—and let me know when my appointment arrives."

"Yes, Mr. Christopher."

The speaker clicked, and then Barbara Webster's voice came through. "Paul? Good afternoon," she said. "I hope your weekend was pleasant." Her words were clear and crisp, despite the distance and the electronic signal scrambling that ensured the privacy of their conversation. *And of course it is our own private satellite bounce,* Christopher thought. His people were freed from dependence upon the uncertainties and eccentricities of foreign telephone systems.

"Hello, Barbara," Christopher said. "I'm fine. How are things going in Buenos Aires?" He rubbed his fingers along the edge of his burnished desktop, feeling the solidity and coolness of the metal surface. A ten-foot cast and polished slab resting upon twin black pedestals, the desk was the product of a Norwegian sculptor whose work Christopher admired. The sculptor had designed the desk for Paul Christopher, and fabricated a perfect copy each time his patron opened another office. There were fourteen long desks now, in fourteen cities around the world. *My empire,* Christopher thought almost bitterly. He could feel the weight of the solidus in his vest pocket, and for a moment the coin seemed to far outweigh the desk.

"It's *all* going wonderfully," Barbara Webster was saying. "These are exciting times. How did the lunch go?"

Christopher had passed three midday hours with representatives of seven of the nation's largest banks. He thought of their faces, of the topics they'd discussed, the size of the sums they mentioned. He had answered all of their questions easily. "As we expected," he said now to Barbara. "The consortium is satisfied. Its members are pleased. And they are in agreement."

"Excellent," said Barbara.

"We went through all the formalities. Handshakes and toasts." The atmosphere in the private dining room had been almost convivial for all the business that had been discussed. The bankers had used *the phrase* again and again. "Christopher Security International 'has their every confidence,' as they are so fond of saying," he related to Barbara.

She laughed softly. "I've heard it myself! Esteban's used it more than a few times. But he always laughs when he does."

"Of course. He should be laughing, Barbara. Esteban's the one borrowing the money, after all. Not lending it." Christopher spoke carefully, a slight accent brightening the edges of some of his words. "A hundred million dollars must have Esteban chuckling all the time," he said.

"You deserve to smile, Paul. Let yourself go a bit. A few days and you'll be holding a hundred million dollars' worth of reins down here."

"Just so long as I don't end up holding the bag."

"I don't think you need to worry about that."

"I have no intention of worrying about it, Barbara. That's why you're in Buenos Aires." She had been with his company for more than a decade. Christopher smiled: that was most of the company's history. Christopher Security International was fourteen years old now, a leading provider of private security personnel and technology. Barbara Webster occupied a place of prominence among Paul Christopher's inner circle of executive advisers. And she was a good friend.

"Thanks, Paul," she said, acknowledging the compliment. "Esteban and I have been cloistered away all morning, going over the final details. I can assure you that everything is fine at the Banco Nacional. We're working with the government now. Believe it or not, they're demanding environmental guarantees."

"We'll be able to provide them?"

"No problem. In fact, it's taken care of. The study will be on the Minister's desk tomorrow morning."

"And after that?" he asked.

"More loose ends, no doubt. Busy work. Details." She gave a throaty chuckle. "Not quite a hundred million details, I'm sure."

"Let's hope not."

"Nothing I can't have taken care of by the end of the week."

"I have no doubts, Barbara. None at all." At

thirty-two, Barbara Webster was perhaps the most skilled and expert negotiator Paul Christopher had ever met.

"I was just talking with Angus. He's ready to get out of London."

A small laugh escaped from Christopher. "I spent two hours on the phone with him Saturday, talking him out of leaving for Buenos Aires then. I've never known him so excited. He wants to make this thing *work.*" Christopher did a passable imitation of Angus Hill's burr. The Scot was currently in charge of CSI's operations within the United Kingdom.

"Oh, it will, Paul. You know that as well as Angus does." Christopher heard papers rustle before Barbara resumed speaking. "And once it does work, everybody involved benefits. CSI . . . the consortium . . . Esteban and the Banco. And the country, as Esteban says. His country benefits."

Christopher smiled then, almost able to forget the coin in his vest pocket. "You tell Esteban that CSI is simply doing its bit to help Argentina's balance of trade."

"I'm sure he'll appreciate that."

"He should. He's the one who brought me the deal in the first place."

"I'll tell him tonight," Barbara said. "We're having dinner."

"Be careful," Christopher advised. He made his voice light. "You know Esteban has quite a reputation for seducing talented corporate women."

"Yes. But is *he* aware of the reputation *I* have for devouring ambitious men?" she asked.

Christopher dropped the banter. "I'll leave you to yourselves, then," he said pleasantly. "With the best of wishes for an enjoyable evening. Now: anything else?"

"Thanks, Paul." She sighed. "Transfer of funds early next week, and we're done."

"Leaving you plenty of time to get to Rome for Maria's wedding," Christopher said.

"Oh, I wouldn't miss *that!* Not the opportunity to see Giancarlo play father of the bride."

"I've no doubts that he'll perform as stylish a job in that role as he does in everything else," Paul Christopher said fondly. He had learned a great deal from Giancarlo Conti, and Giancarlo had been the first to join the executive circle.

"How is the summit shaping up?" Barbara asked.

"As planned. The week after the wedding."

"Wonderful. We're all looking forward to being together," Barbara said. "There's going to be a lot to talk about."

"An understatement," Christopher said wryly.

"You'll be making the announcement from Rome, I assume?"

"Yes," Christopher said. "As we planned. It will be nice to have all of you with me."

Barbara chuckled. "You do hate facing the press, don't you, Paul?"

"I loathe it," he said sharply.

Barbara knew him well enough to tease. "I can see the headlines," she said. " '*Security Magnate Becomes Weapons Czar!*' "

"Please, Barbara," said Christopher. But he feigned a short laugh for her benefit. He would not let her suspect that he was concerned. He felt the coin press against him.

"Sorry, Paul. It won't be that bad. '*CSI Acquires Argentine Manufacturer.*' Do you like that better? And a subhead: '*Seen As Sound Business Move.*' How's that?"

"Yes," said Christopher. "I like that much better."

"Well, I don't know why you're worried. You've handled the press so well through this. Not one hint. No leaks. Esteban's delighted."

"Tell Esteban there's no reason to be surprised. Security companies, after all, have to be purer than pure. And more discreet than discreet. It was our low profile he appreciated in the first place."

"Paul, as far as I'm concerned, after the deal's closed the press can do what it wants. For the next few days, though, let's just hope there aren't any leaks. This is the kind of thing reporters love to play with. Let them play after the funds are transferred." Her voice was firm, full, and even.

For just a moment Christopher was tempted to tell Barbara of the solidus, of who had sent it. But his negotiator had no immediate need to know, and he had reason to keep news of the coin to himself. *For so long as I can,* he thought. *Considering its source.* "I'm leaving for London tomorrow," he told Barbara. "Reach me there through Angus. He'll have my complete itinerary."

"Of course," she said.

"It will be good to see you, Barbara," Christopher said. He felt almost weary. "When this is over. In Rome."

"I'll be there," she said. "With bells on."

"Let's leave the wearing of bells to Giancarlo, shall we?" asked Christopher. He waited long enough to hear a peal of throaty laughter before punching the stud that severed their connection. He swiveled in his chair and stared out at the city.

Christopher sat fifty-seven stories above the streets. His office made a full L, occupying the southwest corner of the building. Some days it struck Christopher as a profligate expenditure of space, but those days were infrequent. He knew well how precarious one's purchase could be at these heights. How easily one could be dislodged. Christopher had seen it happen before. A nudge in the right place at the right time, and any edifice could be brought down. He patted the pocket where the coin reposed. It could wait.

He was pleased with Barbara's report from Buenos Aires, but in no way surprised. The challenges of the acquisition were tailor-made for Barbara Webster's repertoire. Trained in international law and diplomacy, she had been trapped in a low-level State Department post when Paul Christopher first encountered her. He was in Washington, helping develop the security procedures that would guard the Space Shuttle, which then was still being designed.

Christopher had known Barbara Webster for less than an hour before asking her to dinner. The evening culminated with a mutual seduction that moved in easy progression from the restaurant to brandy at the bar of the Watergate, to Christopher's suite in the Watergate. He'd ducked his committee responsibilities the next day, and Barbara had called in sick. They walked Washington's streets, talking, and Christopher had offered her a position with his young firm.

He recalled how suddenly steely and businesslike she had become. It took Barbara less than a minute to accept the job, followed by four hours of hard bargaining over her employment demands. Christopher smiled at the recollection. They had ended their affair not long after she joined the company. There were other stakes—higher ones—to which they needed to apply their concentration.

And we did, Christopher thought. The company

had grown swiftly, from one plateau to the next. Now Barbara was in Argentina taking care of the final stages of an acquisition that would ultimately transform Christopher Security International from a large company into an international titan. A manufacturing as well as a service concern. The stakes now were the highest of all, and he had entrusted the attainment of this next plateau to Barbara Webster. It was in good hands.

Tonight she would dine with Esteban Rojas, and Christopher felt a sudden surge of envy. He found himself recalling the ferocity and abandon with which she surrendered herself to lovemaking. Barbara's performance in bed was the opposite of that in the boardroom. Her very character seemed to change as she shed her clothes. She became unrestrained, without inhibitions. He could recall it all. The convulsive buck of her hips as she ground toward her climax. The taste of her body, her lips and her tongue, the hardness of her nipples, the softness of her cries. It was a powerful memory and for a moment Paul Christopher felt jealous of his friend Esteban Rojas. But the moment passed.

Christopher came back to the present. He drew three deep breaths, slowly. Then he turned in his chair to face his desk once more.

Spread across its surface were magazine and newspaper clippings, three hardcover books, a selection of videotape cassettes. Each of the clippings was neatly labeled by source: *Life, The New York Times Magazine, Le Monde* from Paris and the *Times* of London, *The Wall Street Journal*, others—Christopher had before him a portfolio from the most prestigious and influential publications in the world. The books were handsome trade editions from major publishers. Each book had enjoyed a season on the bestseller lists, each had been offered by book clubs, each had sold millions of copies in paper covers. The video cassettes contained tapings of network documentaries, news broadcasts, interviews and exposés. The byline on each of the pieces was the same: *Miranda Glenn.*

Christopher picked up one of the books, *The Darkness Descends.* Miranda Glenn's first book, it had achieved a large success. Christopher had read the book, and the others, and viewed the tapes, over the past four days, but he had also read *The Darkness Descends* when it was first published. Now he opened the book again and gave a page a cursory glance. He turned to the index. Famous names, ranked and numbered, he reflected. *Names I know.* In the pages of her first book, the young journalist had fashioned a scathing portrait of an electric utility and the industry of which it was a part. *The Darkness Descends* won its author a Pulitzer Prize and, in addition to making Miranda Glenn wealthy and well-known, the book served as the springboard from which were launched a congressional committee, a week of Senate hearings, and the resignations of half a dozen utility executives. All of them were acquaintances of Paul Christopher; some were friends. Christopher had an important client among the utilities attacked in the book. The utility was still his client, and its security needs were still managed by Christopher Security International. Christopher scanned the index, looking at the names of good professional men and women. He thought of how the book portrayed them as avaricious, uncaring exploiters.

He flipped back a page and found his own name in the index. He knew the reference already. Paul Christopher was mentioned in *The Darkness Descends* only once, during a bitter denouncement of the nuclear-power industry. Christopher found the page. He read her words:

As though the environmental hazards posed by nuclear-power plants are not frightening enough, we must not allow ourselves to forget that these plants make very attractive targets for terrorists. Put it bluntly: a nuke is a sitting duck for any fanatic with enough explosives. America's security industry, charged with keeping these installations safe, maintains that it is more than capable of providing foolproof protective systems. But when has that industry succeeded in making *any* client *completely* secure? Any protective system can be broached.

Other questions rise. And many of these questions must be directed at the security contractors themselves. What of their integrity? How do we guarantee that? Fissionable materials are perhaps the most terrorist-tempting materials on our planet. Because their destructive potential in the wrong hands is so nearly infinite, their value on the world's dark markets is equally infinite. How carefully, then, should we the public investigate those charged with the responsibility of guarding atomic installations? How short a leash should we keep on our private watchdogs?

What of men such as Paul Christopher, whose Christopher Security International is a wholly private company, and is thus not exposed to even the *minimal* public scrutiny that any large firm should face. Much less a company that sends its employees into our world *armed*. Or that stands watch over materials from which Armageddon might be constructed. Companies such as Christopher's protect secrets. That does not grant them *carte blanche* rights to secrecy themselves.

Paul Christopher himself, to continue the example,

offers a dilemma. His clients praise him and his firm. According to all accounts, the installations and facilities that his firm guards are well-guarded. But the man himself is an enigma. Obviously, he is a talented businessman. His past, however, is a mystery. Any investigative trails followed into his history run quickly dry. He refuses to grant interviews, and those few gatherings of the press that he has faced have proved unproductive. How can we help but wonder? What covert secrets does the man hide? What unknown allegiances? Should a man of whom so little is known be allowed to stand watch over materials suitable for the fashioning of nuclear bombs?

Christopher closed the book. He knew those words well. They had been read aloud to him in Washington by a United States senator who demanded answers. They had been reworked by less-talented reporters who shouted their questions at him each time he entered or departed the hearing chamber. Christopher acquitted himself well before both sets of inquisitors. To the senators he was the model of a cooperative but articulately independent witness. Questions he felt fair, Christopher answered. Questions he felt were out of line, he identified as such. The press was even simpler to handle: Paul Christopher prided himself on his ability to say *No comment* in every major language, and most minor ones.

Christopher had emerged from those hearings unscathed, his reputation even enhanced by the quality of response and clarification he'd given, while maintaining his personal privacy. He continued to refuse all requests for journalistic interviews, including those requests posed by Miranda Glenn. Especially those. His past was his own business. *Is that still true?* he wondered.

He turned over the book to reveal the author's

photograph. *The Darkness Descends* first appeared nine years ago, when Miranda Glenn was twenty-four. The dust-jacket photograph revealed her as the very image of earnestness, every sophomore's ideal portrait of the muckraking female reporter. In the picture's background huge nuclear-power-plant cooling towers stood stark, capped by plumes of white steam climbing high. In the foreground stood Miranda Glenn, three years out of Princeton, her free-lance pieces starting to appear in the better magazines. The camera captured her idealism and determination, as well as her striking features, her beauty. Her strong face with its high cheekbones was framed by a severe layered haircut, bangs sweeping down nearly to her eyes. She stared straight into the camera. Do not underestimate this woman, the picture said. The journalist was clothed in an olive flak jacket, the uniform of her day, her arms crossed, her shoulders tense.

Christopher turned over the other two volumes. Their pictures served to paint a portrait of Miranda's progress. She had not lost her dedication to the crusade—but money and influence had certainly led her away from the rough costume of her apprentice years. *Manmade Murder*—her second book, in which she created an image of American manufacturing as not only indifferent to environmental concerns but also oblivious to even basic human concerns—showed her standing before a mountain in the process of being decimated by strip miners. To her left towered a huge earth-devouring machine, four stories of steel and strength on tires twice as tall as Miranda Glenn. She'd dressed carefully for the confrontation, though, and was planted firmly on her own piece of Kentucky ground. Miranda wore a simple dress of antique lace, yet she seemed anything but fragile. Miranda Glenn had made herself a mountain flower that was stronger than any machine.

Her latest book had been out little more than a year. Christopher had the week's paperback bestseller list before him, and *Prescription: Death* was number seven. The book consolidated her position. More: she'd been a bright rising star before, but this new success gave the heat that made her a nova. People had known of her; now she was *known*. *Prescription: Death* cast its deadly words about the pharmaceutical industry in sentences that were exhortations, chapters that called clarions to action.

You have come a long way, Christopher thought as he stared at the books. *You have climbed as steadily and perhaps even more rapidly than I.* Miranda Glenn was arguably the most influential independent journalist in the nation, perhaps the world. There was talk in the broadcasting community that her upcoming television special—on the nation's banking system— would burst Nielsen records. *And destroy a few more good careers,* Christopher thought.

After a moment he withdrew the Byzantine coin from his pocket and propped it against the spine of *The Darkness Descends.* The coin glinted in the light and for just a second, the coin seemed to be mocking him. It was almost as if the image had winked at him.

The coin had been returned to Christopher the previous Thursday, early in the afternoon. It arrived via a Christopher Courier whose contract with the client insisted upon hand delivery of an envelope to Paul Christopher. He welcomed the courier to his office and put her at ease. He almost smiled as he signed the delivery receipt that would be returned to the client. Christopher Courier service was expensive, but several people each month were willing to pay the price. They hoped for a moment of his attention, and their couriered requests usually demanded interviews or solicited funds. He'd received several résumés by courier, and a long and highly explicit letter of proposition from a woman he'd never heard of. Christopher Couriers brought him clever invitations to clever parties that he never attended. A lover once retained a courier to bring Christopher a single rose. He had seen all the tricks.

Christopher was startled to see Miranda Glenn's name on the envelope. She tried regularly to reach him, and over the past year had appeared in several of CSI's offices around the world. She was always rebuffed, but pleasantly. He'd thought she would be more original than to use a tactic that less talented journalists had tried and failed. He opened the envelope.

The Byzantine solidus fell into his palm.

Christopher gave nothing away. The courier, waiting patiently, was given no reason to suspect the shock that seized the principal of Christopher Security International. He smiled at her, asked a few questions about Miranda Glenn. The courier had been hired that morning, an in-town assignment. She'd met Miranda Glenn at the journalist's townhouse, accepted the envelope, made the delivery. Was there anything else?

"No," said Christopher. He thanked her and waited until his office doors slid shut behind her before reading the message that accompanied the coin.

If this coin is sufficient to procure an exclusive interview with you, I will be in your office next Monday at 3:00 p.m. Confirm or cancel with my service.

The note was on cream-colored stationery and bore no salutation. Her looping signature was the only other script on the page.

Years earlier, and under another name, Christopher had etched, in such a way as not to deface the coins or decrease their value, a private glyph on each of the coins he had smuggled out of his homeland. He sold the coins carefully in Istanbul's Grand Bazaar. In his office that Thursday his first act was to inspect the solidus for the hidden mark. The inspection took barely a moment. The glyph was as he had made it a decade and a half earlier. The solidus in his hand was one of the coins he'd sold in Istanbul.

Which told him there was likely a traitor among his closest associates.

Christopher felt a stab of pain far more profound than the shock that struck him at the sight of the coin. Only his advisers, those few whom he trusted most, were aware of the coins he'd sold in Istanbul, of the private mark he'd made on each coin. They were under orders to buy any such coins—and return them immediately to Christopher. For one of them to have shared that information was a betrayal that burned his soul.

Years of training took over. Christopher ignored the pain and concentrated upon tasks at hand. He buzzed Diana and asked her to confirm three o'clock Monday for Miranda Glenn. Diana—*bless her*—asked no questions. Nor did she question his canceling all other appointments, save Monday's luncheon with the bankers' consortium. He'd shown the bankers the confident face they most wanted to see, and they had no reason to doubt his confidence. But throughout the meal Christopher had been playing a silent scenario in his thoughts.

Suppose she knows the truth. Suppose she was given . . . all of it. What then? He felt confident that CSI could ride out any storm that might burst over untimely revelations, but that would be less true after the Argentine deal was consummated. With a hundred million dollars riding on his company's name, CSI could afford no scandals, and very little turmoil. *Would it cause a scandal?* he wondered. He already knew the answer.

If Miranda Glenn possessed the complete and accurate story of who Paul Christopher really was, then she possessed a tool that could be used to knock down everything he had so carefully constructed.

Thursday afternoon had been spent assembling his own tools. He assigned members of his research staff to put together a complete dossier on the journalist. Others were ordered to put together a complete portfolio of her work. Any previous interactions between Miranda Glenn and Christopher Security International were to be annotated and brought to him.

His team worked quickly and well, but that was no surprise to Christopher. By Thursday evening he was immersed in her work. The next morning it was revealed to him that, despite her public criticisms of the company, Miranda Glenn used the Christopher Courier service occasionally. By noon Friday the dossier of more private information was coming together on his desk.

Christopher read the dossier over and over. It told him who she slept with, and how often. How much she earned, and how much she was offered. He had transcripts of her grades from college back through elementary school. One summer during her Princeton years she had applied for a newspaper job, and had in the process filled out a long personnel evaluation test. The test was designed and administered by Christopher Security International, and a copy of her responses had rested deep within the memory of the banks of computers CSI operated. He learned her favorite authors, her least-favorite foods. Christopher knew the size of Miranda Glenn's brassiere, as well as the fact that she rarely wore one. Most of the information he perused came from public sources. The rest of it was illegally, but quietly, obtained, and Christopher for once did not give a damn about the illegalities. He had worked too hard and climbed too high to risk having everything brought down by one idealistic reporter. Throughout the weekend he stared at the coin, thought of Miranda Glenn, and considered the source of the coin. There were only eleven members of the inner circle—the only eleven people who knew his story.

A clock's single chime broke the Monday-afternoon silence. Christopher took a deep breath and looked up. On the highest shelf of his étagère stood a squat ship's clock, its brass workings encased in a crystal globe. It was 2:45. He had fifteen minutes.

Christopher gathered the books and clippings and placed them on the étagère. He picked up the thick dossier, wondering what Miranda Glenn would think of it. The information it contained would confirm her every suspicion about CSI, and about Paul Christopher. He had in his hands her past, Miranda Glenn's history with its incidents discreet and indiscreet. How much of his past did she now own? Would she force him to use the material in the dossier? Could any of that material be used to buy her silence if necessary?

He returned to his desk and finished clearing it. It struck Christopher as odd to be putting things away with the sun still high. He was more accustomed to closing up shop while the stars shone, and frequently he met the dawn at one of his desks. That discipline and that drive had earned Christopher and CSI their large share of a frightened world's security business, but Christopher had discovered that it was a pace to which few could acclimate themselves. The hours he kept had annoyed more than a few women over the years: they did not understand his unwillingness to alter his schedule to suit theirs. Christopher could see their faces, the petulance that rose there when he returned them home abruptly after dinner or the theater, depositing them on their doorsteps and lingering only long enough to see them safely inside before departing. He never told them that he found them boring. He never offered any explanations other than the press of important work. And when a woman complained that Paul Christopher cared more for his company than he did for hers, Christopher never disagreed.

With his desk clear, Christopher stepped into the spacious dressing room that adjoined his office. He drew a basin full of cold water and splashed his face. He toweled himself dry, then took the jacket of his dark Cerruti suit from a hanger and slipped it on. Christopher faced a mirror, adjusted his silk tie, drew a breath. He would be dining with Rebecca Devereaux at eight. She was nine years younger than he, and conservative estimates placed her personal wealth at twice his. Rebecca never questioned his schedule, and he never failed to enjoy her company. He was looking forward to the evening.

But first there was the afternoon to get through. Christopher stepped back into his office to await the arrival of his inquisitor.

2

MIRANDA GLENN PAID her cabfare and stepped away from the curb. She felt completely alive. The January air was clear, the temperature biting. She turned to face the skyscraper that housed Christopher Security International. A sudden gust of wind stung her cheeks, but Miranda smiled. She had waited a long time for the confrontation that lay ahead of her. She intended to enjoy everything about the afternoon.

Not that the morning or the night before had been unpleasant, she reflected as she entered the bustling lobby. She'd passed Sunday morning searching for distraction. She'd gone through the *Times* in two hours, could not get interested in a book, did not feel like taking in a play or a movie. There was no point in going over her research again—she had been ready for Paul Christopher for some time. Her notes were organized, the information already gathered was committed to her memory. Sunday, it was simply a matter of waiting for Monday afternoon. But the wait had seemed interminable.

Distraction arrived midafternoon with a call from James Howard Dennis, an Australian journalist and old friend. James Howard was just in from Beirut. It had been years and he thought they might split a bottle, have a bite, swap yarns. His invitation was just the distraction Miranda sought. By sundown Sunday she was seeking more than just distraction. By seven o'clock, on the carpet in front of the fireplace in her townhouse, she had deliciously found it.

Miranda flushed at the memory as she moved away from the revolving doors. She made her way into the building's lush atrium. Covered by a high canopy of glass, the atrium made a calm, sun-drenched glade in the midst of scurrying brokers, attorneys, and executives.

It had been a wild winter night, more intense than either she or James Howard had expected. They'd enjoyed a long late-afternoon lunch at Carolina, laughing at each other's cheerful gluttony as they made their way through racks of perfectly barbecued ribs. Their conversation turned somber as they reminisced over drinks in the Blue Bar at the Algonquin. James Howard Dennis had covered the hell of Beirut during the worst of the fighting. His voice cracked as he described to her the effects of the civil war on Lebanon's children.

"Their little faces, luv," he said in his rangy Australian twang. "Break yer heart to see them. Those big eyes you could drown in. And all the fear there. The chaos." He shook his head and signaled for another double Scotch. "Enough," he said after the drink arrived. "To us. To survivors."

"To survivors," Miranda Glenn toasted, and touched her glass to his. Their conversation turned to other journalists they'd known—colleagues who had fallen while on assignment, whose bylines were forgotten, whose names were carved on tombstones that were rarely visited. James Howard Dennis and Miranda Glenn got slightly drunk.

Not so drunk that we didn't know what we were doing, Miranda thought as she strolled slowly through the atrium. They returned to her townhouse for a brandy and Miranda lit the fire. The seasoned logs crackled, the brandy filled their heads. She'd turned on soft music and they danced slowly together. The pressure of James Howard's fingers on her back grew more insistent. She tilted her face up to kiss him. The kiss deepened quickly.

James Howard moved his large hands to Miranda's shoulders. They looked into each other's eyes. "I'm still taller than you, luv," he said with a gentle chuckle. Miranda stood five-ten in her bare feet; there were not many journalists who could make James Howard's claim.

"But are you still stronger than me?" she asked, and rose on her toes to kiss the pulse of his throat.

"We'll have to find out, won't we?" the Australian said. He kept his eyes locked on hers even as his fingers moved to undo the top button of her Ralph Lauren blouse.

Miranda's eyebrows darted up. "James Howard," she said in a simpering tone. "What are you up to?"

But the Australian merely flashed a crooked grin and said, "You're the one with the reputation for being a great investigator. Why not find out?" He released two more buttons. The edges of his hands brushed her still-covered breasts and Miranda was seized by a shiver.

"It sounds like undercover research to me," she said, reaching up to loosen his necktie. She freed his collar button. She pressed her long fingernails against his throat. She felt his hands slip beneath her blouse to find her breasts. His thumbs pressed against her nipples, stiffening them.

"On-the-spot research, anyway, luv," James Howard said. He pulled her blouse free from her slacks and finished unbuttoning it. He stood tall and allowed her to remove his necktie. Miranda unbuttoned his shirt, combed her fingers through the thick mat of hair that covered his chest.

"You're going gray," she said, and slipped close to him. She pressed her face against his chest, inhaling his rich muskiness.

"Not you," said James Howard, pushing her back gently and sliding her blouse from her shoulders. He caught his breath. He removed his own shirt. He ran his hands over her breasts.

Miranda arched her back, filling James Howard's hands. A purr came from her throat. She breathed deeply as the Australian unfastened her slacks and pulled them easily to her feet. James Howard's thumbs tugged at the waistband of her silk panties, but Miranda teasingly pushed his hands away. Before he could speak she deftly unfastened his belt, unbuttoned his fly and unzipped him. His trousers tumbled down, followed quickly by his shorts. For just a second Miranda clutched the gathering weight of his maleness, then released him and danced a few steps away. James Howard stared at her.

"Well?" she asked as she bent and removed the silk panties.

"Very well indeed," growled James Howard Dennis.

Miranda opened her arms to him. Embracing, they shared a torrid kiss, then sank slowly to their knees in the deep carpet before the fireplace. James Howard's hands roved up and down Miranda's back, massaging her spine, caressing her firm buttocks. She stroked her way down his chest, across his abdomen. Her searching fingers soon found his erect organ, tickled, then tightened around him. James Howard covered her throat and ears with kisses.

Miranda lay on the thick rug before the fireplace. A

soft moan escaped her throat as James Howard's lips found her breasts, teasing her nipples stiff. Her heart began to pound more fiercely, setting a rhythm that grew more demanding when James Howard's fingers found the warm moist heart of her. She rocked her hips gently as the Australian's touch brought her a first, almost tentative wave of pleasure. The next ripple was stronger and Miranda reached to guide him into her.

The logs in the fireplace crackled and hissed. Miranda gave a long, shuddering sigh as James Howard Dennis pushed himself into her. She felt herself rising to meet and welcome him, and they began to flow together. For long moments they moved slowly, seeking the pace that would bring each the most exquisite pleasure. Miranda felt herself churning beneath James Howard, the force of his every thrust lifting her into a region of pure sensation. When at last he swelled within her and erupted, Miranda thought that her own frenzy would not end. But when her pulse finally began to slow, she found herself invigorated rather than drained. When the fire died down she and James Howard moved to her bed.

In the middle of the night she lay in his arms. They were drifting together in the bed, not quite sleeping, yet not fully awake. James Howard's fingers traced patterns on her bare back. "What are you up to now, luv?" he asked her sleepily, his voice hushed.

"What do you mean?" Miranda asked. She moved closer, pressing her breasts against him. Her toes toyed with his ankles. She felt a warmth begin to rekindle itself within her. "Hmm?" She moved her hand across his flat belly.

The Australian swatted her groping fingers away. "Be patient, luv. Only human, you know." He laughed.

"But wonderfully human," Miranda said. Her fingers found him and he offered no further resistance. She felt herself coming more awake. "What did you mean?"

"What I said. What's next for Miranda Glenn?"

She whispered into his ear, and was rewarded by a slap on the rear. "All right," she said, her own laughter mingling well with his. "I'll tell you if you'll be good."

"Fair enough."

"I've got an interview tomorrow with Paul Christopher," Miranda said quickly. "How's that?"

James Howard Dennis whistled softly in the dimly lighted room. "Are you serious?"

"Of course," said Miranda. She tightened her grip.

"How'd you manage that? It's some coup."

"Oh, it is indeed," said Miranda gleefully. "And it's all mine. Tomorrow."

"But, luv, don't you think this story might hit just a little too close to home?"

"I don't know what you're talking about," said Miranda.

James Howard softly stroked her cheek. "Ah, Miranda, don't pretend. Not with *me*. Isn't there a chance that Paul Christopher's just the biggest fish in an industry that you have reason to—"

"Enough!" said Miranda sharply. She did not want any of her old memories stirred up, but it was too late. She stared at James Howard Dennis for a long moment, then turned from him. She shrugged away his hands when he sought to rub her back. Miranda curled herself into a ball and squeezed her eyes shut. But it was no good. James Howard's words carried her back to her childhood, and to her father's ruin.

Born into a family whose wealth and prestige reached back to the Revolutionary War, Miranda

Glenn grew up idolizing her father. Raymond Glenn had been a classically handsome man, dynamic and ambitious. He was one of the bright lights of the State Department, a man whose career gave promise of great things. Her mother had been killed when Miranda was barely two years old, but despite all the demands of his career, Raymond Glenn was a devoted and loving parent. His daughter was as important a focus of his life as his office.

Miranda's childhood was one of privilege and travel, her father's postings carrying them to half a dozen of the world's capitals. Each posting was more influential than the last, and when Miranda was eight her father was named ambassador to Mexico. Within two years he was tapped by a new president to head the American delegation to the United Nations.

The confirmation hearings went smoothly, Raymond Glenn easily fielding questions thrown at him by an array of senators. Glenn even proved himself able to handle the openly antagonistic interrogations of Senator Patrick Thrusher, a demagogue making a name for himself as the watchdog of Washington morality. Raymond Glenn smiled his way through the toughest of Thrusher's questions, winning himself more than a few points for his grace under pressure as well as the shrewd intelligence of his responses. Senate confirmation of Glenn, it was generally agreed, lay only days away.

But on the day confirmation was expected, Thrusher produced a final surprise witness, Lee Lothrop, whose private security-and-investigations company was making its own name in capital circles.

Years later Miranda Glenn obtained a transcript of her father's hearing, and for a time she read it almost obsessively. But the transcript could offer only dead words, and gave no real hint of the agonies her father had undergone in the hearing room that day. They were agonies that would torment him for the rest of his life. The transcript's words may have been dead, but they burned themselves into Miranda's memory never to be eradicated.

Sen. Thrusher: Now, Mr. Lothrop, you've been aware for some time that all of the Ambassador's associations are not entirely . . . professional.

Mr. Lothrop: That's correct.

Sen. Thrusher: And you have evidence that one of those . . . associations is downright immoral, if not dangerous to our nation's security?

Mr. Lothrop: That's right.

Sen. Thrusher: Then I think that in the interests of our great country's well-being you should share that information with us.

Mr. Lothrop: For the past four years Ambassador Glenn has been romantically involved with a woman twelve years his junior, a student at Georgetown University. She is a political-science major, specializing in the study of Marxism and revolutionary movements around the world. Her name is Joyce Reynolds, she is twenty-two years old. She is a member of no less than seven unsavory organizations.

Sen. Thrusher: Would you name those organizations for us?

Lothrop recited the names of the "unsavory groups" to which Joyce Reynolds belonged: study groups, a student task force, an environmental action committee. The sorts of groups, Miranda reflected, to which any concerned young person might belong. Groups no more dangerous than social clubs . . . and far less dangerous than politicians of Senator Thrusher's ilk. Lothrop proceeded to offer dates and locations of meetings between the student and the ambassador, and promised to provide photographs, if such were required. The results were devastating to Raymond Glenn's chances for confirmation.

But not to his character. Given the opportunity to make a statement in rebuttal, Ambassador Glenn exercised his eloquence. He spoke not one word in defense of himself or his actions, but devoted his response to Joyce Reynolds. Miranda remembered those words as well.

> *Mr. Glenn:* The young woman you have singled out possesses perhaps the keenest, most vibrant intelligence I've ever encountered. She is a serious student, and a patriot. It has been her intention to devote herself and her considerable abilities to the service of her country. And our country should be proud to have such young people among its numbers. God knows, we need them, considering the nature of some of their office-holding elders.

On that note the ambassador departed the hearing room, and returned to his home in Alexandria. Reporters were already clustered upon the front lawn, but Raymond Glenn ignored them. Inside, he sat down with his daughter and attempted to explain to the child what had happened. Miranda could still recall the outrage she had felt as her father related the day's events. She had known Joyce Reynolds nearly as long as had her father. Miranda loved Joyce, and it had been a secret hope of hers for some time that her father would marry her. Now, though, there was a cloud hanging over them. Raymond Glenn put his strong arms around his daughter and assured her that everything would be all right. Miranda huddled close to her father.

Shortly before midnight that evening, distraught over the collapse of Raymond Glenn's prospects as well as the damage done to her own hopes, Joyce Reynolds committed suicide. Nothing was ever the same again.

Miranda could not recall her father ever smiling after that long night. It was as though he became a husk of a human, an automaton without a soul. Not even his daughter could cheer him. She found herself raised by a nanny and the household staff. Raymond Glenn passed his days sitting in a darkened room, staring vacantly into space. Miranda visited him twice a day, but he embraced her only wanly, and said little. Each month saw the former ambassador grow more despondent. Sometimes it seemed to Miranda that her father barely knew her. Her heart broke, but she struggled to remain strong, convinced that by her display of bravery she could bring back the father she so admired.

Two weeks before Miranda's twelfth birthday her father suffered a series of small strokes that left him paralyzed. Within six months he was gone. Miranda Glenn, though still a child, had made herself so strong that she did not weep at her father's funeral, nor reveal her grief to any of the relatives in whose homes she was raised. She applied herself to schoolwork and displayed an intense interest in journalism. Not long after Joyce's suicide, she began keeping a scrapbook of newspaper and magazine clippings related to the career of Senator Patrick Thrusher, and a smaller file containing information about Lothrop Security Inc.

Thrusher's career carried him steadily toward higher office, and more than a few commentators felt that he had his eye upon the presidency. But his talent for demagoguery was his undoing, and his reputation collapsed at last under the relentless questioning of an investigative reporter who'd uncovered quite a few skeletons in the senator's own past. On camera, attempting to answer the charges, Thrusher's demeanor broke and he revealed himself as a whining, self-serving coward, a man who, wielding power, could be extremely dangerous.

Miranda Glenn watched the program with a cold eye, taking in every detail of the senator's performance, and noticing as well the way in which the journalist controlled the situation. She felt little joy at seeing the senator ruined: that would not bring her father back. But she did find an interest that would grow throughout her adolescence, guide her choice of colleges and determine her course of study. Miranda Glenn had found her life's work.

At twenty-one she inherited the considerable estate her father had left, but the wealth to Miranda meant simply that she could devote herself fully to establishing her career. She was eager to immerse herself in hard work, and made it a point never to refuse an assignment. Faced at first with innuendos that she was simply a rich girl looking to make a name for herself, Miranda produced work of such high quality that her critics were quickly silenced. Her reputation grew rapidly, and if Miranda had any regret it was that Lee Lothrop died quietly. Not long afterward his partner sold the business to Christopher Security International.

And tomorrow she would meet Paul Christopher.

Miranda felt James Howard's fingers tracing their way gently down her spine. She drew a deep breath, then turned to face him. He deserved some answer. "I know what I'm doing," she said softly. The Australian nodded at her and Miranda moved closer.

"You ready for him?" James Howard asked.

"Have you ever known me to go into any interview unprepared?" Miranda asked, almost angrily.

"Of course not, darlin'," he said. "I didn't mean that. But you must know how hard Christopher's worked to keep himself a mystery. So you can guess how hard he'll work to hold onto that."

"I can guess," said Miranda. "It doesn't worry me."

"No. It wouldn't, of course. Or me, either, if it was *my* interview. But, luv, he's got resources. I don't want to see you get hurt. Or anything happen to you." He tried to take hold of her shoulders, but Miranda, sitting up, pulled swiftly away from him.

"No more than I'd hate to see anything happen to you!" she said. "But I'm not going to hide away from something just because it *might* be dangerous. And I don't like you suggesting that I should." She switched on the lamp beside the bed and glanced at the time. It would be dawn soon.

"I wasn't suggesting anything," said James Howard Dennis. "I was just trying to sound a note of caution. Nothing you don't already know, luv. You're the best in our business. And Paul Christopher's the best in his." He gave her a crooked grin. "It's just that in his business they carry guns."

"But the pen is mightier than—" Miranda began, then broke off. A smile brightened her face. "If you want to worry about someone, worry about Paul Christopher. Because tomorrow—*today*—at three he's going to have to answer *my* questions."

"After a night like this, I wouldn't have the strength to *spell* interview, much less conduct one," said James Howard. He stretched languorously.

"That's because you're not Miranda Glenn," she taunted. Her full breasts bobbed slightly as she moved. "I *told* you I was stronger than you!"

"Why, you impertinent Yank bitch!" the Australian exclaimed. "I'm ready to take you on any day of the week!"

Miranda put her hands on her hips. "Prove it!"

The sun began to rise as Miranda and James Howard clawed and wrestled their way through an arduous, almost violent battle of love. Corded muscles stood out on James Howard's arms as he held Miranda's shoulders against the bed, embedding himself deep within her warmth. He virtually pinned her to the mattress. He growled as he moved over her, his nostrils flaring as he inhaled great drafts of air. A sheen of perspiration covered both of them in minutes.

Miranda Glenn cast her hips up to meet his every thrust. She possessed surprising strengths, and she tensed her muscles, pushing against him whenever she found a weakness. It took long, deliciously exhausting moments, but before they were finally spent, Miranda forced James Howard over onto his back, reversing their positions. She ground herself hard against him, holding him down. As the sun rose she arched her back and milked him dry, her inner muscles clenching fiercely as his heat flooded her. The moan that Miranda released was as much a cry of triumph as of ecstasy.

James Howard Dennis's ego was little bruised by Miranda's victory. He kissed her deeply. They shared a shower and an enormous breakfast before he departed. "You take care of yourself, luv," he said to her at the townhouse door. He pulled his topcoat around him. Miranda was wrapped in her Blackglama mink, wearing nothing beneath it. For a moment she was tempted to ask him to stay just a little while longer. "You watch out for Paul Christopher," the

Australian said. He leaned to kiss her cheek, then stepped out onto the sidewalk. He turned to wink at her once, then hailed a cab and was gone.

In the atrium of the Christopher offices, Miranda turned down the collar of her belted Burberry winter coat. She felt refreshed. After James Howard left, she'd soaked for nearly an hour in a deep, hot bath, then slept soundly until one o'clock.

Miranda had dressed carefully for her meeting with Paul Christopher. She unknotted the Burberry's belt and unbuttoned the coat. She shrugged her shoulders loose and gave her head a shake. This season Miranda wore her hair long, and she fluffed it with her fingers, tossing the curls lightly. She was aware that some of the passersby stared at her. Miranda Glenn was accustomed to stares. Only rarely could she pass through a lobby, or attend the theater, or dine in a restaurant without being asked for an autograph. Over the years, as her fame grew, Miranda taught herself to accept the attention. Ignoring the attention now, she stared at the bank of elevators set into the lobby's far wall. In minutes she would ascend to the fifty-seventh floor. There at last she would meet Paul Christopher.

Anticipation tingled through her like electricity. It was a feeling in its own way as deeply sensual and exciting as those that coursed through her during lovemaking—but there was nothing sexual about this sensation. She knew its currents well; it was her sort of intuition—her journalist's sixth sense—that she didn't completely comprehend, but that she had come to trust completely. Miranda had faith in the accuracy of her intuition. Something was brewing. A story was starting to build. The closer she came to Paul Christopher, the more intense her intuition grew. Soon they would be face to face. Miranda smiled for just a second, but the smile was almost savage. She was onto something.

The corporate offices of Christopher Security International occupied eight floors: fifty-seven through sixty-four. Christopher's company shared an express elevator with the three investment firms that filled the building's highest floors. The illuminated numbers above the elevator indicated that at the moment the car was stopped on fifty-seven. *A client retaining Christopher's company?* Miranda wondered.

She quickly forced such thoughts from her mind. Among the principles that guided her was the determination to enter every interview—especially a key interview such as this—with all the objectivity she could muster. She was a journalist: that was her responsibility. Openly an advocate for the causes in which she believed, Miranda labored hard to ensure that her biases were always well-supported with facts. Any ugly truths she exposed were honestly come by. Any sensibilities she offended with her work probably needed offending. Miranda Glenn made it a point of professional pride to stand in judgment only after she herself had judged all the evidence.

So she would give Paul Christopher the benefit of the doubt. At least—*especially!*—at the beginning. She would be pleasant. Not that it would be easy. She had reason to hate his profession. Already she knew enough about Christopher's business to anger her. She understood his product and his service. Christopher Security International was little more than a global armed force for hire, a mercenary outfit available to anyone able to pay the retainer.

And then, depending upon what she discovered, Miranda Glenn would air Paul Christopher's dirty secrets to all the world.

She moved slowly through the atrium, making her way toward the elevators. At a bench she paused to remove the Burberry. Deeply tanned despite the season, Miranda stood tall. The gray Basile suit she wore established her professionalism without disguising the lushness of her figure. Miranda delighted in the touch of fine wool crepe to her flesh, appreciated the fly-front cut of the jacket, the finely striped gabardine slacks that made her long legs seem even longer. The stares she'd attracted earlier were now multiplied. People were looking her way. Thanks to television, Miranda's face and features were as well-known as her byline. She wore little makeup, less jewelry. A chip of dark jade brooded at each of her ears. Her left wrist was wrapped with a worked-silver bracelet she'd come across in Istanbul's Grand Bazaar. She wore no rings, and carried a Fendi handbag over her right shoulder. The bag was large enough to accommodate the tools of her trade—tiny cassette recorder, camera, notebook—and at the same time offered stylish accompaniment to the figure she cut.

Miranda adjusted the drape of her raincoat over her left arm and began to walk toward the elevators. She had nearly reached them when she heard her name called from behind her. "Miranda! Miss Glenn!" She stopped and turned around.

Approaching from the glass-fronted bookstore that occupied one of the arcade spaces next to the lobby's long escalators were two neatly dressed Japanese businessmen, their hands filled with paperback books and newspapers. Miranda found herself grinning. She was very popular in Japan, and the businessmen had doubtless spotted her when she entered the skyscraper. They'd shopped quickly but well, and Miranda made a mental note to stop by the bookstore on her way out. She wanted to thank them for keeping so complete a stock of her work. The businessmen smiled broadly as they extended their purchases. Miranda removed an ebony Cross pen from her handbag and set to work signing the books, and the copies of *Rolling Stone* that were held out to her.

Her name was splashed across *Rolling Stone*'s cover in type almost as large as Mick Jagger's, the subject of her piece. Although she generally stayed away from entertainment assignments and profiles, Miranda had enjoyed working with Jagger and the Stones. The job had been a pleasant diversion following the publicity tour for *Prescription: Death*. She'd turned in a good piece, and been well-paid for it. But the real reward had come unexpectedly in England when she was approached with the opportunity to purchase a Byzantine solidus that would, it was guaranteed, buy her access to Paul Christopher.

Three o'clock neared. Miranda finished signing the magazines and accepted the Japanese businessmen's bows and handshakes. They stepped back, keeping their eyes on her as she approached the elevators. Miranda punched the button that would summon the express car. Everything was going well. Her intuition filled her with excitement. The autograph-seeking Japanese were the final good omen. She was ready to meet Paul Christopher. The elevator doors opened.

The car's operator was a young blond woman wearing the distinctive CSI guard uniform. A revolver bulked large at her hip. "Fifty-seven, please," Miranda said. The elevator doors closed, and Miranda moved deeper into the car. She leaned against a gleaming metal wall. The elevator whisked her upward.

Miranda kept her eyes on the guard's pistol. She smiled openly as she stared at the weapon. It seemed so ridiculous—and so typical of Paul Christopher.

"Are you afraid someone will steal the elevator?" she asked sharply.

The guard looked at her and Miranda read the nametag on her blouse. *Linda Bradford*. "I'm sorry?"

"The pistol," Miranda said.

Linda Bradford's hand moved almost imperceptibly in the direction of the holstered pistol. "Just a precaution," she said softly.

"Against what?"

"There have been threats. Assassination attempts."

"Assassination? Against whom?" Miranda asked. The car began to slow its ascent.

"Why, Mr. Christopher, of course," the guard said. She turned back to the panel with its numbered buttons. A bell sounded softly. The elevator car came to a halt and its doors opened.

"Thank you," said Miranda as she stepped from the elevator onto the travertine marble floor that marked the beginning of Christopher Security International.

From a central post within a seamless circular white desk, a receptionist fixed Miranda Glenn with a stare and tracked the journalist's approach. Miranda walked directly to the desk and gave her name. "To see Paul Christopher," she said.

"Yes," said the receptionist. "Of course." She busied herself at the controls of the slim modern switchboard, her perfectly manicured fingers dancing over the keys. Miranda glanced around the large lobby. There were no others present, although two spacious seating areas could easily accommodate twenty or more callers. And Miranda knew that the waiting areas were usually quite busy: there was a high demand for the sort of services Christopher sold. During her preliminary research, Miranda had visited several of Christopher Security International's offices —including this one—but never before had she found the reception area deserted. *Of course,* she reflected, *I've never gotten past the reception desk before, either.* She wondered suddenly if Paul Christopher had planned it this way.

Miranda returned her attention to the receptionist, who was speaking softly into the microphone arm of the headset she wore. The receptionist nodded and looked up. "Mr. Christopher's secretary, Diana Lowen, will be with you in just a moment. If you would please sign our register—" She indicated an open visitors' register to her right. Miranda bent, gave her signature, then straightened again. The receptionist held out a clip-on identification badge. "And we must ask you to wear this," she added with a pleasant smile. "For security reasons."

"Of course," said Miranda. She clipped the badge to the fly front of the Basile jacket. "There."

The receptionist nodded, then turned back to her switchboard. Behind her the wall was dominated by an enormous map of the world; the Christopher Security International logo, a gleaming shield flanked by lightning bolts, was prominently displayed at the top. All the CSI offices Miranda had visited seemed sterile somehow, their walls bare of paintings or decorations. As Miranda waited for Christopher's secretary to come for her, she walked slowly from one side of the reception area to the other. The room was sealed at every exit by double glass doors, opaque, with CSI's logo centrally emblazoned. Miranda reached out to touch the door and the badge she wore gave a slight *beep.*

"Excuse me, Miss Glenn?" the receptionist's voice came from behind her. Miranda turned around. The receptionist was smiling, but she was also standing fully erect. She wore her own pistol and her hand was close to it now. "I'm sorry, Miss Glenn," she said, her smile not wavering a bit. "As the badge reminded you, you're not authorized to go beyond reception without an escort. Mr. Christopher's secretary will be with you momentarily. Won't you have a seat?" Her voice was as pleasant as her smile, and Miranda had no doubt that the pleasantries were backed up by solid steel. And perfect aim.

Miranda stepped away from the doors and returned to the seating area.

Before she could take a seat, the doors slid open and a woman came into the reception area. Miranda estimated she was about thirty. Dressed in a severe dark suit, her hair cut short, her brown eyes serious, Diana Lowen approached Miranda Glenn. "Miss Glenn?" she said, her voice frosty and formal. "Mr. Christopher will see you now."

Miranda nodded and stepped toward the doors, following Diana Lowen. Her badge made no protest now. The doors slid easily open before her, and closed as soon as she had passed through. She was *inside*.

They walked swiftly through long corridors. Occasionally others passed, and Diana nodded at them, but said nothing. Miranda accepted their glances, and held her head higher. Let Christopher's employees wonder what she was doing there, she thought. The hallways were color-coded with vertical lines at each branch or intersection. Christopher's secretary led Miranda at last into a comfortably appointed office. "You may leave your coat in my office, if you like," she said to Miranda.

Miranda hung the Burberry on a brass coatrack, then glanced toward the tinted doors that filled the far wall. Almost unconsciously, she hesitated for a second. *He* was through those doors.

"Oh, *do* go ahead," Diana Lowen said. "Mr. Christopher is expecting you."

Miranda nodded at the secretary, and approached the doors. They slid open for her and she walked through the opening, into Paul Christopher's office.

She took a second to get her bearings. Her heart was beating rapidly, a not unpleasant sensation. She was *here*. She was ready for him.

Paul Christopher stood to the left of his desk, his back to her. Miranda moved deeper into the office, the Aubusson rugs muffling her steps. As she moved, her angle of vision shifted and she lost Christopher in the sunlight flooding through the window. He was silhouetted in the brilliant light. She moved closer to him, but he did not turn around. *He will, though,* she thought fiercely, *I will make him take notice of me before we are finished.*

She had nearly reached his desk before Christopher faced her. When he pivoted, his shimmering silhouette became the figure of a man. *Just a man,* Miranda reminded herself. *Nothing more.*

She stepped forward.

_____3

HE STEPPED FORWARD.

"How do you do?" Paul Christopher said, extending his right hand. Miranda took it, her grip firm and brusque. Christopher returned her grip and quickly released her hand. With a wave he indicated the chairs facing his desk. "Please," he said, "do have a seat." He remained standing as she seated herself, then took his own place behind his massive desk. Christopher kept his face impassive, waiting for the journalist to make the first conversational move. He watched closely as she opened her Fendi handbag and withdrew a small cassette recorder. Holding it, she fixed him with an impassive stare of her own.

"You don't mind if I record this, do you?" she asked.

Paul Christopher laughed. "Be my guest," he said. "Of course you may use your recorder." He pressed his fingers together and studied her for a moment more. "But surely you're aware that our conversation is already being monitored. I'll be happy to provide you with a copy of the tape." He smiled. "Or a videotape, if you prefer. It would be my pleasure."

"I'm sure it would," said Miranda. "But I prefer to use my own equipment. I can trust it." Placing the recorder on the edge of the desk, she pressed the keys that started the machine.

For a long moment they stared at each other in silence. "Do go ahead," he said at last. "I assume you had a reason for wishing to see me?"

"Yes," said Miranda. "I do."

"Well?"

"I think you received my . . . *reason* last Thursday. By courier."

Christopher's dark eyebrows darted up. "You mean this?" He held up the solidus. "You know what it is?"

Miranda gave an affirmative shake of her head. "A golden solidus. Coin of the realm for the Byzantines. Its mintmark is Constantinople. It—"

Christopher raised his right hand and brought it down in a chopping gesture, cutting her off. "You've done your homework," he said in his softly accented voice. "But I expected no less. Now. Why did you wish to see me?"

"I thought that was clear," said Miranda.

"From your note?" Christopher shook his head. "Hardly. Explain to me what you want and I will let you know whether or not I will cooperate."

"Oh, I think you will cooperate," said Miranda firmly. "Unless you wish the story of the coin published by itself."

"And you know the story of the coin?" Christopher said.

Miranda merely smiled.

"How did you come by this coin?"

Miranda chuckled softly. "No," she said in an equally soft tone of voice. Her eyes smiled at him, almost mockingly. "But, of course, you're not serious. It *is* my interview, remember? *I* ask the questions."

"Then do so," said Paul Christopher. He placed his

hands flat on the surface of his desk. "But I must make clear to you that my willingness to answer your questions is predicated upon something from you."

"I've already sent you something," said Miranda, gesturing toward the solidus. "And I am here."

Christopher picked up the coin once more. "Indeed you are," he said. His voice acquired a hard edge. "You have sent me this. But I am not willing to play games for it. Understand that. I will not play games. I will call your bluff first."

"But I'm not bluffing," said Miranda, her voice as firm as his.

"All right. What is it you want?"

"I want an interview," said Miranda. "Or, rather, a series of them. I think it will take that. I want to know what makes you work. What drives you to the sort of . . . business that you operate." She spread her hands wide. "I want to know all about you. That's all," she said. "That's not so much to ask, is it?" Her voice was sweet, but her eyes were hard as diamonds.

"It's more than I've ever given," said Christopher. He kept his gaze locked into hers.

"That's one of the reasons it's such a valuable story," said Miranda.

"Why should I?"

"Because no one's ever sent you a solidus before," she said. "Right?"

Christopher said nothing. He drummed his fingers on the metal surface of his desk. "And what do I receive for this?"

Miranda's smile widened. "You've already gotten the coin. What more do you want?"

Christopher toyed silently with the coin. "And the purpose of these . . . interviews?" he said at last.

"To find out the truth," she said simply.

"About what? What truth?"

"About your organization," she explained. "How it functions. What it stands for. How you earn your pay. You're a fascinating man, Mr. Christopher. People want to know about you. About where you came from. How you reached the top." Her eyes narrowed. "About where you're going. What your ultimate . . . goals are." She leaned forward in her seat as she spoke, her eyes shining with enthusiasm. Christopher thought he saw on her face something of the eagerness of a hunter seeking a kill.

"That is, by some distance, more than I've ever given," admitted Christopher. "Such conversations would be at . . . cross purposes with my business." A ghost of a smile passed across his face and was gone. "Especially interviews with so celebrated a journalist."

"I'd disagree with that," said Miranda. "It's to your benefit to talk with me. To make your case before my audience." She gave a slight shrug. "Unless you have reason to *fear* the attention?"

"No," said Christopher simply. "I do not. But I dislike it. Intensely."

Gloating, she said, "But the solidus gives you no choice."

Christopher shook his head forcefully. "Free men always have choices," he said.

Her eyes were unwavering as she said, "Then, Mr. Christopher, I suggest you make your choice."

Christopher's gaze was equally steady. "Oh, my choice is made, Miss Glenn. It has been since the coin arrived. We shall—*talk*." He made the word sound forceful and ugly.

Miranda Glenn nodded. "I assumed that would be your answer. Shall we set up a schedule?"

"I'm leaving for Europe in the morning," Christopher said. "I'll be touring my operations there for two weeks."

"That should give us plenty of time," Miranda interrupted. "To get started."

Christopher did not speak. He thumbed the stud on his console and spoke to his secretary. "Diana. Make another reservation on tomorrow morning's Concorde. For Miranda Glenn."

"Yes, Mr. Christopher," Diana said. Christopher released the stud.

Miranda was shaking her head, the corners of her mouth upturned. "You're very smooth. I'd heard that about you. *European* manners, aren't they?" She placed her hands flat on the arms of the chair. "You take charge very capably, almost before anyone notices. But *I* notice these things, Mr. Christopher. That's my profession."

"What's your point?" said Christopher sharply.

"I can make my own airline reservations—"

"Then do so," said Christopher. His finger stabbed the console. "Only one Concorde ticket tomorrow, Diana. For me. Thank you."

Miranda raised her chin slightly. "All right, Mr. Christopher," she said. "Very well."

"I'll be at British Airways at nine-fifteen. Promptly. I assume I will see you there?" He glanced idly around his office.

Miranda rose from her seat. "I'll be there, Mr. Christopher," she said in a flat, even voice. "I wouldn't miss it." She retrieved her recorder and switched it off. "I'll have my questions for you."

"And I will have mine for you," said Christopher.

Miranda stared at him for a moment. His face was impassive, his eyes unblinking. At that moment, it seemed that he could have been cast from the same metal as his desk. "Thank you for your time," she said, and turned and left the office.

Christopher stared at the solidus for a long moment after the office doors closed. His breathing was slow and rhythmic as he restored tranquillity to his thoughts. She would be difficult to handle, he thought, but having met her he felt confident. The publicity did not matter, the attention would only inconvenience him. But he could live with inconvenience, and overcome it. What mattered was the coin. Who had taken it to her? Who had betrayed him?

When Paul Christopher moved at last, he moved quickly. He put the solidus away, and returned the Miranda Glenn file to his desk. He brought his computer terminal to life and requested the readouts from his meeting with the journalist. He had told her it was being recorded, but he had not informed her of the many levels at which his recording devices worked.

Within seconds he had before him listings of Miranda Glenn's blood pressure, perspiration rate, heartbeat, and rate of breathing, along with other data that verged upon the subliminal. He had *her* on the screen before him.

Paul Christopher set to work.

Shortly before six in the evening Miranda Glenn's telephone rang. "Yes?"

"Afternoon, luv," James Howard Dennis said. "I'm still in town. Thought we might have a rematch," he said with a salty chuckle.

Miranda looked around her bedroom. Her bed was covered with Vuitton luggage and articles of clothing. Her closets were open, drawers extended. But she could be done packing in an hour, and have the rest of the evening with James Howard. She thought of the touch of his hands and lips, the warm feel of him within her. *No*. That had been yesterday's diversion. Now she had met Paul Christopher. Now she had to work. "I'm sorry, luv," she said, mimicking his accent. "I've got an early flight in the morning."

"You met with Christopher this afternoon?" James Howard asked.

"Yes."

"Well?" Ice clinked in a glass. "Share a few secrets with an old friend? How did it go?"

Miranda's laughter was rich and full. "Oh, James Howard. I'll sleep with you. Anytime. But you can't seriously expect me to share a story?"

The Australian's laughter echoed hers. "No. No, I don't," he said, and sighed. "But, luv, I *do* expect you to take care of yourself. You know that."

"But I'm a big, strong woman," said Miranda Glenn distractedly. Her mind was already returning to the tasks she had ahead of her. She folded a wool skirt into a suitcase.

"You're flying out with Christopher?" James Howard Dennis asked.

"Between us?"

"Yes."

"Then you're right. I'm flying out with him."

"Well . . . you just make sure he doesn't dump you out of the plane at fifty thousand feet."

It earned a chuckle from Miranda. "It's a *public* flight," she said.

"Yeah. And it's Paul Christopher sitting beside you, too."

"Just wish me luck."

"All of it I've got, luv. You know that. I'll be waiting for the book."

"I think a lot of people will," said Miranda as she hung up and returned to her packing.

Paul Christopher had decided not to let his preoccupation with Miranda Glenn spoil his evening, or at least not his appetite. He and Rebecca Devereaux sat at the quiet, private table they preferred at Le Cirque. They'd begun the meal with cold Moroccan rock lobster served with mayonnaise and tarragon. Rebecca had insisted upon champagne, and although Christopher found himself in anything but a festive mood, he ordered a bottle of Krug. Its dry effervescence helped refresh him, and before the waiter removed the *langouste de Maroc* he was feeling improved. He watched Rebecca as she ate.

Watching Rebecca Devereaux do anything, he reflected, was a pleasure. She smiled at him as the rock lobster shells were removed, the waiter unobtrusively replacing them with a parfait of foie gras and black truffles. The loveliness of Rebecca's low-cut aqua Dior could not compete with the lace of diamonds that glittered at her throat. There seemed to be hundreds of stones. Christopher shook his head, almost as though noticing the gems for the first time. "I've warned you before about wearing that sort of thing in public," he said softly. "You might as well wear a sign inviting the thieves in."

Rebecca swallowed a bite of foie gras and followed it with a sip of champagne. Her dark eyes laughed like diamonds themselves in Le Cirque's soft lighting. "Surely I can get away with it tonight," she said, an edge of teasing in her voice. She batted her eyes at him with a false demureness. "If a girl can't wear her diamonds when she's out with Paul Christopher, whom can she wear them with?" she asked. Her voice dripped honey.

"No one," said Christopher. "It's unfortunate, but that is the nature of our modern world. Have some good imitations made, and seal these away someplace *safe*." He shrugged. "Think of them as an investment."

Rebecca pouted. "Paul, you're no fun," she said. "Sometimes you just *have* to get out the good stuff and show it off. You should know that." She winked seductively at him, cocking her head forward so a long blond curl tumbled down and covered her left eye. "Can't you understand that, darling?"

"I can understand that you don't take this very seriously," said Christopher. He ate some foie gras. "But you should, Rebecca. You really should."

She raised her bare shoulders. "Paul, what is it?" she said seriously. "What's troubling you?"

Christopher waved a dismissive hand. "Nothing at all," he said. "How could there be—in your company?"

"You're sweet," said Rebecca Devereaux. "But I think sometimes you forget how well I know you. Oh, don't protest. We've known each other too long."

"As you say."

"You're sure there's nothing?"

"I'm fine," said Christopher. He raised his glass to her. "To pleasant company," he toasted.

"And companionable evenings," Rebecca answered him. Crystal clinked over the table. They drank.

"You leave for London in the morning?" Rebecca asked.

Christopher nodded. The foie gras was removed. A moment later the waiter returned with their main course, *petit faison rôti aux baies de genièvres*. The rich aroma of baby pheasant and juniper berries, chestnuts and vegetables, complemented by delicate fresh quail eggs, filled the air around the table. The conversation dwindled as the couple savored each bite.

"Are you going to see Rita Sue when you're in London?" Rebecca asked.

"Yes. In fact, we're dining together tomorrow evening."

"Give her my best," said Rebecca. "I haven't seen her in ages. How's she doing?"

Christopher gave a short chuckle. "You know Rita Sue. She does what she wants to do."

Rebecca touched her lips with a napkin. "And whatever she wants to do turns out best for Cedri-Chem."

"It never misses," said Paul Christopher. "*She* never misses." Rita Sue Cedric was an old and valued friend. Since the death of her husband a decade ago she had been the head of one of Europe's largest pharmaceutical firms, CedriChem.

"How long will you be gone?"

"A couple of weeks," Christopher said as he finished his meal. "I'm doing a grand tour. And finishing up in Rome for Maria Conti's wedding."

"Your friend Giancarlo will at last be related to royal blood," Rebecca said. "At least by marriage."

"But only, as Giancarlo himself says, when the first male grandchild is born!" Christopher's smile was genuine. The meal had relaxed him. "He'll be disappointed if Maria bears only girls. He wants to bounce a baby count on his knee."

"A royal wedding," said Rebecca.

He looked again at the diamonds at her throat. "And there will be guests there wearing the same sort of jewelry, and they'll be sending signals to every thief in Rome."

Rebecca clapped her hands together. "The more

business for your company, Paul," she said. "Let's have our coffee at home, shall we?"

They returned to her Fifth Avenue townhouse silently in the back of Rebecca's limousine. Her hand brushed against his as they rode, and Christopher closed his fingers gently around hers. She gave them a squeeze, which he returned, but his mind was filled with thoughts of Miranda Glenn and the solidus. He gazed out the limousine window as they rolled through New York's streets.

The drawing room of Rebecca Devereaux's townhouse was beautifully appointed, and its heavy drapes were drawn tight against the January chill. Rebecca's butler took their wraps and ushered them toward the crackling fire. The butler disappeared for a moment, and returned pushing a cart on which were arranged coffee and a selection of liqueurs. The butler bowed and left the room, closing its massive wooden doors behind him. Christopher unknotted his tie and opened his collar. Rebecca poured the coffee and, bending down, gave him a soft kiss on the cheek after placing his cup beside his armchair.

"Poor Paul," she said, standing once more. She walked to the fire, and sipped her coffee. She placed the cup and saucer on the mantel, and touched a rheostat there that dimmed the room's lights. "Rest your eyes, darling," she said. "You seem so tired."

Christopher shook his head. "Some . . . changes in the company."

"Growing again?" Rebecca said.

"Always trying," said Christopher heavily. He pressed his fingers against his eyes. When he looked again, Rebecca's hands were behind her back. She unzipped the Dior and returned one hand to her breasts, holding the dress up as she walked slowly toward the chair where Paul Christopher sat. Four paces from him she stopped and stared down at him for a moment. "Poor Paul," she said again. Her tongue darted across her lips. She removed her hand and the dress stayed for a moment, covering her, then slipped from her body. Rebecca stepped out of the dress. The silken undergarments she wore concealed little of her slim body, but she took some time removing them. When she was nude except for her necklace, she crossed the space between them and sank slowly to her knees before the chair. Rebecca leaned forward and unfastened Christopher's belt, then opened his pants. He said nothing.

Rebecca took him in her hands and brought her face close. Her breath was warm. She looked up at him, her necklace still in place, the facets of its gems sparkling brilliantly in the firelight. "You are full of tensions, Paul," Rebecca said in a voice that was a purr. Then, her mouth closed around him and for a time Paul Christopher forgot about the world.

As midnight approached, Miranda Glenn reclined in a bubble bath. Her hair was tucked into a towel, and she placed a hot washcloth across her eyes. She wanted to drain away all the tensions—and excitement—of the past few days. There would be tensions and excitement enough in the days to come. She let a long, deep sigh escape slowly, and took steam deep into her lungs.

Her bags were packed and stood in a neat row beside her front door. Miranda had put her notes in the Gucci briefcase that she favored for long trips. Her mind was clear. Meeting Christopher face to face had seen to that. Since leaving his office she had grown increasingly pleased with the effectiveness of the solidus. The coin had accomplished everything its seller promised. *More*. Christopher had acquiesced so easily—he had surrendered too much too soon. Miranda wondered why.

During the course of the evening she had replayed the tape of their first meeting several times. Miranda was not quite certain what she hoped to hear, but as a journalist she found his words—and his strong, deep voice—fascinating. The subtle hints of accent intrigued her, and she had made it a priority to find out exactly what the source of the accent was. Where had he been born? What tongue did he grow up speaking? She was aware that if she could discover his nationality, she might have discovered the true key to his secrets.

But the coin had proved the only key necessary to get his attention, she thought as she climbed from the tub. She used three fresh, fluffy towels to dry herself. Miranda took a long time rubbing herself down. When her skin glowed she padded from the bathroom and crawled naked between the sheets of her bed.

She had no trouble getting to sleep. Miranda Glenn slept soundly.

The ship's clock, perched on a high shelf, chimed four A.M. Paul Christopher ignored it. He stood in a small room off his office. The room was wood-paneled and dark; its walls were heavy with bookshelves and dark paintings. A writing desk and chair, along with a leather armchair, were the room's only furniture. Christopher stood at the window.

He had a similar room attached to each of his offices. It served as a study, a tranquil place for contemplation. Christopher used the rooms infrequently, although he valued their presence. He never carried paperwork into the studies. He went there only when he needed repose—and when he needed to think.

On a shelf to the left of the door stood a Baccarat crystal decanter of Remy Martin Louis XIII, flanked by a single snifter. The cognac was reserved for times of greatest triumph or tension in Christopher's life. He walked to the shelf now and, with careful and precise movements, poured himself a snifter of the Remy. He waved it beneath his nose, taking in its full and comforting bouquet, then took a careful sip.

The hours he had spent making love with Rebecca Devereaux had been exquisite, but despite heroic efforts she had failed to drain his tensions. At midnight he tucked her into bed and gave her a final kiss. Rebecca was asleep before he left her bedroom. Christopher already knew that he wouldn't get to sleep tonight.

He was accustomed to night thoughts. Standing at his window, cradling the crystal snifter in his right hand, he stared out at the city. How many Christopher employees were at work there now? How many of his people stood guard over property or people tonight? Christopher could have the answers in minutes at his computer terminal, but he was not interested in statistics. He looked out into the night, wondering what moved in its shadows. The shadows were what he and his employees stood on guard against.

Christopher considered Miranda Glenn's reactions during their conversation. She had entered the room already excited, and when he first displayed the solidus, her pulse jumped. The peak had come when he invited her to accompany him to Europe. Had she been surprised? What had she expected?

He took another swallow of the Remy and after a

moment refilled his snifter. He wondered exactly how much Miranda Glenn knew of the solidus and its particular history.

Five chimes came from the ship's clock. Christopher walked to the bookshelves and slid aside a collection of Shakespeare. He touched the paneling behind it in a special way, and a section of the wood swung open, revealing a small safe. Christopher pressed his thumb against a small scanner on the safe. The ProTech chip that he had helped design read his thumbprint, along with his skin chemistry, and the safe's door swung open. Christopher drew a slow breath, then removed three objects from the safe. He carried them to his writing desk and centered them on the leather blotter.

There was a small wooden box, lined with velvet. Inside the box rested golden coins from ancient eras and empires. The solidus would be at home among them, Christopher thought: it had been among them when he stole the coins and smuggled them from his homeland.

Beside the box lay a thin book, leather-bound. Stamped in gilt on its cover was Cyrillic lettering identifying the volume as a history of ancient coinage. The author, Father Josef Martinu, was also identified in gilt. *Father Josef fancied himself a scholar,* Paul Christopher thought. He remembered sitting as a boy at the priest's knee and hearing wonderful stories of the history of the precious metal, of alchemy and ancient lore. Underlying all of the stories and coloring the words the priest used was a love of gold that even a boy as young as Paul could tell bordered upon the obsessive. That bright light that shone in the priest's eyes as he spoke of gold was far brighter than the light which shone during Mass.

They collected coins together, the priest and his favorite pupil. Their funds were limited, their acquisitions meager. It was easier for them to justify the expense of numismatic magazines, and the boy raced to the church on days when a new issue was due. Together he and Father Josef scoured the pages carefully, determined that their eagerness not cause them to overlook a piece that might fall within their means.

From time to time the priest attempted to temper their enthusiasm. "These coins are, after all, *worldly* goods, my boy," Father Josef would say. And the boy would nod in agreement, and then bow his head to pray with the priest. But Paul had been a perceptive youth, and he had not doubted that the priest spoke for his own benefit as much as the lad's. Soon after praying they would be turning the pages of the coin catalogs once more, speculating over the worldly joys of owning any of the exotic pieces listed there.

But we could never have dreamed of owning coins as wonderful as these, Christopher thought bitterly. He looked at the mound of coins in the velvet-lined box. *How could we have ever afforded them?* After a moment he picked up the book, *Father Josef Martinu*'s name glittering in the small room's soft light. *You found a way to these coins, didn't you, Father?* he thought. *You had to have them no matter whom you betrayed. Would you have taken them had you known how high their price would finally be?*

The third item on his desk was a small hinged picture frame. Paul Christopher hesitated a long moment before opening the frame to reveal the photograph held within. He no longer looked at it often. But few days passed when he did not think of the girl in the photograph, of how deeply he had loved her. Of how she had died and the part Father Josef played in that death.

Captured in the photograph forever was Maria as Paul had known her. They grew up together in the small village not far from Prague, the village whose church and priest were the center of all activity. *We all looked up to him so,* Christopher recalled. *Which made it so simple for him to guarantee the Soviets little trouble from our region.* As the crisis of 1968 built, the priest grew increasingly passionate in his advocacy of restraint. And virtually everyone in the village listened to him. *Except for me,* thought Paul Christopher. *And my Maria.*

He stared for a long time at the photograph, then abruptly left the desk and walked to the window. He finished the snifter of Remy and poured another. Below him Manhattan winked colored lights like gaudy gems. Christopher cradled the snifter in the palm of his right hand.

He and Maria were to marry in September, and the village hummed with excitement at the prospect. In the larger world troubles brewed. Dubcek's reforms became the focus of gathering tensions between the Soviets and Czechoslovakia. In the early weeks of August talk circulated that the Russians would invade. Paul, with his passionate belief in freedom, argued with Father Josef; the friendship that reached back to Paul's childhood began to crumble. "Can't you understand, my boy, that there can be no defense of violence?" the priest asked. "That any resistance would only make matters worse for our people?"

"Can't *you* understand that to behave like . . . *sheep* would be worse than death?" Paul responded. The memory still made him angry. Father Josef's insistence upon docility maddened the university student. Paul was no longer a village boy whose primary contact with the world was through coin magazines and a priest's conversations. His studies at the university had introduced him to larger ideas. How could Father Josef ask that Paul remain calm when the whole world was tumbling down?

That world collapsed when Soviet tanks rolled through the streets of Prague. *And my corner of that world died forever with Maria on those streets.* Christopher returned to his desk and looked once more at the photograph. The last time he saw Maria her face was bloodied, her body lifeless. He had been swept away from her by the crowd, retreating in the face of overwhelming Soviet superiority. Maria died the day freedom died in Czechoslovakia.

And later that night Father Josef died, Christopher thought. He glanced at his watch, at the scars radiating beneath it. *And I came into my . . . inheritance upon his passing.* He ran his fingers through the coins, listening to their clatter. He had sold most of them within a year of escaping his homeland, and used the proceeds to finance his new life. But Paul Christopher had always known that he would regain possession of the coins. Each of them was marked in a way that only he could identify. And he had passed on the knowledge of those identifying marks to his closest advisers, and instructed them to be alert for the coins, the secret symbols of his escape from oppression. *These coins paid for Paul Christopher's creation,* he thought. *And my people have been under orders to watch for any of the coins, to buy them and return them to me. There are very few pieces of the collection missing now.* A bitter laugh escaped him. *The souvenirs of my past.* He picked up the solidus. *Now this one is being used against me. Once more a coin lies at the heart of a betrayal.*

But who has betrayed me?

Christopher returned the items to the safe. He took his snifter and stood by the window to wait for dawn.

4

SHORTLY AFTER SEVEN in the morning Paul Christopher placed a call to Miranda Glenn. She answered on the second ring. He could tell from her voice that he had not awakened her. "Yes? Hello?"

"This is Paul Christopher," he said.

"Good morning," she said evenly.

Christopher had been unable to leave the solidus in his safe. Something about it compelled him to keep it with him. Its presence forced him to play an unfamiliar role. He spoke slowly, carefully selecting each word. "I thought we might have gotten started badly yesterday," he said.

"I thought we did all right," replied Miranda.

"Yes. I'm sure you did." He made his tone pleasant. "At any rate, I wished to begin today on a cooperative note. Would your integrity be too terribly compromised by a ride to Kennedy? Obviously, I must go that way myself."

There was a moment's pause. Then Miranda gave her answer. "I feel sure my integrity can stand up to one free ride."

"Excellent. Shall we say an hour?"

"Fine." After only a second's pause, Miranda added a soft "Thank you."

Christopher hung up. He left the solidus on his desk

and stepped quickly into the dressing room that adjoined his office. Years of late hours and early mornings had impressed upon him the necessity of keeping a fresh wardrobe close by his desk. He smiled as he laid out his clothing: more of his suits and jackets hung in office dressing rooms than in his homes. His luggage had already been packed and picked up by his driver from the penthouse apartment that Christopher rarely saw.

In the bathroom he drew a basin full of hot water. Taking an ivory-handled shaving brush, Christopher worked the soap into a rich lather. He shaved slowly and closely, drawing the razor hard against his heavy dark beard. He'd reached no answers during the night, but the prospect of a new day and having Miranda Glenn where he could keep an eye on her invigorated Christopher more thoroughly than ten hours' sleep would have. By the time they reached London, even at the globe-shrinking speed at which Concorde hurtled, Christopher intended to know some things about her acquisition of the solidus and her timing of its delivery. How much did she know? Christopher finished shaving and stepped into a scalding shower.

When he was dressed, he stepped to his desk and punched Giancarlo Conti's Rome telephone number. He was surprised when Maria Conti answered the call. "Little one," he said warmly, "what are you doing in your father's office? You should be readying yourself for your wedding."

"Uncle Paul!" Maria exclaimed. "You sound wonderful!"

"I always feel wonderful when I'm speaking to you, little one," Christopher said. "But you haven't answered my question."

Giancarlo Conti's rich voice came over the speaker.

"She is here preparing for the wedding, Paul. She is trying to bankrupt me preparing for the wedding!"

"Good morning, Giancarlo," said Christopher.

Conti's daughter spoke up. "Is not true, Uncle Paul! What he says. There is a dress, nothing more. I think it would look so wonderful on me, and there is a party this weekend that—"

"You see, Paul," Conti interrupted. "What am I to do?"

Christopher grinned. "Here is what you are to do, Giancarlo. Permit me to purchase the dress for Maria. Call it an early present."

"Oh, Uncle Paul!" the girl exclaimed. "Thank you!"

"Paul, you'll spoil her," Conti said.

"No more than you, Giancarlo. No more than you. Maria—you go and buy that dress and whatever else you need to go with it. And I'll see you at the wedding."

"I'm on my way, Uncle Paul," said Maria.

"You should have seen her smile, Paul," said Conti. "So beautiful it would break your heart."

"I have no need to see it," said Christopher softly. "I can imagine it clearly." Maria's girlish smile reminded Christopher of his own Maria, of what it had meant to love a girl so full of life. He drew a breath. "What I can't imagine, old friend, is that the girl I bounced on my knee is suddenly old enough to be marrying. Where have the years gone?"

"Where indeed, Paul?" said Conti. He chuckled. "But we still have plenty of good years ahead of us."

"Oh, yes," said Christopher.

"Still, Paul, it does not seem so long since we first joined forces. I was thinking last night of when we met, of our early years together. Like yesterday, no?"

"Just like yesterday," said Paul Christopher. Giancarlo Conti had been operating a small detective agency in Rome when Paul Christopher first encountered him. Maria had been a child, and at first Christopher had found an almost painful amusement in her name. His own Maria was dead only two years when Paul Christopher bought out Giancarlo Conti's agency and began the creation of Christopher Security International. Conti and he grew close quickly, and Conti became the first of Christopher's advisers. And a very close friend.

"It will be good to see you, Paul. Not just for the wedding. It's been too long since we had the opportunity to sit and talk."

"Not like the old days," said Christopher. He and Conti had passed long hours planning the strategy by which they'd made the company grow, establishing a firm European base of operations before expanding to the United States. Once the company made a name for itself in America, the pressures of rapid growth had kept Christopher and Conti too busy for more than occasional relaxation together. "The price of success," Christopher said.

"*Si*, Paul. But not too high a price for such great success."

"No," said Christopher. He glanced around his office. He'd called Conti intending to inform his oldest associate of the coin Miranda Glenn had sent, to warn Giancarlo that there was a traitor among the advisers. But Christopher found himself hesitating, and his hesitation burned like a betrayal itself. He'd never kept information from Conti before, and it was difficult to do so now. Perhaps after another conversation with Miranda he would feel more comfortable about letting Giancarlo know of the threat to the company. "I'm leaving for England shortly."

"Ah, to see Angus," said Conti with a laugh. "Tell

him I look forward to shooting skeet with him after the wedding. Tell him he owes me a rematch."

"I'll do that, Giancarlo," Christopher promised. "But keep your bets low. He's the best there is."

"Ah, Paul, but I've been practicing. Angus might have a few surprises in store."

"And I'll look forward to watching from the sidelines. I might even place a wager myself."

"Bet on me, old friend, and you cannot go wrong!"

"I know that, Giancarlo," said Christopher. "Always have."

"*Si*, Paul."

"And I'll see you at the wedding. Father of the bride."

Conti sighed heavily. "My daughter the contessa," he said. "Who would have thought."

"You've done well with her, Giancarlo," Christopher said. "You are a good father."

"I've tried, Paul. You know that."

"Of course I do. See you in a week or so."

"*Ciao*, Paul," said Conti, and the connection was broken.

Christopher turned his attention to a pair of memos directed to James Helmers, head of Christopher Security International's Washington operations. He was not pleased with Helmers's performance lately, and the memos made his displeasure clear. Of all his advisors, Helmers was the one with whom he felt least comfortable. But of all his advisors Helmers was also the one whose relationship with Christopher was the most distant. A seat on Christopher's inner circle had been among the demands Helmers made before selling his company to Christopher. Christopher had granted the request, but had never felt a full measure of trust for Helmers.

As he worked, Christopher was also aware of the connection between Helmers—Lee Lothrop's partner —and Raymond Glenn. *Suppose he and Miranda—* Christopher cut the thought short. He forced himself to concentrate upon the memos, and dispatched them before readying himself to fetch Miranda.

An hour later Thomas Gardner, Christopher's New York driver, guided his employer's custom Bentley to the curb in front of Miranda Glenn's building. "I'll get her, Thomas," Christopher said. "I won't be long." He left the car, approached Miranda's door, and pressed the buzzer. She did not keep him waiting.

Miranda was striking in the gentle morning light, Christopher realized when the door swung open. Even more striking than yesterday. Christopher made an effort to force such thoughts away. He would not grant her even her physical beauty; he would not concede even that. There were too many beautiful women who did not wish to bring down all that he had built. "Good morning," he said. "Is there anything I can help you with?" He made his voice open and friendly, hoping to get their journey off to a good start. *And to gain what conversational advantage I can,* he considered. *Let her think that my conciliation flows from fear of her knowledge. Perhaps she will lower her guard.* He moved forward, into the entryway of her townhouse.

"I'm packed and ready," Miranda said, smiling. "You didn't think I wouldn't be, did you? You didn't expect me to make us late for our plane, did you?" She did not wait for an answer as she fetched her Burberry from the coatrack. She folded the coat over her right arm for the ride to Kennedy. Miranda picked up her two bags. He moved to open the door, and their hips brushed.

"Excuse me," said Christopher.

Miranda shook her head. "Not at all." Their eyes met for a moment.

"Shall we go?" he asked. They descended to the sidewalk.

"You're already dressed for London," Miranda observed idly as the driver stowed her luggage along-side Christopher's in the Bentley's roomy trunk. Christopher wore a gray Harris tweed jacket, gray silk knit necktie against light blue shirt, dark flannel trousers.

"It's a nation I enjoy," Christopher said. He held the door open for Miranda. She entered the automobile and settled herself against its luxurious leather seats. Christopher took his place beside her. "You look as though you're dressed for big game," he said to her as the driver put the Bentley into gear and pulled away from the curb.

Miranda grinned easily. "Maybe I am," she said. Her khaki Calvin Klein safari jacket was belted tight at her waist, but flared open boldly at the line of her breasts. Beneath the jacket bulked a navy wool turtle-neck. The hem of her pleated skirt fell to mid-calf; dark Botticelli boots climbed higher. "My working clothes," she said with a chuckle.

"And I'm to be the prey you stalk?" asked Christopher. For her benefit, he gave up a chuckle of his own.

Miranda's smile did not fade, but she raised her shoulders. "The only prey I *ever* stalk, Mr. Christopher, is the truth," she said, grinning. Her words were warm despite their message.

Christopher nodded. "Of course it is," he said. "I'm familiar with your work, Miss Glenn."

"Is this a longstanding familiarity, Mr. Christopher?"

"Most of it I've only read or seen recently," he said. "But I'm an attentive reader, Miss Glenn."

Her eyebrows arched upward. "I'm sure you are. And I prefer *Ms.*"

"I'm sure you do," said Christopher, and they both smiled.

"Why not just call me Miranda?" She spread her hands. He had nothing to fear from her, the gesture indicated. "Most of the people I interview do."

Christopher paused for a moment, considering her request. "All right," he said. "Miranda." He said nothing more. *Let her ask.*

A moment later she did. "Well? May I call you Paul?"

"Please feel free," he said. Christopher thought to add a slight dig: "So long as you will be more formal in print."

"Oh, I will be," Miranda promised. "You may depend upon that."

A silence fell between them. Christopher broke it at last, asking, "Are we ready to begin . . . Miranda?" He forced himself to sound tentative.

Miranda smirked. "Paul, *I* got started the moment I opened the door this morning."

"I see." He said nothing more, staring at Miranda and waiting for her to speak.

"Do you see?" the journalist asked. "Do you really?" She leaned closer. "Had you been expecting something different?"

Christopher shrugged. His face remained impassive.

"Tell me," she invited. "What *had* you been expecting? How did you think I would handle this?"

I did not expect to be blackmailed with a coin, Christopher thought bitterly, *I did not expect to be betrayed.* He could not voice those sentiments to her. Not yet. Christopher took a moment to choose his words. "A more formal interview, perhaps. Questions from a prepared list, I suppose. I thought—"

"That it was still the nineteenth century, it sounds to me!" Miranda exclaimed. She gave a giggle. "Well, Paul, all I can say is that what you see is what you get." She hunched her shoulders.

At Kennedy he asked for her passport. "Thomas will check our bags through," he explained, guiding her through the British Airways terminal. The couple caused quite a stir as they passed through the airport. People pointed at them, nudged their companions and whispered recognition. Paul Christopher did not doubt that it was Miranda the public recognized. He maintained a much lower profile. *So far,* he thought. Christopher stood patiently to one side while Miranda signed an autograph. He was reimbursed for his patience when the cassette recorder that nestled in one of the large pockets of Miranda's jacket triggered the metal detector through which they passed. A bell cut through the terminal, and the attendant requested that Miranda empty her pockets. That a security device should stop her was too ironic. Christopher managed not to laugh out loud.

Despite Christopher's composure, Miranda sensed his amusement. She glared at him as she handed the guard her recorder and passed once more through the security gate. This time no alarm sounded. Miranda glanced at the manufacturer's colophon on the side of the security gate. "Not CSI, I see," she said as she retrieved her belongings.

"No," acknowledged Christopher. "But effective nonetheless, you must admit." Christopher allowed himself his own trace of smugness.

They walked side by side to the Concorde. Thomas

Gardner returned their passports, and Christopher and Miranda boarded the plane.

The aircraft was less than fully booked for the morning flight, allowing Christopher and Miranda to sequester themselves in relative privacy. They remained silent through the sleek aircraft's taxi and takeoff, accepting coffee from the stewardess after they were airborne. Christopher was curious. Time was being wasted.

Eventually Miranda spoke. "You thought it funny that I was stopped by security at Kennedy," she said. "Didn't you?"

"Not at all," Christopher said after a swallow of coffee. "I always find myself pleased when security procedures work as they should. Even when the equipment involved is not of my own design or manufacture."

She studied him for a moment, the barest hints of a frown line creasing her forehead. "You passed through the gate without difficulty," she observed.

"As do you on most of the flights you take, I would wager." He tipped his head toward her. "No?"

It took a moment for Miranda to nod, but she did at last. "Tell me something, though," she asked, brightening momentarily.

"Of course."

"Why is it, Paul, that I have trouble believing that you're not armed?"

"Because you approach me with your mind already made up," Christopher said. He sat straighter.

Her eyes flared. "Go on," she said.

"Because of my profession—and your distrust of it, Miranda—you *assume* that I am carrying weapons of some sort. Despite the fact that such an action is in flagrant violation of more laws than we could count." He raised his coffee cup toward his lips, but paused halfway. "But those . . . *preconceptions* were something I *did* expect from you. So, please. Go on with your questions." Christopher finished his coffee.

Miranda tossed her head. The golden Bulgari hoops on her ears gleamed. "You would admit, however, that you know ways to circumvent security systems." She patted the pocket where her recorder resided. "I get caught for a recorder—it's running, by the way—yet *you* could board an airplane armed to the teeth, and—"

"To what end? *Why* should I do such a thing? Or admit to you that I had?" Christopher asked. "The answers are self-evident. I design those systems. I manufacture them. I market them throughout the world. Obviously I could, as you say, circumvent them." He smiled innocuously at her. "Not easily, you understand. And it grows harder each year to bypass the systems we develop. Soon it will be impossible."

"Except for the people who design the systems," she insisted. "And that gives you a great deal of power, doesn't it?"

Christopher did not answer.

"And you still haven't answered me!" She made her request a demand. "Aren't you carrying weapons?"

Christopher sighed patiently. "Is that the story you seek? Something so lurid? 'Paul Christopher Captured Smuggling Guns'?" He shook his head and blinked. "Miranda," Christopher said in an almost paternal tone as though taking her gently to task.

A flush colored Miranda's cheeks. Christopher noticed that the rise of color was not unattractive. "Be careful," she said. "You'll make me angry."

"I have no wish to do that," said Christopher. "I've

read your books. I've seen what you can do when your . . . *anger* is roused."

"Remember it, then. And don't patronize me."

Christopher ignored her instructions and went on speaking. "Nor do I wish you to think in any way that I set myself or my company above the laws of any nation in which we serve." He showed her the palms of his strong hands. "I carry no weapons."

She stared hard at him for a long moment. "All right," she said slowly. "I'll accept your answer. For now." She relaxed a bit into the comfortable seat. Miranda nervously fluffed the lapels of the safari jacket she wore. For a moment her attention seemed to wander as she glanced distractedly around the Concorde's cabin. "Tell me one thing?" she said without returning her gaze to him. "How many weapons could *I* conceal beneath this outfit?"

"That would depend upon the purposes to which you wished to apply the weapons," Christopher said easily. "Are you planning on changing careers? Becoming an assassin or a terrorist? A . . . blackmailer, perhaps?"

Christopher watched Miranda fight the impulse to smile, the corners of her generous mouth turning up slightly despite her efforts. "No, Paul, I'll stick with journalism. Sorry to disappoint you." She pressed her fingers together and for a moment gave them her attention. "Really, I'm simply a little curious. Look around at the rest of the passengers. What are they carrying?"

Christopher kept his eyes on Miranda.

She continued to speak, slowly, abstractly, as though pursuing no particular point. "Isn't that what we're supposed to think? When we get on a plane. Or go into a bank. Or—anything? That those around us might be somehow dangerous to us."

Christopher had no reply to make. He watched as Miranda rubbed her palms together.

"Isn't that what you sell? That fear? Those thoughts about our fellow men and women? That's your product—the fear that they—or *I*—might be a murderer in disguise. That the person next to you might be a killer? That the briefcase he carries might hold a bomb?" Now she raised her eyes and looked at him. "That fear—isn't that your product?"

"Not at all," said Paul Christopher evenly and without hesitation. "Quite the opposite, in fact."

"The opposite?" she said with a soft laugh. "What do you mean?"

Christopher drew a deep, pensive breath. When he spoke, his words came slowly, despite their being a speech he'd made before to audiences official and otherwise. "We respond to the needs of a dangerous world. Christopher Security International provides its clients and their concerns with the confidence that the persons next to them, as you put it, are *not* likely to be dangerous. At least to them. There is, of course, no way to guarantee absolute safety. Any who think there is are mistaken." He fell silent as the stewardess approached and refilled his coffee cup. Miranda passed her own cup back to the stewardess. She reached to stretch past Christopher, and taut muscles rippled at the line of her jaw. *I must get her to underestimate me,* Christopher reminded himself. *While being careful never to underestimate her.* The more acquainted he became with Miranda, the more difficult that task became.

"CSI does more than that," Miranda said when the stewardess was gone. "You do much more." Again, her tone was vaguely taunting.

"Of course we do," Christopher said conversationally, deliberately overlooking her dare. "CSI helps ensure that employees are honest, that their backgrounds are meticulously investigated and that their representations of themselves check out completely." He smiled at Miranda, and wondered if she could suspect why he did so. Christopher thought of the long personnel form she'd filled out years ago. And of the discrepancies he'd discovered between her answers on the form and her real history.

"Go ahead," she said, prodding him. "Tell me more." Her eyes were cold and she did not shift her gaze from Christopher.

"Besides personnel and private investigations, CSI provides perimeter, facility, and data security services for many of the world's largest corporations, and for government agencies and services in eight nations." He laughed. "Of course, you're already familiar with our courier service."

"I must admit, it works well," Miranda said with a wry smile.

"CSI also manufactures products in a growing number of security-related fields, and we market those products worldwide. Christopher Security International has earned—"

Miranda cut him off with a toss of her head. Thick auburn curls flounced over her shoulders. "I've read your literature. I've studied the public information. What little of it there is. Please don't waste time recapitulating advertising copy. I'm asking you a different question. You answer it."

"My apologies," said Christopher, hoping the words did not sound as thick as they felt in his throat. He could not take his eyes from her. Color flourished in her cheeks at the intensity of his stare. *Is she always this easily rattled?* he wondered. *If so, my problem may be easier to handle than I'd thought.*

"Fine," said Miranda, accepting his apologies as

sincere. She drew herself up in her seat and straightened the folds of her skirt. She took three slowly measured breaths. "I think, Paul, that you have made your fortune promoting and then selling fear to your clients. Once you've persuaded them that they should be frightened of the world in which we must, after all, live, your firm moves in at generous—*more* than generous—retainers." She looked hard at him for a long moment, the smoldering in her eyes beginning to blaze. *"Security* needs," she said harshly.

When Miranda remained silent for a moment, Paul Christopher spoke up. "I'm sorry," he said. "But what *is* your question?"

Her eyes sparkled with anger. "You try to have it both ways," she said, accusing him. "And I must admit that to a certain extent you succeed. You make the claim that the world is dangerous beyond belief. You make that claim persuasively . . . constantly. And once your clients have accepted that . . . once they are frightened and terrified, you get to charge them dearly for protection." Miranda moved in the airplane seat to face him more fully. "And in turn, they grow frightened, ultimately, of the very services they pay you to provide." The speech had left her slightly breathless, but she added, "You wanted a question. All right. Paul Christopher—you promote fear, don't you? Isn't *fear* the real product you and Christopher Security International distribute?"

Christopher did not move. "No," he said with simple firmness. "Of course that's not true."

Christopher said no more, but took up his copy of the *Times* of London, unfolded it with a snap, and began to read. Surprisingly, Miranda left him to his newspaper, but she studied him for a long time. At last she turned her back to Christopher, rummaged in her briefcase and withdrew a large notebook. She

opened the notebook and after a moment's consideration began to write quickly. She did not look up.

The Concorde hurtled faster than sound toward
London. Paul Christopher applied only a fraction of
his attention to the newspaper he held before him.
Inside, he thought furiously, taking stock of his exchange with Miranda Glenn. He did not think her
silence would last long, and when she broke it he
intended to be prepared. *I must hold onto my upper
hand,* Christopher thought. He was convinced he had
the edge so far, and he was determined to maintain it.
*What I would not give, though, for the chance to set her
straight—and turn her over my knee!* The thought gave
rise to a flush of his own. He felt his face redden, and
he drew the newspaper closer.

The anger that Christopher would not allow loose
boiled inside him, but his composure was such that
Miranda could detect nothing of her companion's
turmoil. The newsprint faded into a blur before
Christopher and he tightened his grip against the
edges of the *Times. Who provided her with that coin?*
He had to know, and soon, just how much besides the
coin had been given to Miranda, and he set about
developing a plan for obtaining that information.

But as he did so he also recreated for himself the list
of individuals who knew of his passion for specially
marked ancient coins. Of the people from the same
list, only five of them knew the *full* story of the
coins . . . and the full story of the man who called
himself Paul Christopher.

High over the Atlantic he tried to envision one of
those people—*friends* more dear and counsel more
trusted than any he had allowed himself since his
youth—taking the coin and, knowing fully what she
would do with it, providing the coin to Miranda
Glenn.

He saw Angus Hill betraying him. And Giancarlo Conti, David Glise, Rahjit Desai, Barbara Webster, James Helmers.

Christopher couldn't believe it of any of them, and he sought to chase them from his thoughts. How could he consider Barbara Webster to be his betrayer? Even now, he thought, she worked hard for Christopher Security International, and for Paul Christopher. No one save Christopher himself faced a greater loss than Barbara Webster should any untimely publicity result from Miranda's possession of the coin.

Christopher closed his eyes for a moment and a vision of Barbara came into being in his thoughts. He saw her in all of her moods, from her steely control during tense negotiations, to her mouth slack with passion during the frequent, fevered lovemaking that had filled their short affair.

In none of her faces could he find any hint of treason, any indication that he should have anything other than absolute trust in her and her integrity. Not Barbara Webster, not her. Christopher turned his attention to the other names on his mental list, wondering as he did just how Barbara's evening with Esteban Rojas had turned out.

In Buenos Aires the clear morning was already warm and the city's streets were already crowded.

Barbara Webster had grown very fond of Buenos Aires over the past few weeks. She enjoyed its rapid pace, the sense of excitement and ambition that ran along its busy streets like an electric current. The sense of wealth and vision that flowed through its corridors of power. Under the tutelage of Esteban Rojas she had come to see that hopes still flourished in Buenos Aires, indeed throughout the nation, despite the precarious, debt-ridden state of the Argentine economy. Perhaps, she thought, deals like the one on which she and Esteban Rojas had worked so hard would help make those hopes more real. Certainly Esteban believed that.

And what of my hopes? she wondered in the brilliant Argentine morning. *Has he any idea of them?*

Barbara rode beside Esteban now, in the huge and comfortable rear seat of a vintage Cadillac, lovingly restored to mint condition. "A passion," Esteban had admitted when Barbara first saw the limousine and admired it. His broad grin threatened to consume his face as he showed off his car. "All of my life I have truly loved only four things," he said, and raised his fingers to count on as he explained. "My nation. My Banco: my *bank*." Esteban held up the third finger and his grin grew even wider. "And big, shiny American automobiles."

"And the fourth thing?" Barbara had prodded when the banker said nothing further.

His teeth had shone like torches as he grinned. "Women . . . in all their wonderful variety."

Then why did he spurn me last night? she wondered this Tuesday morning. On the opposite side of the seat Esteban Rojas concentrated upon a sheaf of flimsy papers he'd drawn from the overflowing briefcase that was his constant companion. The seeming disorder implied by the state of the banker's briefcase was, Barbara knew well by now, an illusion. Esteban Rojas was a man who attended every detail of his life and business, as well as being possessed of great vision. Beneath the surface chaos (his desk was more disordered than his briefcase, and the shelves in his office were a disaster) worked one of the most precise and cultivated minds she had ever encountered. As precise and attentive a mind as her own, she had long since realized with the honest self-appreciation that was one of her trademarks. She had a great deal in common with Esteban Rojas.

Which was one of the reasons she was so attracted to him. And one which made it all the more difficult to understand Esteban's rebuff of her the previous evening.

Unless he was not attracted to her, she thought. Unless he did not share the feelings that gathered in her stomach when she came close to him.

But, if Esteban Rojas did not share those feelings, why had he asked her out? Why had he shown her so happy and relaxed an evening? She thought of the warning Paul Christopher had given her during their telephone conversation, and of the joking response she'd offered. But she had not been joking—she had hoped to spend last night in Esteban's arms.

Monday night, Esteban had treated Barbara to a hectic, delightful evening in La Boca, Buenos Aires's dockside Italian district. Its streets were filled with restaurants and cafés, shadowed by abandoned traveling crane bridges that had been used, a century earlier, to pull barges along Riachuelo. La Boca offered an atmosphere far removed from the environment in which Barbara Webster customarily moved.

"The change will do you good," Esteban encouraged when she offered slight resistance to his invitation. "And I think you and I should get to know each other better. It would be a shame, Barbara, if our business concluded without our knowing each other as . . . friends as well as business associates. Say you'll come?"

Shortly after sundown Barbara, dressed casually in silk slacks and a matching blouse against the warm Argentine evening, followed Esteban through streets crowded with stalls and vendors, dining establishments and small shops. She found herself slowly responding to the relaxed, happy atmosphere of the waterfront. After weeks of restrained meetings and meals with American and Argentine bankers, attorneys, and government officials—meals at which official protocol was far more important than food or conversation—Barbara at first was nearly overwhelmed by the zesty exuberance of La Boca. She felt as though she was being carried along by the frenzied mingling of laughter, of chatter in Italian and English as well as Spanish, by the happy music that echoed, it seemed, from every door. Esteban held her hand warmly and guided her easily through the crowds. She had never felt more safe than she did at that moment. Perhaps he was right. Perhaps this was just the change of pace she needed.

She needed more than that. Her thoughts strayed uncontrollably to what might follow this evening. Of a slow undressing of each other, a slower exploration of the newness of his body, and his exploration of hers. Of the building need that could be satisfied by coming together more fully than is possible in any other way. They rounded a corner, and Esteban gave her hand a squeeze. Barbara's heart jumped.

She was between affairs. Barbara had enjoyed the attention—and twice, the love—of several men. But at an early age she had found that she was capable of fending for herself in the world. She discovered as well that the ambition that was as natural to her as breathing, served to distance or even disappoint most of the men she met. So she had raised her guard against that sort of male response. She selected her lovers carefully. None of the liaisons lasted more than a few months, and in recent years the partings had all been amicable and friendly. She never ventured more on a romantic entanglement than she was willing to lose. And for a long time, the size of her emotional wager had shrunk with the beginning of each affair. Perhaps Esteban would be different.

They paused occasionally to peer through restaurant windows, but each time Esteban beckoned her onward. Barbara was hungry, and the Italian fare on several of the tables they'd spied had looked delicious. But she followed him and at last he took more than a moment at a window. Esteban turned to face her. "Here," he said happily. "I think you will find this most entertaining. Not to say delicious." He put his hand gently at the small of her back and ushered her into the cramped confines of the restaurant.

The air was filled with irresistible aromas and thick with the music of a guitar-and-piano duo. The tables were covered with simple checked cloths, and huddled close together. It was virtually impossible to move without bumping into someone, but the atmosphere was that of a large, happy family. Esteban found a table near the rear of the restaurant.

Barbara and the banker found themselves sitting on the same side of the table, nearest the wall. They adjusted their seats even closer together as the center of the restaurant was noisily cleared to make room for a spur-of-the-moment dance. The waiter proved more than efficient and in seconds had brought Esteban and Barbara tall glasses of rich dark wine. Other diners began to clap and sing along with the spirited music, and the first dancers moved to the cleared space. Esteban raised his glass in a toast that Barbara could barely hear over the restaurant's din. He brought his face close to hers, and Barbara fought the impulse to close her eyes and press her mouth against his.

"To business relationships," Esteban toasted, and moved closer, until his glass clinked against hers. Before Barbara could respond, the banker flashed his grin, drank deeply, and raised his voice with the rest.

Plates and platters of pasta, shellfish, and beef, crusty bread and wonderful vegetables in thick sauces passed before them. Barbara sampled everything, and all but gorged herself on some of the dishes. Each bite offered its own surprises and delights.

After they had eaten their enormous meal, Esteban exclaimed, "Now it is time to dance!" He bounded to his feet.

"Oh, no—" Barbara was not given time to complete her protests. Esteban took her hands and pulled her deftly to her feet, guiding her easily through the crowd of tables, chairs, and diners until they reached the improvised dance floor. A conga line began to grow, curling like a snake back upon itself. They joined the line and Esteban turned to look over his shoulder at Barbara.

Her smile radiated her happiness. The heaviness that had accompanied the meal left her. She felt light as she swayed in rhythm with the line of dancers. And with Esteban. Impulsively she gave his waist a squeeze. The impulse deepened and she pressed her cheek against his strong back.

Within an hour their arms were around each other as they joined in song after song. Barbara sang as energetically as she could, taking in great deep drafts of air. She put all of her enthusiasm into singing songs whose lyrics were Italian and whose words she did not know. No one seemed to mind.

Their revelry lasted well past midnight, and the restaurant was still crowded when they at last took their leave. Reluctantly they bade good evening to new friends. Esteban and Barbara faced a morning meeting with yet another minister. They walked back to Esteban's car.

Barbara walked close to him. He held his right arm loosely around her shoulders, and as they walked he hummed softly one of the songs they had sung that evening. Barbara accompanied him, her voice softer still, a feeling of warmth spreading through her each time he gave her shoulders a squeeze, or allowed his thumb to graze her neck. She wanted to taste him, to fill herself with him.

She held Esteban's hand as they walked through the lobby at the Elevage. How many times had she met him in the hotel's lobby since the negotiations for the acquisition began? And how often lately had she wished that he would come with her, as he was now, to her suite?

But at the door Esteban faced her squarely and said, "Barbara. It is my hope that you enjoyed yourself this evening half as much as I did. You are a wonderful companion, and I thank you."

"Won't you come in?" she asked, surprised.

The banker gave a slight shake of his head. "I must review my papers. Attend to details. You tempt me. But I must decline." He bowed to brush his lips against the fingers of her right hand. Barbara reached up with that hand to brush her fingers against Esteban's ruddy cheek.

And then he was gone, walking slowly along the corridor, not looking back. Barbara could hear him begin to hum one last chorus of the song she had almost thought of as *theirs*.

Barbara went into her suite, closing the door behind her, and with it hoping to seal off the feelings that hurt more than she cared to admit.

But those feelings would not go away. The car pulled to a smooth halt before the government office building where they would have to face the minister and answer his foolish environmental charges. Esteban stacked his papers neatly, then spoiled the orderliness by shoving them into his briefcase.

He smiled at Barbara. "It keeps my . . . perspective," he explained, patting the swollen sides of the leather case. They climbed from the Cadillac. "It reminds me that it is possible to drown in paperwork. I refuse to. Business is more than just *paper*. Although *government* may not be," he added with a wink and a wave at the government building. They started up the steps. "There are hearts and minds at work. Paper is simply the leavings. The rest—the *real* work of those hearts and minds—why, that is what runs the world."

Barbara smiled at him across the discreet distance she kept between them. There was no need for Esteban to know he had hurt her. "You sound like Paul Christopher," she said.

Esteban nodded vigorously. "I take that as a high compliment, Barbara. He and I are of the same breed, I think. As are you. You know the esteem I hold him in." He paused for a moment. "And you know the feelings I have for you."

"Do I?" Barbara asked. They entered the building.

Esteban did not answer her. They called for an elevator, and as they waited, Barbara glanced at her gold Cartier watch. She silently made the adjustment for time zones, placing in her mind the present position of Paul Christopher. The calculation took barely a second for her. Christopher was aboard Concorde, approaching London.

Miranda Glenn watched him sleep. She had held her peace for fifteen minutes after he opened his newspaper, but when she looked up to provoke conversation once more, she discovered that he had fallen asleep. She was tempted to wake him, but the relaxation that spread across his face intrigued her. She could sort her thoughts as she watched him.

The muscles that lined his strong jaw were at ease. His nostrils flared as he breathed in a steady, slow rhythm. Close up, Miranda could see strands of gray threading the jet hair at Christopher's temples. He was, she had to admit, an extremely handsome man.

And an annoying one! She had to admit that she hadn't done as well during their first long conversation as she'd hoped. Often her provocative, hard-hitting style worked well, generating quotable material almost faster than she could take it down. It had failed with Paul Christopher, though, and she took advantage of his slumber to seek a new one. The Byzantine coin had pierced the protective walls Christopher kept around himself in the form of his company. Now she had to break down the armor that was more personal, that shielded whatever vulnerabilities he himself possessed.

There may not be many of them, she realized as she stared at Christopher. *He even sleeps with determination!* Miranda thought, grinning in spite of herself.

Why am I letting him sleep? she wondered. It was to her benefit to keep Christopher awake. If he were so enervated that he could not keep his eyes open—well, Miranda had never minded taking advantage of exhaustion to prize stories from subjects preoccupied with the need for sleep. Usually, as their self-control wavered, they tended to say things—quotable things —that they might not under other circumstances.

Christopher gave a slight start, every muscle in his face growing suddenly tense. His gray eyes came open immediately, and he sat up straight. He looked refreshed although he'd slept far less than an hour.

"Good morning again," Miranda said to him.

Christopher turned to face her, and in the cabin light of the Concorde there was something in his face that sent a surge of unexpected curiosity through

Miranda. This was not curiosity about his past, or his attitudes, or any of the things that she intended to expose. It was a curiosity about *him,* rather than his *story.* She did not know where the feelings came from. And she shuddered to think that her professionalism could so quickly develop so serious a crack.

Just as unexpectedly, the sensation vanished, leaving her a bit disconcerted, more than a bit concerned. She had something to guard against now, and something told her that she would have to work very hard to keep that guard up.

"Hello, Miranda," said Christopher, the soft accent making her name into a wonderful word that she might never have heard before.

"Did . . . did you have a nice rest?" she asked inanely, wondering furiously where her organization had gone.

"I feel quite renewed," said Christopher. He glanced at the Corum gold-piece watch on his left wrist. "We should be approaching Heathrow shortly," he said. "Do you have your hotel reservations in order?"

Miranda nodded. She could not keep her eyes from his, and his eyes seemed deep enough at that moment to dive into and lose herself. "Claridge's," she managed to say.

"Of course. I'll be happy to drop you there. And we'll adjourn for the evening, shall we?"

His question was phrased politely, but there was something in its tone that brought back the hard edge that Miranda feared was lost. Tiny hairs on the back of her neck stood up, and she wondered if he had been asleep at all. What trick or sorcery had Christopher employed to fluster her so?

Miranda felt more herself by the moment. She felt anger beginning to build inside her. She had no idea how he had manipulated her for those few moments, but she knew that she detested the feeling. "I'd thought we could work tonight," she said in an icy voice.

"No. I have a business engagement," Christopher replied casually. "We can resume our work in the morning." He looked toward the front of the aircraft.

The stewardess made an announcement that Miranda did not catch, but she noticed Christopher straightening the back of his seat and fastening his seat belt. She did the same. Keeping her own eyes forward, she spoke softly. "We have a lot of work ahead of us."

"Do we?"

The question irritated her. "Or maybe not," she snapped. "I can take the coin and tell its story now. If that is what you would prefer."

"I have no preferences," said Christopher. He could not tell if she was bluffing. "Other than to have my privacy disrupted as little as possible."

"That's nothing new," said Miranda. The inexplicable momentary closeness she had felt to him was completely gone. Now she wanted only to grind him down. "You've always been private. Your whole life has been your industry, your company, and nothing more."

"You think so?" said Christopher calmly.

His calm struck her like a slap. "I *know* it is so!" she said sharply. "It's one of the things that most frightens me about the power you wield."

"I see," said Christopher.

Miranda was at a loss for words. She could not stand the look in Christopher's eyes. It frightened her. But she could not look away. He had a charm and a charisma that could be devastating, as she was coming to realize. "And you say you carry no weapons," Miranda muttered almost inaudibly.

Christopher smiled. "I carry no weapons," he agreed. "But I never go anywhere unarmed."

Concorde dipped at subsonic speeds toward Heathrow. Miranda was eager to reach ground, to secure herself amid the plushness of her suite at Claridge's. She had a great deal to think about.

5

PAUL CHRISTOPHER DEPOSITED Miranda Glenn in the
competent care of the desk manager at Claridge's.
Returning to his Rolls-Royce he instructed Tony
Earnhardt, his London driver, to take him directly to
the tower that housed the London offices of Christopher Security International. It was half-past seven
when they departed Claridge's, moving into a gray
and mist-shrouded night. London's lights sparkled
like multicolored gems in the fog.

Christopher took the mobile telephone from its
compartment and dialed Rita Sue Cedric's Belgravia
townhouse. Randolph, her butler, informed Christopher that Lady Cedric was occupied late at her office.
Christopher called CedriChem.

"This is Paul Christopher for Lady Cedric," he said
to the switchboard operator.

"One moment, sir," said the operator.

As he waited for Rita Sue to come on the line,
Christopher watched London pass by. The city never
disappointed him, and its mood always seemed to suit
his own. Tonight was no exception. The flight with
Miranda Glenn had left Christopher bleak, her very
presence a reminder that he had been betrayed.

London gave Christopher an evening to match his

bleakness. As the night deepened, so did the chill drizzle, raindrops beading on the Rolls-Royce Silver Cloud's windows. Through the rain he could see the familiar skyline. Others might decry the skyscrapers that now dominated London. Not Paul Christopher. Their lights broke the horizon, their height a clear indication of the bold new order of which he was a part. His own office suite occupied a good bit of the sixtieth floor of one of the city's newest and tallest structures.

A voice came from the telephone. "Paul?"

"Hello, Rita Sue," he said, shifting his attention back to the phone. "I've just gotten in."

"We rolled out the weather for you, Paul, didn't we?" Rita Sue asked, her Texas accent no less thick for all the years she'd spent in England. "Good, cold rain. Thick, wet fog. What more could a man like you ask for?"

"One thing more," said Christopher.

"Name it."

"A bit more time before we dine this evening. There are a few things I must attend to at my office."

"There are indeed," said Rita Sue, a sudden coldness in her voice baffling Christopher.

"I beg your pardon?" he said.

"Explain it to you later," Rita Sue said.

"You don't mind the delay?"

"Oh, you'll make it up to me," she said with a sly chuckle. "And I've got a passel of papers spread across my own desk at the moment. What say we get together around—ten? And let's just meet at the restaurant. You take care of reservations."

"Any preferences?"

"Oh, I think I could work up an appetite for Le Gavroche," she said.

Christopher laughed. "And you know that I have just enough clout left to get us a table there on such short notice," he said dryly.

"You just use up that clout and don't you worry about it," said Rita Sue. "I expect it'll be worth it to you."

"Your wish is my command, Lady Cedric," Christopher said.

She gave an unexpected whoop of laughter. "Call me *Lady* again, *boy,* and I'll have your head! I was wrestling steers when your mama was still powdering your behind!" Actually, Rita Sue Cedric was forty-two, although she looked easily a decade younger. Only five years older than Paul Christopher, Rita Sue Cedric nevertheless enjoyed playing the role of wizened Texas frontier woman. It was a role she played with panache, and it had brought endless delight to Sir John Cedric, not to mention the world's press. She was a character—and characters made good copy.

As well as attractive targets, Christopher could not help thinking. Sir John had been killed by a terrorist bomb five years earlier. Operatives of Christopher Security International had identified and located the assassins and, when the British government failed to deal justice, their fates had been attended to by CSI, at Paul Christopher's personal order. Close before, Christopher and Rita Sue had grown more intimate since she was widowed. "Le Gavroche at ten," he said now.

"I'll be looking forward to it," Rita Sue said. "So will you, Paul."

"I already am," said Christopher, but the connection had been broken.

Angus Hill greeted Christopher in CSI's sixtieth-floor lobby. The broad-shouldered Scot stepped forward as the elevator doors opened, a big hand out-stretched. Handsome dark handlebars curled upward before his ruddy cheeks, punctuating his thick red beard. Christopher noticed that beneath that beard Angus Hill's mouth was drawn downward into a grim frown. "Welcome back to England, Paul," Hill said as he shook his employer's hand. His grip was strong as steel. "It's good to have you here."

"Even better to be back, Angus," Christopher said. The two stepped away from the elevator, Christopher nodding at the uniformed guard who stood watch over the otherwise deserted reception area. It was nearly eight o'clock. Christopher and Hill walked through empty corridors to Christopher's office.

Christopher left his briefcase on a shelf of his étagère, and hung his jacket in the dressing room. The office suite all but duplicated his quarters in New York. Christopher seated himself behind his massive desk and waited for Angus Hill's report.

The Scot got straight to business. "We have a situation, Paul," he said, his heavy burr thickening his words. "And it's with Alphasome."

Rita Sue's ambiguous warning became clearer to Christopher. Of all the many projects and products that CedriChem currently had in development, Alphasome was by far the most exciting. Its potential profits were literally inestimable, and the revolution it would effect upon the world's treatment of disease would be overwhelming. The development process had devoured most of the past decade and millions of pounds in funding. The expectation was that Alphasome would be introduced within the coming year. Christopher Security International was responsible for all of CedriChem's security systems, and since the project's inception both Paul Christopher and

Angus Hill had been deeply involved in establishing the procedures to guard CedriChem's proprietary interest in Alphasome.

"How bad is the breach?" Christopher asked, completely alert.

"We're not completely certain there *is* a breach, Paul. Only an anomaly." Angus Hill's forehead wrinkled, but he did not pause as he recounted the facts. "Nigel Hemmings is a day overdue returning from a vacation. Do you recall Hemmings?"

"Of course," Christopher said, nodding. He did not know the scientist well, but he had met him on a few occasions and was familiar with his reputation as one of the most skilled and brilliant biological engineers in the world. Dr. Nigel Hemmings's abilities had played a tremendous part in the synthesis of Alphasome, a synthetic hormone that could be used to program the body's immune system against a wide range of infection and disease—including cancer. "What's happened to him?" Christopher asked.

"He took off last Monday for a week tramping through the Lake District. Left London by train, disembarked in Penrith, spent the night there and set out the next morning. He was dressed and equipped for a long tramp, even in winter weather." He frowned. "But he has not been seen or heard from since."

"Giving him up to a week's lead if he has gone over to a competitor."

"Aye. But we cannot overlook the possibility that something's simply happened to him. His profile—"

Christopher brought his computer terminal to life, quickly calling up the pertinent data on Dr. Nigel Hemmings. The scientist was forty-seven, single, never married, no living relatives, a physical-fitness fanatic who also placed a high value on privacy.

Hemmings had consistently used his vacation periods and weekends to get off in wild country by himself. Often he returned from such solitary jaunts refreshed, filled with new ideas and approaches to problems in the laboratory. On several occasions, as a precautionary measure, CSI had maintained surveillance of Hemmings throughout his vacations, and each time the scientist had followed his plans to the letter. He simply camped and hiked. No clandestine meetings with competitors. No attempts to smuggle priceless information from the country.

Christopher spoke up. "Of course, his timing could not be better than right now. It would be worth the wait to take the full process, rather than the pieces that have been accumulating over the years. Alphasome's essentially ready, isn't it?"

"Aye. But we cannot overlook the possibility that something's simply happened to him, delaying his return."

"Without any notification?"

"That's wild country he's walked into, Paul."

"But well-traveled."

"Less so at this time of year. And he has a reputation for loyalty to CedriChem. He's turned down every offer that's ever come his way. Teacher, lecturer, research scientist for other firms. He's stayed with CedriChem."

Christopher nodded. "His profile is that of a scientist. But also that of someone likely to be open to manipulation. He's a loner." He glanced back at the screen. "And he's never been late before. He's always returned precisely when scheduled."

"Aye."

"Any reason to suspect politics?" Christopher asked. "To suspect that he may have defected?" *Your firm promotes paranoia*—Miranda Glenn's accusations came back to Paul Christopher for an instant, stinging him. He brushed the words aside. "Alphasome would be valuable behind the Iron Curtain, too."

Angus Hill shook his head. "No. Nor really much reason to suspect he sold out. He was well-compensated for his time at CedriChem, and Lady Cedric is personally fond of him. He'll have a piece of Alphasome when it reaches the market. It will make him a very rich man." He brought his huge hands together with a clap. "The only trouble is, we can't find him!"

"You've taken care of the details of the investigation?" Christopher asked.

"Of course. We've put every resource on this. We're covering the territory he'd intended to hike through. We've got the competition under surveillance. We're watching his house, we've got a monitor on his phone lines, and we're screening his bank balance." For a moment the Scot nearly smiled. "We're breaking a few laws, but we're going to find the bugger!"

"Of course you will, Angus," Christopher said. "I leave it in your hands. You know I'm dining with Lady Cedric at ten?"

The chief of CSI's United Kingdom operations nodded. "I've been in touch with her throughout the day. She's concerned, but more about Hemmings's welfare than the possibility he's gone over. She refuses to take that possibility seriously."

"She's a good judge of character," Paul Christopher observed.

"Aye. But, lad, her butt's not on the line if we've let Hemmings walk away with Alphasome. Think how that'll make CSI look."

Christopher managed a smile. "Angus, I expect

Lady Cedric stands to lose a good deal more than we if Alphasome is gone."

"Ah, sure, you're right, Paul. But the timing is—"

Christopher shook his head, cutting off the conversation. "Let's find Hemmings. The rest . . ." He sighed. "Things will fall as they may, and all we can do is endeavor to ride out any storms." He leaned forward and placed his palms flat on the cool surface of his desk. "What else need we deal with?"

The two men attended quickly to the remaining items on Angus Hill's agenda. At the moment Alphasome was the only area of concern within Hill's purview.

"You'll be pleased to know that things proceed very well on the Argentine front," Christopher said as they reached the end of their review. He was pleased by the size of the smile Angus gave him. "You'll be there before the month is out, I feel certain."

"Oh, I'm looking forward to it, Paul. I've got plans for *WISP* and *ASP* that I think you'll like."

"No doubt, Angus," said Christopher, rising from his seat. "I've no doubts at all."

"First, though, we'll find Nigel Hemmings. You can count on that!" Grim determination showed on Angus Hill's face.

"Nor do I doubt that, Angus," Christopher said. "You've never let me down."

"And I won't this time, Paul." The Scot's eyes were clear and his determination shone in them as well.

Christopher stared at him for a moment. He drew a breath and sought the proper phrasing for what he must ask. "By the way, Angus?"

"Yes?"

"How . . . has the market for old coins been of late?" he asked quickly, feeling a deep pain as he spoke.

"I've seen nothing, Paul." He looked curious. "You've not asked in some time. Is everything—"

"Everything is fine, Angus," said Christopher, ushering the Scot to the office door. "We'll talk in the morning." He remembered Miranda. "And I'll have someone with me for a tour. Perhaps we'll spend the afternoon at the armory."

"A prospect?" Angus Hill asked.

Christopher laughed. "Hardly. A young woman," he said, and laughed again as Angus's face brightened. But he did not reveal Miranda's name. "You'll meet her in the morning. I think you'll be surprised."

"I'll see you then, Paul," Angus Hill said, and left Paul Christopher alone in the sprawling office.

Christopher set about preparing himself for his dinner engagement with Rita Sue Cedric. He was displeased with the way he'd attempted to trap Angus into some sort of revelation about the solidus. Not only because he'd made the inquiry in so clumsy a fashion—*Miranda's presence has made me an amateur!* he thought angrily—but also because of his great affection and respect for Angus Hill. Hill was one of the five people who held the secret of Christopher's history; one of that official inner circle which knew the truth. And Hill would soon be taking charge of Argentine operations; more specifically, he would manage the marketing of *WISP* and *ASP*. Those reins would be his within a very few weeks. There could be no percentage in Angus Hill selling out Paul Christopher's trust, confidence, and friendship.

But, still, Christopher could not help thinking, Miranda was in England not long ago. Christopher was aware from the dossier assembled on her that the London office of CSI was one that Miranda had visited in recent months. But there was no evidence that she'd met with Angus Hill, and he could not conceive of Angus betraying him. It was unthinkable. *No!*

Christopher cleared his mind during a quick, hot shower. Outside it was dark, although, thanks to Concorde, only a few hours had passed for Christopher since he met Miranda at her townhouse. He suffered no jet lag, but was aware that its effects— coupled with the full night of concentration and Rebecca Devereaux that preceded it—would not escape him long.

Soon he must face Rita Sue Cedric. On most occasions, that was a quite pleasant prospect: she was a strikingly beautiful woman, possessed of a sensuous way of moving and a voluptuous figure. *And I have enjoyed the richness of that figure unclothed on more than one evening,* he thought as the spray beat against his skin and its steam roiled upward around him. *We've given each other some pleasure since Sir John was murdered by those bastards,* he thought. And then brightened: *Not that our relationship has ever grown deep enough to affect our business dealings. Nor will it ever. Rita Sue remains as much a tigress in the conference room as she does in bed. But in the privacy of her heart I'm sure she still mourns for John.*

Paul Christopher and Rita Sue Cedric had established their sound business relationship long before they became lovers. Their lovemaking was infrequent; more often they saw each other in boardrooms, or spoke by telephone. Those exchanges were professional beyond question and always would be. What they shared on a few evenings was something else. Something personal, but not love. Rita Sue Troxler from Tyler, Texas, had been a devoted wife to Sir John Cedric. Christopher knew her well, and felt certain that the depth of that devotion would last until the end of her life. She'd never again share too much of herself with another man. Who could take Sir John's place? He'd been dynamic, a giant of the pharmaceutical industry who'd held onto his company through assaults from the British government as well as attempts by hungry conglomerates to snatch CedriChem for their own. Sir John was also a first-rate scientist, and a man of no little social conscience. He'd met Rita Sue Troxler, in fact, while on an expedition deep into the heart of a Brazilian jungle, in search of rare plants whose medicinal properties might be synthesized. Rita Sue was a coltish botanist, just graduated from Stanford. Her Texas twang gave a shading to Latin taxonomic terms that captivated Sir John from the moment he met her. They were married by expedition's end, and were inseparable thereafter. Rita Sue had brought the middle-aged businessman profound delight, and had proved an exceptionally gifted student as Sir John instructed her in the intricacies of the modern pharmaceutical industry. She'd learned well. CedriChem had not faltered in its growth and success under Lady Cedric's guidance. She'd achieved triumphs of her own, and was held in high esteem by her industry. Rita Sue put in long hours in her office, guiding CedriChem's growth and managing its performance. Her own feelings reached out as had her husband's: she maintained those social projects and concerns that had been dear to him, as well as initiating good works of her own. Despite her presence as a fixture on the social scene, there was nothing trivial about Rita Sue Cedric or her handling of the wealth and power delivered into her hands by assassins.

Christopher toweled himself vigorously. He knew

that in the middle of the night, with him, Rita Sue had wept more than once for the decades of love stolen from her by a terrorist bomb. *She never blamed CSI for the bombing. Nor was it our province: Sir John always refused bodyguards.* Two CSI plainclothes guards had hovered unobtrusively close to Rita Sue Cedric in public since her husband's death. *At least I can protect her,* Christopher thought. He missed Sir John himself, and despite the reassurances Rita Sue had offered from the beginning, Paul Christopher continued to hold himself in some ways responsible for the bombing. *We should have kept watch anyway, despite John's objections. Then he would be here with her. She could fill her arms with him rather than with poor, temporary substitutes such as myself.* He knew the names of a few of her other lovers. The list was not long. Those few men that Rita Sue welcomed into her bed were men who could accept what she had to offer, and give back what they were able. They were no threat to her, nor was she to them. Love was not an element in their relationships. Respect, affection, trust, were.

As well as a healthy sense of fun and an enjoyment of the most strenuous of intimacies, reflected Paul Christopher with a grin. He tore open a Turnbull & Asser wrapper and withdrew the crisp new white shirt that rested within. As Christopher dressed he replayed his conversation with Angus Hill, readying himself for his meeting with Rita Sue. She had made no mention of the Hemmings situation during their brief telephone conversation, and Christopher did not know quite what to make of that. Obviously, Rita Sue would be concerned, and if things went badly there was the possibility that CSI's relationship with CedriChem would be damaged. *If Hemmings has stolen*

Alphasome, then Rita Sue would be foolish not to order an immediate review of all security systems. And perhaps order our dismissal as well. Alphasome was too vital for her to behave otherwise, Christopher knew. *It is as much a feather for CedriChem as is Argentina for CSI.*

He knotted his silk necktie and pulled on the jacket of the navy Saint Laurent suit he'd selected for the evening. Christopher left his office and, once settled in the Rolls, instructed Tony Earnhardt to take him to Le Gavroche, where he would meet Rita Sue Cedric.

In her suite at Claridge's, Miranda Glenn seethed. The great hotel, as always, offered its variety of comforts, and a delectably laden room-service tray lay almost untouched on the table to the left of the armchair in which Miranda sat. She was not particularly hungry, although she had not eaten since a small breakfast in New York. Occasionally she selected some morsel from the tray and nibbled it absentmindedly along with sips from the dark Amstel beer she'd ordered to accompany her meal. Otherwise she simply sat and seethed, furious at herself for failing to draw Christopher more fully into confrontation. The flight had provided her with more than three hours' uninterrupted access to him, yet now she felt Christopher was a greater enigma than ever.

And that's no one's fault but my own, she thought. *I must shift my tactics.*

To that end she had chosen to remain in Claridge's on this, her first night in London. Christopher would not be specific about how long they would be here; two days at least, he had told her, and her reservation of the suite was open-ended. Before leaving her at the hotel, Christopher had agreed to Miranda Glenn's request that they share breakfast. He invited her to come to his office at nine, and offered to send the car for her. "I can find my own way there," asserted Miranda. "After all, I've been there before," she had added with a sweet smile to which Christopher merely nodded.

So here she sat in Claridge's, feeling more than a little disappointed in herself, dressed only in a sheer pink teddy despite the winter rain that pressed against the hotel windows. Claridge's rooms, Miranda had discovered years ago, were islands of warmth regardless of the conditions outside. Miranda curled her long, bare legs beneath her. She placed a bit of good Stilton cheese on a wheat cracker, and chewed slowly, paying no attention to the rich taste. For a time after she'd unpacked, Miranda had thought about dressing warmly against the chill evening and stepping out to one of the watering holes her journalistic colleagues were likely to be frequenting on an evening like this. It was always good to see old friends, and there was the added excitement of possibly bumping into an old lover—or encountering a new one. The prospect was tempting and Miranda pondered the temptation through a long, languid soak in the suite's overlarge bathtub. The thick bubbles and heavy clouds of steam brought her to the edge of drowsiness, and she almost dozed in the tub, a languorous, sensual sleepiness suffusing her. She brushed hot water against herself, and rubbed slowly her most sensitive spots with a soft washcloth. She stretched her legs, tautening their long muscles. She stroked herself, flowing with the water, drawing more hot water every few moments to extend the mood. She thought fleetingly of James Howard Dennis, of the other men who in recent months had shared her bed. Her breathing quickened.

She thought of Paul Christopher. He came into her thoughts uninvited and unstoppable, in her imagination taking her by the shoulders, pressing his lips roughly to her breasts, and then pressing himself into her more fully than any man ever had. She felt herself on the verge of frenzy. A low cry escaped her lips.

The noise brought Miranda back to reality and she sat up straight. She shook her head. The steam-filled air had made her giddy, she thought. She'd lost control of her thoughts. She could still see Paul Christopher, so darkly handsome, looming above her, sending pulsating waves of pleasure through her. Miranda shook her head more forcefully to clear it of her maddening fantasies. After a moment she climbed from the tub, hoping to leave behind her all memories of passion—especially those connected with Paul Christopher. Miranda rubbed herself harshly with a thick towel. She felt angry and, in ways that she did not wish to consider, achingly unfulfilled.

She should have awakened him on the plane this afternoon, she told herself for perhaps the tenth time since landing at Heathrow. That had been a mistake. Not just letting Christopher sleep, but watching him as he slept. Something had happened to her as she spied upon him, something had clouded her objectivity. She did not trust herself to go out into the evening—there was too much chance that she would seek to quench the fire that still smoldered deep within her. Professional instincts took over: better to force that fire to blaze in Christopher's direction. Better to stay in the hotel room and work.

Nude, Miranda brushed her hair energetically. Her skin glowed pink from the hot bathwater and the harsh toweling. She pulled on the teddy and caught a glimpse of herself in the mirror. She was some tidy package for a man to unwrap, she immodestly admitted, and for a moment a wave of desire coursed through her again. She drained a glass of dark Amstel and settled into the armchair. But just sitting still did no good. Too many stray thoughts wandered through her mind. At last she rose and pulled on a long silk kimono over the teddy. She pushed the chair to face the table, and moved the tray aside to make room for her work. From the Gucci briefcase she pulled three bulging file folders of information and placed them on the table. Miranda took a couple of grapes from a crowded stem and popped them into her mouth. Their liquid sweetness reminded her how hungry she was, and she seated herself at the table once more, alternately eating from the tray and scribbling ideas into the large notebook where she outlined her new line of attack. She worked for hours, the energy that might have been expended in passion now transformed into hard concentration. Miranda would show Paul Christopher tomorrow. He would know that he was under pressure from the best in the business. And she would direct that pressure until she located the weakest points in his psyche.

Miranda turned to a fresh page in the notebook. At the top of the page she used her large, looping handwriting to form a single question. *Who is Paul Christopher?* Miranda Glenn did not intend to leave the question unanswered for long.

Under Tony Earnhardt's expert touch, the Rolls-Royce slid easily through the Chelsea traffic, delivering Paul Christopher to Le Gavroche at precisely ten o'clock. Christopher dismissed his driver. "No need for you to wait, Tony," he said. "And I won't need you again until late tomorrow morning. We'll be running out to the armory for the afternoon. Let's say around . . . eleven. And ask Elena to pack a lunch for two. There will be a young woman with me."

"Very good, sir," said Tony Earnhardt. Christopher left the Rolls-Royce and entered the restaurant.

Le Gavroche's unassuming facade belied the comforts within. The maître d'hôtel stepped forward to greet him, his black tie severely formal and his manner matching his wardrobe. Christopher followed the maître d' to the table. "Lady Cedric has not yet arrived, sir," he was told. Christopher ordered a Bombay gin martini with an olive. He sat back to wait for Rita Sue. As he waited, his eyes roved among the paintings on the wall, from Chagall to Buffet. His drink arrived and he took a sip, pronouncing it perfect. Christopher waited.

Rita Sue Cedric made her entrance at ten minutes past the hour. A blond whirlwind in a deeply cut Balenciaga dress, there was no mistaking her arrival. Her voice overrode the restaurant's restrained and conversational tones when she spotted Christopher. "There he is!" she said, pushing past the surprised maître d'. "There's my man! You stand up, Paul, and give Rita Sue a good hug!"

Christopher, who sometimes considered Rita Sue Cedric as undeterrable as a force of nature, did as she requested, folding his arms around her and drawing her close. "I always offer you as an example to my clients who wish to know how to behave subtly in public," he said softly to her, pressing his face against her cheek. "So as not to draw attention to themselves."

Rita Sue stepped back. "Paul," she said, her accent making his name seem several syllables long, "you know that's a damned lie!" She gave him a bawdy wink. "Now, let's sit down and eat." The maître d' held her chair. After they were seated he poured glasses of Malvern water for them: among the purest waters available, it was intended to clear the palate. Rita Sue smiled up at the maître d'. "Bourbon on the rocks," she said. "A double. And would you be a love and get me some real water to chase it with? This other doesn't have much taste." She smiled dazzlingly at him.

"Of course, Lady Cedric," said the maître d', stepping aside to whisper instructions to a white-jacketed waiter.

Rita Sue placed her hands flat on the damask tablecloth and stared at Paul Christopher. Around them the other diners, the distraction for the moment grown silent, returned to their food and their own conversations. "How are you, Paul?" she asked warmly. Her tone was entirely different from that with which she'd made her entrance.

Christopher nodded. "I'm fine. I've been in conference with Angus."

Rita Sue nodded. She remained silent as her drink —with a glass of water doubtless just drawn from the kitchen tap—was served. She took a deep sip and placed the squat glass back on the tablecloth. "I've known Hemmings—" she began before Christopher cut her off with a wave of his hand.

"Rita Sue, please," he said evenly, his voice audible only to her. "Not here. It's too public—the tables too close together. We'll talk after dinner." He drew himself up straight. "Or skip dinner and get straight to business."

Rita Sue shook her head, her blond hair bouncing at the gesture. "You're not going to get out of feedin' me, Paul," she said with a calculated crudeness.

"Waiter, pass me that menu that hasn't got any prices on it."

After that, the meal passed pleasantly, and Rita Sue restrained her exuberance. For their first course they both chose *papillote de saumon fumé Claudine*— slivers of smoked salmon encircling smoked haddock and truffle. They ate the salmon slowly, savoring the texture and taste of each bite. Rita Sue spoke quietly, telling Christopher of a new project she was starting.

"It's back to botany for me, Paul," she explained. "I'm having a complex of greenhouses built in Crouch End," she said, her glee apparent.

"People shouldn't build glass houses in that section of town," Christopher said glumly. They finished their first course and awaited the arrival of the next.

Rita Sue was untroubled by Christopher's lack of enthusiasm. "That's why I'm having them built *there*," she explained. "Because it *is* an . . . undesirable section." She raised her head almost as though to look down her nose at him. A trio of large emeralds made dark pools against her creamy neck. The cleft between her full breasts formed a dark shadow beneath the gems. "There are children in Crouch End, too," she went on. "Children who see nothing but grimness. I'm going to show them flowers."

"More loose stones and bricks there than flowers," observed Christopher as the waiter served their *caneton Gavroche*, following the restaurant's custom of serving the duckling's breast first, pink and deliciously undercooked, followed barely twenty minutes later by the roasted legs, dark, crisp, and succulent. Lightly buttered vegetables and large rolls complemented the duckling. "They'll break every window you put up," Christopher said.

Rita Sue merely laughed. "Not at the fees I pay you for the security you provide." Her smile may have been a taunt. "Or try your best to provide."

"To what end are you doing this, Rita Sue?" he asked as he took a small bite of duckling.

"Crouch End, I told you."

"Rita Sue."

She nodded, and pressed her napkin to her lips. "To give something back in a place where it's needed. And don't worry. This is one social program that's going to flower in the form of profits. That's a promise."

"It's a promise Sir John made, too."

Her gaze grew wistful for just a moment. "Maybe that's why I enjoy making it so much," she said. She raised her wineglass and sipped the 1959 Haut-Brion. Once with Christopher at Le Gavroche she'd ordered a beer, and he swore throughout the evening that he'd seen a tear in the maître d's eye at the request.

"Send me the specifics, Rita Sue, and Angus and I will take a look at them."

"I knew you'd see it my way," she said slyly. "I already bought the property." The waiter lifted her plate out of the way and Rita Sue laced her fingers beneath her chin and stared dreamily into space. "It's not going to be another Royal Botanic Gardens or anything," she said. "But it'll be close!" Her eyes sparkled with laughter.

They declined dessert. It was well past eleven when Christopher and Rita Sue left their table. Christopher was startled to find that Rita Sue's bodyguards were not waiting for her before the restaurant. "Where are my men?" he asked, his breath frosting in the night air.

"Why, darlin'," she said, coming close to him and drawing her long mink tight around her. "I gave them the evening off. I figure I'm as safe as I'd possibly want to be. With you." She leaned near and softly kissed the lobe of his left ear. "Even though we got business to discuss."

"You let your car go, too?"

"Sure did," she said, smiling.

Christopher hailed a taxi and they climbed into its spacious passenger area. Christopher gave the driver Rita Sue's Belgravia address. She sat close to him as the taxi began to move. "Can we talk now?" Rita Sue asked.

"Let's wait, Rita Sue," Christopher said. The meal had made him sleepy, and he drew deep breaths, attempting to reinvigorate himself.

Rita Sue curled against him, saying, "It's good to have you back in England, Paul. Even without this other . . . problem." A sigh escaped her, and turned into a yawn. "To which Angus is overreacting. I've known Nigel—"

Christopher silenced her by placing his mouth on hers, and their kiss grew ardent. Rita Sue's long-nailed fingers traced patterns on the back of Paul Christopher's neck that made him shiver. He pressed his body into hers, surprised at the depth of feeling—of need—that came over him. They were still entwined when the cab arrived at Rita Sue's door.

Randolph took their wraps. He had laid out coffee and brandy in the drawing room. A fire crackled in the grate. "Rebecca Devereaux sends her regards," Christopher said, reminded for a moment of the young heiress. Then Rita Sue came near him and he was reminded of nothing save her.

"Let's talk business," she said after pouring coffee for them.

"All right," said Christopher.

"Nigel's a day overdue," she went on. "Two days, come tomorrow morning, provided he doesn't turn up. Not like him. Not like him at all."

Christopher carried his brandy to the fireplace and stood there in its radiant warmth. "We have . . . surveillance in place," he said slowly. "If he has gone over, we shall know as soon as anybody. Of course his trail is more than a week old, making it—"

Rita Sue Cedric's eyes blazed with anger. "You get to that in just a minute!" she said sharply. "You just take your time, Paul, and march yourself through what you people are doing in case—in the *likely* case that Nigel Hemmings hasn't gone *over!*"

"Of course," said Christopher. He sipped brandy, taking its heat deep inside him where he felt a chill. "Everything that can be done is being done, Rita Sue. I assure you of that. We're working quietly with local authorities in the area where Dr. Hemmings disappeared. We've got searchers of our own covering the area. And we're searching through the night, using certain . . . special equipment that we have at our disposal."

"I see," said Rita Sue.

"More than that, I cannot tell you. That's all we have thus far. But we should prepare, I think, a plan for containing any damage, should our worst fears be realized."

"*Your* worst fears," corrected Rita Sue fiercely. "I have fears of my own, but they're about Nigel's safety. I *know* that man. Nothing you can say will convince me that he's sold out to my competitors. My people do not betray me."

Nor do mine, thought Christopher. Bitterness flooded through him, and the exhaustion of the past few days began to catch up. He seated himself on a sofa facing Rita Sue. "We must simply wait, then," he said.

She finished her coffee. "I know you and Angus, and your people, are doing everything you can, Paul." She drew breath. "And I know that you have no choice but to consider every alternative. That's how you earn your fees. That's how CSI has grown. But you can't know Nigel Hemmings the way John did and I do. He's a good man. If he's hurt, I want him found."

"We'll find him, Rita Sue," Paul Christopher promised.

"I know you will, Paul," she said with genuine warmth. Her eyes grew misty. "He will be found, Paul. He was with John before I was. He's part of CedriChem's team. He can't be gone. Find him."

Christopher repeated his promise, and moved to sit beside her, offering his arm for comfort. It was past midnight, he realized. *And I must face Miranda in nine hours*. He felt a trifle guilty at that thought. CedriChem, being a British company, had escaped much of the journalist's ire in *Prescription: Death*. But not all of it. Miranda Glenn had some carefully crafted words for CedriChem and the woman who ran the company. He wondered sleepily what Rita Sue would say if she knew.

Her fingers stroked his cheeks and he looked deeply into her eyes. "You're tired, Paul," Rita Sue said solicitously.

"And I have an early morning tomorrow, I fear," he answered her. "I must go shortly."

"Where?" She leaned to him for a quick kiss. "Back to your office, where you'll work all night?"

"You know me too well, Rita Sue."

"Paul?"

"Yes."

"Sleep here. Please. With me." She pressed her face against his neck, her breath warm. Christopher thought he felt as well the warmth of tears against his skin. He stroked her bare shoulders, running his fingers up and down her spine. "We'll find him, Rita Sue. Everything will work out."

"It's just that I don't like to lose people," she said, kissing the pulse of his neck, pressing the tip of her tongue against its steady beat. "Stay with me. Sleep here."

"Yes," he said.

She extinguished the lights in the drawing room and they walked up the long staircase hand in hand to the second floor. Rita Sue's bedroom spread its thickly carpeted floors over much of that second story, the huge canopied bed seeming small at the far end of the room. It offered, Christopher had thought more than once, what seemed nearly an acre of firm support and silk sheets full of pleasure.

Tonight, that pleasure came slowly, with exquisite gentleness. Christopher removed his jacket and unknotted his necktie. Rita Sue unfastened the buttons of his shirt, then stripped the shirt from his broad shoulders. She took a step back and reached behind her neck to unclasp the emeralds. She placed the gems carelessly on a night table and faced Christopher once more. She shrugged the straps of her dress from her shoulders, and turned so Christopher could unzip the back. His hands brushed across the small of her back before she stepped away from him, turning to give him a view of her as she removed the dress.

The fullness of her figure took Christopher's breath as it always did. The heavy weight of her breasts rode proudly and without hint of sag above her flat abdomen. She stepped out of silk culottes to display firm thighs and the rich nest that lay between them. Christopher removed his trousers, socks, and shorts as Rita Sue watched. Then she came to him and they stood for a moment beside the enormous bed. He filled his arms with her, and she pushed hard against him, the tips of her breasts boring against him. Christopher's hands roved downward to cup the curve of her buttocks and draw her even closer. Rita Sue raised her face to his and their mouths opened, their tongues met. Christopher's arousal heightened and his hips moved insistently against Rita Sue.

They found their way onto the bed without interrupting their embrace. Christopher kissed Rita Sue's neck, ran his tongue over her breasts, flicking the nipples with the tip of his tongue. They grew even more firm beneath his ministrations, and soft, sweet gasps escaped Rita Sue's lips. Christopher used his tongue to trace a torturously slow route down and across her stomach, its muscles rippling as if of their own volition as his kiss passed. He nibbled the cream of her thighs, and with his tongue tickled the underside of her left knee before he moved his attention to her right leg and began to trace his way once more upward. Rita Sue cried out as his tongue and lips found their ultimate goal and began their exploration of it. Her hips rose and fell, tidelike, in the sea's own stately rhythm until the storms within her body broke loose and Rita Sue thrashed beneath him wildly, her churning hips unable to guide her free of his mouth's demands. She called his name over and over. The biggest wave of all broke and she cried out explosively, and said, "John," just once.

Paul Christopher waited until the storm's force was spent before taking his warming mouth from her flesh.

He moved up and kissed her mouth. Rita Sue breathed heavily, clutching at him, guiding him into her. The evening's first storm soon proved to be its mildest, and together they rode out three more, but were asleep within an hour and slept soundly in each other's arms until dawn.

6

BECAUSE OF HIS appointment with Miranda Glenn, Paul Christopher had to refuse Rita Sue Cedric's offer of an enormous Texas-style ranch breakfast. "Put some meat on those ribs of yours," she teased as they lay close together in her bed. The sun rose over London, fingers of light poking through gaps in the heavy drapes. Christopher felt more refreshed than he had in days. He stroked his hand down Rita Sue's spine. She moved against him. Her fingers found him. "Last night was lovely," she said. "Very sweet. But I always like to start the day off with some *exercise*." Paul Christopher joined her.

By eight he was in his office with Angus Hill. There had been no further news of Nigel Hemmings. Search and investigation proceeded, both suffering from the coldness of Hemmings's tracks. Nor was the weather in the Lake District cooperative: heavy rain was falling there. The ground was sodden. Christopher asked Angus to call Lady Cedric and bring her up-to-date.

"Of course, Paul," said the Scot.

Christopher glanced at the gold Corum coin timepiece he wore. Miranda, he knew well by now, was punctual to a fault. He had three-quarters of an hour before she arrived. That was more than enough time.

Christopher was ready for her; he was looking forward to the meeting, in fact. After a hot shower and a shave, a fresh suit and shirt, Christopher felt invigorated. *More likely it was last night that recharged me,* he thought wryly. He'd rarely slept better, or been awakened more delightfully.

He turned his attention to Angus Hill and gave a few instructions. "I'd like you to greet our guest this morning and bring her back to me," Christopher said. "And clear your schedule. I want you to join us for breakfast. I think it's important that you be there."

"All right," said Angus, his puzzlement obvious.

"She's Miranda Glenn," said Christopher flatly, and did not blink as he watched Angus Hill's face. What was he searching for?

"Well, then," said Angus in a voice that might have been a grumble. "I see." It was clear that he did not.

Christopher stared at him for a long moment. "If you wish to ask me whether or not I know what I'm doing, Angus, please go ahead," he said with a ghost of a grim smile.

"No, Paul." Angus Hill stood up and made his spine straight, as though at attention. With his big fingers he gave the lapels of his tweed jacket a sharp tug, then lowered his arms to his side like a military man presenting himself for review. "Lad," he said in a serious voice. "I'll not question your judgment—you've never given me cause before. We've known each other far too long and worked far too hard for me to question you now. I just want you to be aware that if there's anything I can help with—"

"I know, Angus," said Christopher softly. "And I do appreciate it." He drew a breath before speaking more vigorously. "Now, call Lady Cedric and bring her up-to-date. Have someone monitor the Hemmings thing, and tell them to call you away from the table if anything comes in while we're meeting." He smiled more pleasantly. "No need for her to find out everything."

"Aye." The concern had not completely left his face.

"It's all right, Angus," Christopher said. "I can handle Miranda."

The Scot cocked his head oddly toward his employer and good friend. His brow wrinkled. *"Miranda,* is it?" he said with a bold wink. "Lad, all of a sudden I'm not worried at all."

Hill's broad smile coaxed one from Christopher. "Neither am I, Angus. We deal with what we must."

"Aye. We always have."

"Then I'll leave the Hemmings matter in your hands," Christopher said.

"Don't worry about a thing. We'll find him." Angus Hill left Paul Christopher's office.

Christopher turned to his terminal. There was good news from Buenos Aires. Barbara and Esteban had successfully dealt with the government's environmental concerns. Neither *WISP* nor *ASP* was particularly energy- or materials-intensive in manufacture, and a good portion of the thirty million dollars that Christopher would pump into new facilities for Christopher Defensive Systems—formerly Sistema Defensa— would guarantee a manufacturing installation that cooperated with its environment rather than violating it. The plant would be a showpiece, and its products would alter their world. Barbara Webster's electronic memorandum reported that with the governmental hurdle overcome, things would begin to move even more rapidly than they had in recent weeks. The transfer of funds and title could come quickly, perhaps within the next forty-eight hours, barring complications. Everything was now in place.

Including Miranda Glenn, Christopher thought. *And excluding Nigel Hemmings. Either one could, should they choose, bring all this down.* He looked out over London.

Despite the pressures of Miranda Glenn and the disappearance of Nigel Hemmings, Christopher felt absolutely calm. He sensed a renewed strength in his muscles, a gathering of the powers and the forces that he possessed, that he had mastered in himself over the years and focused upon the problems he faced. Paul Christopher did not believe in insurmountable obstacles, whether they assumed the shape of an escape under darkness and gunfire from a homeland grown hostile and oppressive, or the carving of a corporation that commanded the world's respect. Certainly he could handle Miranda Glenn.

At nine o'clock his communications console chimed. "Miranda Glenn has arrived in the lobby," his secretary, Victoria MacDonald, told Christopher.

"Angus will meet her and escort her back. We'll be having breakfast in the dining room at nine-thirty. James has everything prepared?"

"Yes, sir."

"Good," said Christopher. He sat back to await her arrival. His desk was clear, his terminal blank. Christopher breathed deeply.

Moments later the doors to his office opened and Miranda Glenn entered, followed closely by Angus Hill. Christopher rose to greet them and as he did so he was taken once more by Miranda's loveliness. Something about her went far beyond her striking features, the soft frame of rust-colored hair providing a perfect setting for a face that could have been sculpted. But those were merely physical details, he realized. There was more to it. Something burned within her, a fierce flame whose heat colored her cheeks and gave luster to her eyes. Christopher understood the source of the flame, and its fuel: idealism was what burned within Miranda. Her belief in the truth shone in her face; her desire to uncover it shone behind her eyes. *I possessed that flame once myself,* Christopher thought as he extended his hand to her. *But that was in another country, and the boy I was then has been dead for many years.*

"Good morning, Paul," Miranda said. Her tone was gloating as she said his name, and Christopher had no trouble forgetting that she was a beautiful woman with a strong spark of idealism. Miranda became once more a beautiful annoyance with whom he must deal. He showed her to the comfortable conference chairs clustered around a low glass-and-chrome table.

"Before we begin, Miranda," he said, "I'd like to explain to Angus exactly why you are here and what it is you wish to accomplish."

"Oh, I think I would be very interested to hear your version of that, Paul," she said sweetly.

Christopher took a moment to stare at her, but he was smiling as he did so. "Miranda is an . . . *investigative* reporter, Angus. A profession at least half of which you and I should appreciate."

"Aye," said Angus Hill softly, muttering something under his breath.

"And it would appear that she has elected to investigate *us.*" Christopher looked directly at her as he spoke, his gaze unwavering. "Am I correct so far, *Miranda?*"

She tipped her head to him. Her thick hair tumbled over her shoulders, the yellow sweater and green Hermès scarf complementing it perfectly. "I could not have said it better myself, Paul."

"Good. I wish to be . . . accurate."

"No more than I," she said.

Paul Christopher nodded. "I decided to cooperate with Miranda's curiosity about CSI. And so, Angus, here we are. I'm sure she has a list of questions for us?" he said, directing his comment to Miranda.

She did not answer him immediately, but opened her Gucci briefcase and withdrew a slim manila folder. She opened the folder and placed it on her lap. Methodically she extracted her pen from her pocketbook and took a moment to study the contents of the folder. "Yes," she said at last. "I have some . . . *prepared* questions." Her glance at Christopher became a glare.

"Then, please go ahead."

Miranda tapped her pen against the edge of the folder. "Christopher Security International is responsible for protecting all manner of valuables," she said in a brisk and professional manner. "From industrial secrets to radioactive wastes. And yet, little is known about you, personally, Mr. Christopher. How healthy do you think that is?"

He made her wait a moment for his answer. "It's quite healthy for my sense of privacy," he said.

"I'm sure it is," said Miranda with a sniff. "But I'm not willing to trade parries and banter with you today."

Christopher spread his hands wide. "Nor am I interested in talking about myself. My company is another matter."

Miranda met his gaze for a long moment, then looked away as though lost in thought. "All right," she said unexpectedly, and turned over the top page in her folder. "Isn't it true that Christopher Security International will provide, at a fee, an armed guard for anyone who can pay the price?"

Christopher shook his head. "You know better than

that. We select our clients carefully. At every level. Our uniformed guards no differently from our plain-clothes operatives or our security analysts. We insist on establishing legitimate need for armed-guard service." He turned to Angus Hill. "Anything to add, Angus?"

"Aye," said Angus, his burr becoming a bit more pronounced. "We take as much care in establishing our relationship with a client as we do in providing our service. That's why we have the reputation we do. That's why you'll find far fewer complaints against Christopher Security personnel than is the industry norm. And—"

"But you *will* admit there are complaints against the company, Mr. Hill?" she interrupted.

"Call me Angus," he said. "Aye, there are complaints. Show me a business—even yours—without them. But before you cut me off, I was going to say that if you'll check the record, you'll find that CSI has responded to each of those complaints. And when we have gone to court, the settlements have been in our favor ninety-eight percent of the time."

Miranda was unpersuaded. "Which only proves that you can hire the best legal talents to win your victories on technicalities," she said forcefully.

Angus shook his head. "Perhaps you should be investigating the judicial system," he offered.

Christopher listened to them debate the question for a few moments. He gave it only half of his attention. He was thinking ahead, planning the tour he intended to provide Miranda, considering the questions he would ask her as they made their way through his British operations. There were things he wanted to know quickly. And at the same time he hoped to keep her sufficiently interested in him so that the Argentine deal would clear without difficulty. As long as she remained at his side and not at her typewriter, he felt safe. As for the Nigel Hemmings situation, there was little that he could do, and he tried to put the matter out of mind. Looking at Angus, he realized again how fortunate he was to number such people among his closest employees. And winced a bit inwardly at the thought that he could have doubted the large Scot. *But it was one of them,* he thought with a momentary sadness. Then he turned back to the conversation.

At nine-thirty the trio adjourned to the executive dining room. The long dark table was set with Wedgwood china and Reed & Barton silver. Angus outmaneuvered Christopher to hold Miranda's chair as the journalist sat down. Christopher looked at him, and thought he detected a twinkle in Angus's eye. *She fascinates as readily as she annoys,* Christopher thought as he took his own seat at the head of the table. Angus sat facing her, and was no sooner in his chair than he resumed the point he'd been making.

"Miranda, you can't indict an entire company—an entire industry!—on the basis of hearsay. On the basis of unresolved charges, or personal opinion." He sighed heavily. "I'm with you—the world *would* be a better place did it not need professionals such as ourselves. I'd give up my own job in an instant could I be assured that the world would enjoy peace and tranquillity." He fluffed his beard and gave a short laugh. "But, lass, that's not the way the world works. I live in London. Bombs go off here with frightening regularity. Christopher Security International provides a valuable service. Perhaps an *invaluable* one during these times."

The long speech seemed to leave Angus depleted. He sat back in his chair and watched Miranda, waiting for her response.

Miranda gestured at the dining room's dark paneling, its elegant fixtures and trappings. "The *value* of your services is made obvious by the quarters you maintain," she said. Her accusation was directed as much at Paul Christopher as at Angus Hill. "You cannot deny that you are well-compensated for your work."

Christopher smiled pleasantly. "And what was the size of your most recent advance?" he asked. "How much will the story of Paul Christopher command on today's market?"

Miranda did not answer. Breakfast was being served, and for a few moments the three busied themselves with the exquisitely prepared thin slivers of smoked salmon, the perfectly poached eggs, cups of rich Jamaican Blue Mountain coffee. Christopher caught Angus Hill's eye and was not in the least surprised to find the gleeful twinkle still there. Angus appreciated spirited argument, even when—or perhaps especially when, Christopher thought—it was directed against him.

Breakfast done, their conversation became more sedate, moving away from the abstract arguments that had occupied them during the meal, and on to the more concrete details of Christopher's London operation. They went on a tour of the six floors that comprised the nerve center of CSI's United Kingdom business. Mostly, Christopher explained as the tour proceeded, it was dull stuff: management, accounting, data processing. He introduced Miranda to several employees; others seemed to recognize her on their own. Thankfully, no one sought her autograph. Angus might be charmed by the journalist—however much he disagreed with the views she held and espoused—but Christopher doubted if the Scot could tolerate a fan among his people.

Shortly before eleven they returned to Christopher's office suite. They seated themselves briefly in the conference area. Throughout the tour, Miranda had said little, except for her occasional comments and questions about minor details regarding the corporation. Now, though, she once more took the offensive. "Quite impressive, gentlemen," she said to them. Morning sunlight streamed through the long office window, striking the fiery highlights of her hair. "All the properly dressed people with their neat columns of figures. Not a gun in sight."

"You're not going to be satisfied until you see a weapon, are you?" Christopher asked. He mused for a moment, smiling. "Were I an investigative reporter, perhaps I would feel the same way. It's not an unreasonable wish."

"What do you mean?" Miranda leaned forward a bit, holding her notebook at an angle before her, like a shield.

"I mean to comply with your desires," said Christopher, and turned to address Angus. "We'll be going to the armory this afternoon. Ask Edmund to have everything in readiness, if you would."

"Certainly."

Christopher looked thoughtful. "We have an *ASP* there, don't we?"

Deep furrows crossed Angus's broad brow. "Aye," he said in a voice almost a whisper.

"Tell Edmund I'd like to demonstrate it this afternoon."

For a moment it appeared the Scot would object to Christopher's request. He began to rise out of his seat, then checked himself and settled slowly back down. Angus drew two deep breaths before speaking. "It'll be ready for you," he said.

Miranda watched the exchange carefully, her fascination and curiosity obvious. "What is . . . *ASP?*" she asked.

Christopher faced her. "I believe I'll let it speak for itself," he said. And added mysteriously, "It can, you know."

"What *are* you talking about?"

"Ask *ASP*, Miranda," said Christopher. He rose smoothly to his feet, casting his long shadow across her and bringing an end to the conversation. Angus stood up, and after a moment's hesitation so did Miranda. Christopher stared at her for a moment, as though expecting her to speak. When she did not, he extended his hand to Angus. "Thanks for joining us this morning," he said as they shook hands. "And lending your *perspective* to our discussion."

Miranda shook her head, as though clearing it. "Of . . . of course," she said. She stood straighter, and offered Angus her own hand. "It's been a pleasure," she said. Her composure and charm returned. "If not the education you might have wished."

Angus took her hand and bent slightly at the waist, an inch's worth of bow in her direction. "I hope we can resume our debate at some time," he said warmly.

"Of course," she said.

Christopher touched her arm slightly, and she turned her head toward him. "We have about an hour's drive ahead of us," he said. "Perhaps you'd care to freshen up before we depart?"

"Yes," said Miranda.

Christopher stepped to his desk and summoned Victoria MacDonald. She appeared promptly. "Miss Glenn and I will be leaving for the armory. Please show her where she may refresh herself for the ride."

Victoria nodded crisply. "Of course," she said, and stepped toward the doors, pausing a moment for

Miranda to join her. The journalist looked back once, sharply, but did not speak. Escorted by Christopher's secretary, Miranda left the room and the doors closed behind her.

Angus did not speak. Christopher waited him out, the two of them staring at each other until, after a long moment, wide grins broke over their faces. Angus shook his head and wagged a finger at Paul Christopher. "Of course, there can always be a first time for you to be wrong."

"I'm not wrong," said Christopher. "Considering the circumstances."

"Which are?" Angus inquired.

But Christopher shook his head. "I can't, Angus. This one's for my shoulders only," he said with a curt laugh.

"Can I ask how bad it is?"

"Potentially?" Christopher shrugged. "A worst-case scenario would be about as you would imagine, no doubt. Bad."

"On the inside of the company?" Angus asked.

"At the top," Christopher said. "Be alert," he warned in a grim voice, and said no more.

"Are you sure it's wise to keep it all on yourself?"

"I have no choice," he said. "Except for me and thee. And I must admit that I gave no quarter at first to thee," he said in dark paraphrase of an old joke. He looked solemnly at the Scot.

"I appreciate your honesty, Paul."

"Not half so much as *I* appreciate *yours,* just now," Christopher said. He raised his right hand and brought it down hard. "Enough. But be wary."

"I will." Angus Hill took a step toward the door, then stopped and glanced back at Christopher. "But are you sure you want to show her *ASP?*" he asked.

Christopher smiled. "She will see what she wants to see," he said. "So why not show her? She need not know that soon it will be our product."

Hill smiled back, and raised a thumb of good luck before he left the room.

"We'll lunch at the armory," Paul Christopher said to Miranda Glenn as they arranged themselves in the back seat of the Silver Cloud. Tony Earnhardt steered the car smoothly into the late-morning London traffic. The day was surprisingly clear, and the previous night's rain had left the air fresh. By the time they'd left the city, the sky gave promise of becoming glorious by afternoon.

"An armory," Miranda said casually as they sped along.

"A testing ground, really," Christopher said. "It's perhaps a bit stodgy of us to call it an armory." He smiled at her. "But the word has a pleasant resonance."

"To *you*, perhaps," she said.

"As you will," said Christopher. He relaxed into the leather seat.

Miranda was silent for a moment. When she spoke again, it was to change the subject. "Your accent is curious," she said. "I can't quite place it."

"Let me know if you do," said Christopher. "Or perhaps you'll have a lucky guess."

For a moment Miranda seemed about to make a guess, but she fell silent once more. Christopher watched her as she formulated her next approach. "What sort of things do you test there?" she asked finally.

"Security systems, mostly," Christopher began. He then launched into an explanation of some of the systems he and the research-and-development team he'd assembled had created over the years. He spoke quickly, but carefully, even as he led the conversation deeper and deeper into technical information. Miranda responded with interest of her own, somewhat to Christopher's surprise. But she did not attempt to steer their dialogue back to the more sensitive or provocative areas she'd previously sought to explore. Rather, she addressed him on technical points, revealing the depth of study she'd applied to Christopher's field. He was impressed. *But she's an impressive woman,* he thought. *With a rare combination of abilities. It will be a challenge to keep those talents focused on me these next few days, rather than on what storms may break around me.*

He watched her as she spoke, at the flash in her eyes as she asked a question, the curve of her lips in concentration as she considered his responses. *Of course,* thought Paul Christopher, *that challenge is also a rather pleasant prospect.*

The Rolls-Royce moved through the gently rolling English countryside in the direction of the estate which served as the armory for Christopher Security International.

7

"Christopher Defensive Systems," said Esteban Rojas to Barbara Webster. "So soon to become a reality."

"Are you placing any precise wagers on the exact time?" Barbara asked. She sat a discreet distance from him in the conference area of his office in the Banco Nacional.

Esteban shrugged. "Twenty-four hours," he said. "Thirty-six. By this point I am willing simply to watch the forces come together. I am a patient man with such a show to observe." He shrugged diffidently. "Whenever it happens will be fine with me." A smile illuminated his dark features. "After all, we have the best seats in the house."

Barbara gazed at him, considering his words. "I don't know that I've ever thought of you as . . . *patient*, Esteban," she said after a moment. "Your energy, your personality—they radiate such a sense of ambition, of drive."

"No more than you do, Barbara," the banker said. "And you know what I mean by patience. The wait and the way we handle ourselves during it. Whatever its duration, whatever the final results. The final days before something such as this comes together can be quite pleasurable. The final hours." His voice was the only sound in the office. "The final moments. And then—it is done." He pressed his hands together in a clasp. "And if it is done well, it lasts," he said. "No?"

Barbara nodded her agreement. "Yes. It will last."

Esteban took an expansive breath. "So the wait becomes a part of the process itself, and one must derive from it what one can." He sipped from a cup of strong, dark coffee. "You share my attitude, Barbara?"

"Yes, Esteban," she said.

"Good." He revealed to her another smile. "I enjoy it when we are in . . . agreement." Esteban stared piercingly at her for a moment, then looked away.

"And so we wait," said Barbara softly. She looked beyond him at the clear summer sky that arced high over Buenos Aires. Soon she would return to New York winter. "And then the wait will be over," she said. "And then . . ." Her voice trailed off. *Is it the excitement of the acquisition that I will miss the most? Barbara wondered with sudden intensity. Or the players involved?*

"And once it is over we move on to the next challenge," Esteban Rojas said, offering his own finish to the sentence she'd begun. "For this is the kind of person I am, Barbara. And the kind of person *you* are. It is demanded of us. We demand it of ourselves."

"I've been curious before," Barbara admitted. "Why do we push so hard? What is it we want?"

"Our natures," Esteban said matter-of-factly. "We are driven. To exalt in the heights at which we climb. To be fulfilled by the levels at which we work." He sighed. "You know as well as I that without challenges our lives would be empty." He looked at her with dark eyes and repeated the word. *"Empty."*

"Yes," said Barbara, hearing herself as though by echo, her voice distant and small. "I know."

She and Esteban had shared dinner the preceding evening. Last night though, she recalled, had been a far more formal occasion than the hours of revelry they'd passed in La Boca. No songs were sung last night, no endearments exchanged. But the time spent at table at La Veda with Esteban proved no less disturbing to Barbara than had their dancing. In the restaurant's soft light she thought she saw something smoldering in Esteban's eyes. And she thought more than once she saw the embers there blaze up as he gazed at her. She had never seen eyes so intense, and their intensity was completely directed toward her. Barbara had been bathed in Esteban's gaze all evening. By the time the meal was finished she found herself in a wonderfully drowsy, almost dreamlike state, waiting only to draw Esteban close to her, to envelop him and reveal herself to his overpowering eyes.

Barbara had thought no words were necessary, and she stood close to Esteban in the elevator at her hotel. He looked at her and, as the doors slid open, had taken her hand. Before she could speak, he bowed to her at the door of her room, and his grip tightened briefly. He touched his lips to her hand and departed.

Now in his office, Esteban continued to discuss the final hours before the multinational transaction was completed. "There are, of course, ways to fill the hours of waiting. The pleasant distraction of—"

"Yes?" Barbara heard herself prompt him almost eagerly. Inwardly she winced. She did not enjoy the sense of foolishness that came over her around

Esteban lately. It was a loss of control. She was determined to keep her emotions from him. They'd worked together too long and over too difficult and complex a deal for her to behave like a schoolgirl. "What sort of distractions, Esteban?" she said with a calculated coolness that sounded almost convincing.

"Details," replied Esteban with a cool grin of his own. He hefted his briefcase. "There are still some things that must be . . . *satisfied* before all can be consummated."

Barbara kept herself from stiffening, and ignored the thoughts that his choice of word inspired. There was business to attend to. She lifted her own briefcase, nor were its own sides flat any longer. "One habit I've picked up from you, Esteban," she said, and forced a smile. "One thing you've given me."

"But not the only thing, I hope," Esteban said. He spread papers before him. "How can you be concerned about the wait when there is so much for us to do? Together."

She stared at him, but did not speak.

Esteban smiled at her. Did he have any idea what emotions churned within her? He gave no evidence. He tapped his pen against the papers. "Shall we busy ourselves with details, Barbara, you and I? And while we move papers, the money will move, and all will be well. None of the things that could happen will happen." He reached over and gave her hand a gentle pat. "Only the things we *hope* for." He bent over his work.

Barbara Webster stared hard at the Argentine banker. There were many things she wished to say to him, and for just a moment she thought that she might find words with which to express herself. But the moment passed before she acted upon the impulse.

Suddenly she could see no way to make her feelings clear without also embarrassing herself. Barbara felt herself go cold, wholly professional once more. "Let's get to work," she said in a distant voice.

They tackled the contents of their briefcases, interrupting their concentration only long enough to monitor the transfer of funds in New York, the acceptance of those funds in Argentina. The only conversation that passed between Barbara and Esteban dealt with the business transaction that was, Barbara understood and made herself accept, the essence of their relationship.

Nothing more.

Some days James Helmers's loss of independence burned him like an open wound. This was one of those days. He sat at his desk in CSI's Alexandria, Virginia, offices, studying two long memos from Paul Christopher. The memoranda spelled out in no uncertain terms a variety of operational changes upon which Christopher insisted, and outlined the increases in performance that Christopher expected. There was a patronizing tone to the memos that Helmers heartily resented, an aura of superiority in Christopher's words that put Helmers in his place. In short, the memos were telling James Helmers how to do his job.

As though I weren't in this industry when Paul Christopher was still speaking Czech, Helmers thought angrily. He shoved the memos to one side of his spacious desk. *But I can't expect it to be otherwise,* he thought. *After all—it's his company now.*

In its day Lothrop-Helmers Protective Services had been the largest of the Washington-area security companies. The merger between Lee Lothrop and

James Helmers had proved a sound move for both: their success and wealth grew rapidly. *After Lee died I made the company even more successful. But not successful enough to protect us from Paul Christopher's takeover.* That was not entirely true. Helmers could have turned Christopher down. But there was too much money involved—as well as the promise that Helmers would remain in charge of Washington operations, as well as holding a seat among Christopher's executive advisers.

The reality was different. *I shuffle papers all day, I get to be charming when entertaining clients, I make my reports directly to Paul Christopher himself.* Helmers placed his hands on the armrests of his comfortable executive chair and gripped them tightly, as though fearful of falling. He squeezed his eyes shut. *And Paul Christopher tells me what I must do and I follow his instructions most carefully. This is the life I have made for myself: I am Paul Christopher's errand boy.*

The deal he had cut with Christopher had looked very favorable, but its emptiness became quickly clear to Helmers. He was in charge of capital operations, so long as he did what Christopher wanted. And the seat among the advisers was even more powerless. He was not an old friend of Christopher's, like Giancarlo Conti or Rahjit Desai or Barbara Webster. Christopher's conversations with Helmers at executive meetings always struck Helmers as perfunctory at best. The one time Christopher had seemed genuinely appreciative of Helmers's abilities had been the occasion when Helmers had come across one of the ancient coins Christopher was so keen to possess. Christopher had thanked him deeply, and they'd passed a long and talkative dinner together. *But that was only one dinner out of years of doing business together. And Christopher had seemed more interested in that stupid coin than in any of the suggestions I made.* Since then Helmers had come across two more of Christopher's coins, but he had deliberately kept them to himself. It was a small revenge, but one that gave him an inordinate amount of gratification.

Helmers would not deny that Paul Christopher had exerted an effect on the private security industry. The standards Christopher set for his company, the sums he poured into the development of new security technology, the global vision Christopher possessed, dwarfed even the grandest of Helmers's ambitions. But Helmers was also aware that the larger the company grew, the more easily it could be brought down. He had wondered from time to time what any of the government contractors for whom CSI provided security would think if they knew that Paul Christopher had been born and raised in a Soviet client state. That knowledge was valuable. Made public, the shock waves would reverberate for months.

After a moment Helmers pulled the memos back to the center of his desk. There was work to be done, and Helmers prided himself on always completing jobs he undertook. At sixty-three he no longer allowed himself many hopes—the patterns of his life were too well-established for that—but there was one hope that flared with occasional brilliance. And that was the hope that, for all Christopher's confidence and ability, for all of his genius at business, for all of his . . . *arrogance,* something would happen that would teach Paul Christopher a lesson in humility.

And if that lesson brought down Christopher Security International, James Helmers did not think that he would be terribly distressed.

There were protesters outside the New Delhi offices of CSI, and Rahjit Desai pushed his way through them, ignoring their charges that the company was a tool of American imperialism. Their cries almost amused Desai: the placards they carried and the epithets they shouted echoed words he himself had shouted as a student in Paris in 1968. The fire in the protesters' eyes blazed no more brightly than had the fire in Desai's own eyes when he was a student. *So many years ago,* he thought, and paused in the lobby to look back at the knot of angry students.

In a way, he sympathized with their anger. Christopher Security International provided guards for a large chemical plant outside Delhi. In the wake of the tragic accident at a similar plant, the entire Indian chemical industry had come under suspicion. A protest march against the gates of CSI's client had resulted in a clash between the students and the security force. *Those were CSI truncheons cracking idealistic heads,* Desai thought, and wondered how he had come so far from his own days as a radical that he could give the order to disperse the protesters with whatever means were required. *Now I order the use of teargas against children,* he thought, *where once I stood tall against such tactics myself.* He stepped into the elevator. His thoughts roved back to his own student days, to Paris and his first meeting with Paul Christopher.

By October 1968, the worst of the student riots were over, and DeGaulle was busy trying to restore tranquility to the French economy. The air around the Sorbonne was no longer acrid with teargas, and most of the students were returning to their classes. Young

Rahjit Desai, a student in the history of law, found himself missing all the excitement. What a thrilling month May in Paris had been!

But by October everything was going gray. Still under the spell of the more charismatic of the student leaders, Desai tried to rally others to the cause, but there was little enthusiasm for revolt left among the students. The May revolution might as well have been ancient history—it would be remembered, but not recreated. His classmates were paying more attention to grades than revolutionary ideals, and the rhetoric around which so many had rallied was increasingly heard only in small groups over bottles of cheap wine. It was in one of those groups that Desai first met Paul Christopher.

They were the same age, their birthdays within a month of each other. Desai, though, saw in Christopher's gray eyes even then a world-weariness that bespoke far more knowledge of life and death than that possessed by the bold-talking self-styled heroes of the student revolution. Paul's left wrist was wrapped with gauze, and Desai could see pain blossom across the Czechoslovakian's features when he moved his hand too quickly. But Christopher never complained, and Desai had known him for weeks before he learned the story of how that wrist had been injured, of Paul's escape from his homeland under cover of darkness, pursued by Soviet security police.

Increasingly, they spent their time together, two foreigners filled with ideals that fueled their lives.

But we burned that fuel quickly, Desai recalled as he entered his office. *We watched as our revolutionary leaders revealed feet of clay. They were so willing to order others to the barricades, so fearful of being harmed themselves. Their cowardice dampened our*

*own revolutionary flames. And once the flames died we
saw how empty our heroes' hopes had been. Always
tear down, never build. Well, Paul has built something
now, and I share the responsibility with him.*

That responsibility included the bloodied heads of
Indian students. Desai had been unable to take his
eyes from the newsreel footage that played again and
again. Desai had not slept well. He could not forget
the students' faces.

By Christmas 1968, Desai and Paul Christopher
were fully disillusioned with the radicals with whom
they associated. They shared Christmas dinner at an
inexpensive restaurant, and Paul insisted upon paying.

"What are your plans for the next term, Rahjit?"
Christopher had asked as they lingered at the table
over brandy.

Desai shrugged. "It is time to begin studying once
more, I suppose. There is a great deal of work to be
done in my country, you know. I must learn as much
as I can and return home to put my knowledge to
work for my people. They need so much." The Indian
sipped his brandy. "And you?"

Paul took a long time answering. "I came here
looking for something, Rahjit. I thought that I might
find . . . in the movement, something that might
sweep across the world. Something that might make a
difference to my homeland." He spoke slowly, almost
tentatively, his accent still heavily Slavic. "But there's
no difference between the revolutionaries here and
the bastards who rolled through Prague. It's not
freedom they're after at all." He fell silent.

"What are you after?" Rahjit asked softly.

Paul shrugged. "Who knows?" he said with a slight
smile. "I'm no idealist. Not anymore. I can't afford
that." He toyed with his snifter for a moment. "But

there are many things I can afford. I have . . . funds. I imagine I'll be leaving Paris soon."

It took Rahjit by surprise. He had not known the Czechoslovakian long, but he had grown attached to him. "Where are you going?"

"I can't say just yet. I have a few ideas. I'm looking for something I can do that might make a difference." His laugh was curt and harsh. "More of a difference than sitting in smoky rooms with unwashed rabble cursing some establishment that's oppressive." His eyes were hard and clear. "I know about oppression, my friend."

Rahjit nodded. "When will you be leaving?"

"A week or so. After the first of the year." Paul finished his brandy. "Don't look so glum, Rahjit. I'll be in touch with you. Who knows? Perhaps we can find some work together."

Rahjit Desai did not see his friend for two years. And when Paul Christopher did reenter Desai's life, the young Czechoslovakian had shed virtually all traces of his accent, along with his rough edges. The Paul Christopher who stopped by Rahjit's Left Bank room two years later was immaculately dressed in a Saville Row suit, his hair neatly cropped, an expensive watch all but covering the scars on his left wrist. "Hello, old friend," Christopher said when the Indian answered the door. "I told you I'd be back."

For a moment Desai was speechless. He had wondered from time to time what had happened to his friend. "Come in," he said at last.

Christopher took a look around the cramped quarters. "The life of a student," he said almost wistfully.

"For a few weeks more," said Desai. "And then I'm finished."

"And then?"

The Indian shrugged. "Back to my home to apprentice at the law, I suppose."

"And pass your life handling papers for the wealthy?" Christopher asked. "Or eke out a living as an advocate for the poor?"

Desai said nothing.

"Let me make you a proposition, Rahjit," Christopher said. "Let me tell you what I have been doing."

Desai listened carefully as Christopher told him of the past two years. It was the first time Desai had heard Giancarlo Conti's name, and when he discovered that Paul Christopher was in the business of providing private security guards to wealthy businessmen on the Mediterranean, he could not hide his surprise. "You are guarding the very people we used to curse," he said almost angrily.

Christopher shook his head. "I just listened, Rahjit. Remember that. When I came to Paris I thought that ideals could change the world. But then I began to listen to the idealists." He chose his words carefully. "This is a dangerous world, my friend. It grows more deadly every day. What I offer my clients is some assurance of insulation against those dangers. That they might go about their concerns without fear. Things are not likely to grow better in the years to come. You know that as well as I. Tell me that there aren't any number of companies and individuals in India who wouldn't pay well for quality security services. Good companies, my friend, who provide employment and investment in areas that need it."

They talked through the night. Gradually, Rahjit Desai found himself persuaded by Paul Christopher, and when Desai finished school, he traveled to Rome, where he passed a summer beginning to learn the intricacies of the profession Paul Christopher had selected. By fall Desai was in Delhi, opening the first of CSI's offices in Asia.

And now I am a wealthy man, thanks to Paul Christopher, Desai thought. *And our company has done a great deal of good over the years. I believe that. I truly do.*

But Rahjit Desai was a man of imagination, and he was unable to free his thoughts from images of young Indian idealists being clubbed by CSI security guards. He sat at his desk and sought calm, wondering all the while how far he would be willing to go in the defense of his clients against the idealistic anger of Indian students. *Have I come so far from Paris?* he wondered. *Has Paul?* Desai felt slightly sick, and he knew that sooner or later he and Paul would be forced into a confrontation over this matter. He could not at that moment say where his loyalty lay.

Angus Hill looked out at the unexpectedly mild and sunny January morning. *At least we've got good weather for the search,* he thought. He had just spoken at length with Lady Cedric. As always, Angus found her to be professional in her understanding of the reality of a situation, and uncompromising in her demands that Christopher Security International change the reality to one that suited her more fully.

"Find Nigel," she said firmly before hanging up. "You can do it, Angus, I've no doubts."

"Lady Cedric," he said, and drew breath. "We've got a large search under way now. And we're watching the likely places he might turn up if he's taken Alphasome elsewhere."

"No," she said, her voice becoming hard-edged. "Find him safe in the Lake District. *Don't* find that he's betrayed me. Do you understand, Angus?" she said.

"Aye, Lady Cedric," said Angus Hill. "I'll do my best. We all will."

"I expect nothing less, Angus," she said before hanging up.

He paced the length of his comfortable office. The Hemmings matter concerned him, but far less than Miranda Glenn did. Angus had been completely sincere when he told Paul Christopher that he had confidence in his abilities. *But there are some things that no one, not even Paul, can deal with. And a wild card in the form of a traitor in our own highest echelons—*

Angus clapped his hands together, cutting off the thought. He could not avoid it: if there was a traitor, he or she must be found and the threat removed. But it would do no good to dwell upon it. Nothing could be accomplished by brooding over what he would have sworn a day earlier was an impossibility. *To betray Paul!* Angus Hill swore softly and prowled about the room.

The chime of his telephone interrupted him, and Angus stepped swiftly to his desk, hoping that the caller might bear news of Nigel Hemmings. But it was Giancarlo Conti, calling from CSI headquarters in Rome.

"Angus?" said the Italian in his careful English.

"Aye, Giancarlo. I'm here."

"Ah, good. How are things in London?" he asked.

Angus Hill made himself cheery. "Could not be better, lad. Paul's in England, as you know."

"Yes, Angus. I'd called for him."

"He's at the armory, Giancarlo. On his way there now, in fact. By car, though, not helicopter today. Try him there early afternoon."

"Not important," said Giancarlo Conti. "Planning the summit, a few details to attend to."

"Aye, your turn this year. We're anticipating your hospitality," Angus said. The summits of Christopher's executive advisers were filled with hard work, interrupted by elegant distractions. *Now I will be able to look at none of them without wondering—* He cut off the thought. "Are you ready?"

"Of course!" laughed Giancarlo. "After all the preparations for Maria's wedding, the summit is a dream." A deep chuckle came over the telephone. "And for the summit I do not have to consult with Maria's mama on every detail!"

Angus laughed heartily. "How is Maria?"

"Nervous as a—"

"Bride?" said Angus with another laugh.

"Si. Yes!" Giancarlo sighed. "She will be a beautiful bride. My Maria."

"We're looking forward to it, lad," said Angus. He glanced at his watch. Christopher would be nearing the armory.

"Tell Paul that I called," Giancarlo said.

"Aye."

"And I will see you when you arrive in Rome!"

"I cannot wait," said Angus. The conversation ended.

Angus had not lied to Giancarlo. He was eager to see all of the advisers gathered together. He wanted to stare into their eyes, and find among them the betrayer. And then?

Eliminate him, Hill thought. There was no alternative for Paul. How could there be? Angus would kill the traitor with his own hands if he could. He hoped Paul would be equally ruthless.

A bitter taste flooded his mouth. Angus stepped

away from his desk and looked out over London. He reviewed in his mind the faces of each of the advisers, and attempted to picture them betraying Paul Christopher—to whom they owed so much. None of the pictures was pleasing, none of them made any sense. *If I could get my hands,* Angus started to think. Then he realized that to have his wish would mean grappling with Barbara Webster, or Giancarlo Conti, or Rahjit Desai, or David Glise—

He stopped himself from such thoughts. They were too painful. He'd known each of those people for years, would be willing to have any of them at his back in a dangerous situation.

It was not Angus Hill's habit to drink during working hours, and his dour Scots discipline caused him to decline alcohol at most business meals or engagements. Now, though, he seated himself in the Brayton chair behind his desk, and pressed his thumb against the ProTech seal that guarded the desk's deepest drawer. The drawer slid open, and Angus extracted from it a sturdy glass and a bottle of Glenlivet. He poured a healthy drink of the smoky Scotch, and replaced the bottle in the drawer. He thumbed the ProTech seal into action, and carried his whiskey to the window.

To have put Paul Christopher in jeopardy, he thought as he took a swallow of Scotch. The whiskey's taste matched Angus's mood: the blending of flavor and bite filling him for a moment. He raised his glass toward the sun. He watched the light rays as they were made diffuse by the golden liquid. Angus thought of Paul Christopher, and his already deep admiration for the man grew even more profound. Looking at him over breakfast that morning, it had occurred to Angus

Hill that no one could have detected any trace of concern on Christopher's face. He might have been talking to a young associate, rather than one of the world's most glamorous and hard-hitting journalists. Paul Christopher radiated nothing but confidence and ability and charm.

Angus sighed and sipped his whiskey. The Argentine transaction alone would have proved sufficient to inspire anxiety in most men. Add to that not only Nigel Hemmings's disappearance, but also the prospect of a betrayal from within the organization that Christopher had so meticulously constructed . . .

Yet he sat comfortably throughout breakfast, eating heartily, laughing, speaking in almost casual tones with Miranda Glenn. That had not been hard to do, Angus thought, as he considered his own relaxation in her presence. That was part of her journalistic gift, he supposed, that ability to put people off their guard, make them join her in conversation rather than confrontation. But Angus knew that Paul Christopher had controlled the conversation and its direction from the moment she arrived in the office.

Now Christopher and Miranda would be approaching the armory, Angus realized. Was Christopher still in control? Of course he was, thought the tall Scot as he drained his glass. But to show a journalist *ASP* might be going too far, he thought, especially *this* journalist.

Angus put the glass down and stalked back to his desk. Brooding would accomplish nothing. There was work to be done. He activated his computer and began, once again, to review all available data pertaining to Nigel Hemmings, his professional career, his hobbies and interests, his romantic involvements, his passions. And only occasionally as he worked did Angus Hill stop to think that in another CSI office somewhere in the world, one of his counterparts was even now living with the fact that he or she had betrayed Paul Christopher.

"*Damn,*" said Angus softly. "Damn the traitor."

8

PAUL CHRISTOPHER SPOKE to his driver over the intercom. "Tony, why not take the long route in? The course."

"It's a lovely day for it, Mr. Christopher," said Tony Earnhardt. "We should have a good view."

"Fine," said Christopher. The Rolls-Royce turned onto a white driveway, and came to a halt before a glass-walled guard booth staffed by two Christopher Security International uniformed employees. "Look sharp," Christopher teased Miranda. "You don't want to miss this. Your first two guns are passing on the right."

Miranda gave a musical laugh. She had enjoyed the ride from London, although her attention had been focused upon Paul Christopher rather than the lovely day through which they drove. Miranda took pride in her abilities as a researcher, and that pride had earned a reward as she and Christopher talked technology. Miranda had made it quickly clear to Christopher that he need not talk down to her—he'd better *not!*—or couch his explanations in layman's language. She assured him of her ability to follow any line of discussion he chose to follow. Christopher took her at her word.

Not that she trusted him yet. Having achieved the

influence over Christopher that the Byzantine solidus had purchased, Miranda still had no idea how deep that influence went. Certainly Christopher still refused to answer personal questions with anything more than vague quips. Nor would he give any quarter to her discussion of professional ethics. But as far as the details and hardware of his industry, he displayed a remarkable openness and accessibility. He was not giving her what she wanted, yet she realized that he was giving her far more than another man in his position might be willing to surrender. That impressed Miranda. She raised Christopher a notch or two in professional respect, at least. *I can give him that much,* she thought, *without giving away too much of myself.*

The uniformed guards smiled as Christopher exchanged a few brief pleasantries with them. Then Tony Earnhardt steered the Rolls-Royce past the guard booth and through the mechanically opened gates of a tall perimeter fence.

"The fence is electrically charged," Christopher explained to Miranda. "As well as being vibration sensitive, and in communication by way of fairly smart sensors with an even smarter perimeter security system. Being a proving ground, we have it all here," he said with a smile. "Like wearing a belt *and* suspenders."

"Which do you wear?" Miranda could not resist asking.

Christopher shook his head slightly. "That's private information," he said, smiling.

Miranda glanced at his waist and saw the narrow belt with polished buckle that Christopher wore. "I'm an *investigative* reporter, remember," she said. She raised her eyes, only to blush at the realization that Christopher had watched her inspection of his midriff.

He did not mention it, though, but went on about the security systems through whose surveillance they passed. "There's a microwave fence in place as well, at the moment, going through some tests. And it communicates with the central system also. Should our perimeter be breached—or for that matter, too closely approached—we grow aware almost instantly."

"And come out guns blazing every time a rabbit hops into your territory, or a bird violates your airspace, no doubt," Miranda said.

"I must admit that we're perhaps more accurately and constantly aware of the size of our wildlife population here," Christopher admitted easily. "But I've mentioned that it's a fairly intelligent system. We can generally tell whether our interlopers are human or not." He sat in silence as they moved along the drive and into a thick, well-kept stand of tall trees. "The entire four thousand acres is a wildlife preserve, by the way," Christopher said to Miranda.

"I see," she said, unpersuaded. She would only give him so much. "Admirable."

Christopher did not answer her. "Keep your eyes open and perhaps you'll spot some of our wildlife. I've seen families of foxes," he said. "A stag or two. I've asked Tony to give us a scenic tour today. This road is one of our test courses."

"Testing what?"

"Drivers and cars," said Christopher. "Mostly drivers, although I'm sure you're aware that CSI does a good amount of automotive work, preparing vehicles for the . . . challenges they may face."

"I've seen the literature," said Miranda sharply. "Bullet-proof, bomb-proof . . ."

"Our driver-training course is one of the best," said Christopher calmly. "A number of governments have enrolled their drivers here, as well as corporations and private employers." He grinned. "Anytime you see a dignitary in a procession, just think! I might have made money for training his chauffeur."

Miranda was less amused. "Good for you," she said dryly.

"At any rate, we have a good course here."

"What is it you teach?" Miranda asked.

The Silver Cloud emerged from the woods into a long meadow. The road was a typical double-lane country asphalt thoroughfare. Earnhardt held the Silver Cloud at a steady thirty kilometers per hour as they climbed a gentle hill. From its crest they looked down upon a valley with a broad stream bisecting it. The stream was crossed by a narrow bridge, at the far side of which workmen were busy at a smoldering overturned car. Christopher thumbed the intercom. "Pursuit vehicle or target?" he asked Earnhardt. "Can you tell from here?"

The car moved a distance down the hill, nearly approaching the bridge before Earnhardt spoke. "Hard to say," the driver mused. "But pursuit, I'd wager," he said. "Shall I stop and ask?"

"No," said Christopher, laughing. "You might be wrong, and we wouldn't want Miss Glenn to get a bad impression of our school." He turned to Miranda. "Unless you insist."

"No, I'll take your word for it," she said. She gestured at the overturned Fiat. "But aren't you going to see if anyone was hurt?"

Christopher shook his head. "If anyone is injured during a driving exercise, we leave the wreckage in place for a week. With a red flag on it." The Silver Cloud moved across the bridge. "We have very few injuries here." He nodded at the workmen as they rolled past the wreckage.

"I will ask you to confirm that it *was* the pursuit vehicle," Miranda insisted.

"Of course," said Christopher. He watched her make a note in her pad.

Miranda finished jotting down her impressions of the scene. "A very realistic course," she observed, casting a quick glance back at the wreckage before the curtain of woods closed once more around them.

"There are very realistic dangers to which drivers today must respond," Christopher said. "But we don't want to get lost in debate again, do we? We'll have time for that later. Today you wanted hard facts and weapons. So I am happy to oblige."

Moments later the Silver Cloud left the woods once more, and they were given their first view of the quarters which served to house the armory of Christopher Security International.

The house rose out of the ground like an enormous Romanesque sculpture, a home suitable for giants. Of roughly squared dark stone laced with lighter mortar, the main building sprawled in several directions. It shot out long wings like spokes from its massive central body. Their peaked roofs were of heavy slate, as was the long patio that stretched from the house to the edge of a large parking area. Miranda counted five chimneys, the tallest of which towered over the four-story pinnacle of the main building. Beyond the house were outbuildings and large solid barns.

"From here we have, of course, the rear view," Christopher said as the Silver Cloud made its way down the hill and toward the house.

"It looks more like a fortress than a branch of a modern corporation," Miranda said.

"Well, I wasn't around to supervise the original construction," said Paul Christopher with a laugh. "But I don't think I would change anything. The main building was put up by a nobleman in the fourteenth century," he said. "Other wings have been added by successive owners, and the original style has been preserved."

"It's impressive," said Miranda without irony. "Massive."

"It's solid as a mountain," Christopher said, and Miranda noticed his pride. "We've made some changes, of course. But little that's . . . obtrusive." He shrugged. "Not far from here, but well out of sight, we have a more modern metal, modular installation. Where the devices tested here are made. But I love this place."

"I look forward to seeing it," Miranda said honestly.

"And I to showing it," said Christopher. He gave a smile that struck Miranda as almost boyish and bashful. "Showing off the . . . armory is one of my favorite things."

He could be charming, Miranda thought, and immediately raised her guard. It was one thing to respect Christopher's professionalism; quite another to be charmed by his personality. "And you're going to show me . . . *ASP?*"

"*ASP*, as you will see, Miranda, is more than capable of showing itself. Although I doubt if *ASP* derives as much delight from the display as do I," Christopher said.

Miranda looked at him curiously as Tony Earnhardt parked the Silver Cloud in Christopher's designated space. Christopher and Miranda got out of the car and were greeted by a well-dressed young man who approached from across the patio. "Mr. Christopher, so good to see you here," he said, extending his hand.

"Edmund Patterson," said Christopher. "This is Miranda Glenn."

151

They shook hands, Patterson speaking enthusiastically. "I do *so* enjoy your work, Ms. Glenn," he said in a carefully cultured British accent, forming his words with precision.

Miranda was flattered, but hard to convince. She detected Christopher's hand in the compliment. "That makes one of you," she said to Patterson with a laugh and look toward Christopher. Together they walked across the patio to the French doors that would admit them to the manor house. To one side of the patio was sunk a shallow pool. Christopher and Patterson stepped aside to permit Miranda to enter the house first.

She found herself in a long softly lighted hallway. Its dark wooden walls were hung with tapestries, with crossed long swords, with great ancient fighting implements. Tall suits of armor stood guard over pools of shadow. Incongruously, flowers added splashes of color, sprouting from slender crystal vases on mahogany occasional tables. Miranda permitted herself a soft whistle. "It's the most atmospheric armory I've ever visited, anyway," she said.

Christopher came to her side. "You've visited others?" he asked.

Miranda shrugged and smiled at him. "I've covered war zones," she said. "I've seen children standing guard over munitions dumps, if that counts."

Christopher's gaze grew grim. "It counts," he said.

"But—yours is so *stylish!*" Miranda said, her voice laced with sarcasm. Heavy, carved oak doors broke the corridor at a couple of places. The ends of the corridor were sealed by immense double doors whose substantial brass fittings glowed dully even from a distance.

Edmund Patterson took a step down the corridor. "We've arranged a tour for you," he said to Miranda, although he seemed to be seeking Christopher's approval with his eager words. Christopher's face remained unreadable. Patterson could not be more than twenty-five, Miranda realized. She and Christopher fell in step behind the young man.

His back to them, Edmund Patterson continued speaking. "We've arranged rather a full afternoon of it," he said. "Each of the department heads here will be joining us, in succession. We thought we might have a high tea this midafternoon." He cast a quick glance back over his shoulder, showing them a toothy smile. "But with everything going on here at the moment, we'll have to move rather briskly."

Christopher waited until Patterson was not looking their way. He slowed his pace, and took Miranda's arm to slow her for a moment. He leaned close to her and whispered, "English efficiency at its *best*." Miranda laughed under her breath, and Christopher released her arm.

Behind the huge double doors stretched another corridor, less formal than the first. In places its walls were splashed with eclectic contemporary art. Miranda recognized a Pollack, a Rouault. Its walls were also more frequently broken by less ornate doors than those of the entryway, each fitted with a nameplate identifying its occupant.

"I thought we'd begin with one of the training classes," said Patterson. "In fact, there's one in session just now." He glanced back at Christopher, who nodded curtly. Patterson moved briskly down the corridor, Christopher and Miranda following at their own, slower pace. Miranda glanced at the nameplates as she passed them, recognizing some of the names from her research.

Patterson paused before a door and waited for Christopher and Miranda to join him. "I think you'll enjoy this," he said to Miranda as he opened the door. They entered a large classroom. They stood against the rear wall. Christopher did not interrupt the instructor. There were perhaps half a dozen students, men and women. Their attention was focused upon the instructor, a tall and classically handsome woman in her late forties. Miranda squinted to read the words written on the blackboard. *Willingness* was one of the words, and in even larger letters was written *Determination*. The instructor's pleasant voice reached them clearly at the back of the classroom.

"Your willingness must be equaled and exceeded by your determination," she said. "For that, ultimately, is what our clients pay for: our determination to provide our services completely and without hesitation. To place ourselves, if need be, between any of our clients and any threats that they may face. But more than that. You must be willing, as you understand, to *die,* if need be, for the client. Your *determination,* though, must be to avoid any situation that might call for such a willingness."

Miranda only half-concentrated upon the lecturer. The instructor's words could be considered more closely later, when Miranda replayed the tape recording that was being made by the unit in her pocketbook. She glanced at Christopher, but his eyes were directed toward the head of the class. Patterson's eyes remained upon her, his expression almost offensively solicitous. Miranda thought of Christopher's description of Patterson and almost giggled again. The lecturer pressed on with her words about the ethics that must guide a Christopher guard. After a few moments Miranda nudged Christopher gently. He looked at her and nodded. They quietly left the classroom.

Patterson was undeterred in his own fierce determination to guide them on an exhaustively comprehensive tour of the facility. His enthusiasm for its every cranny was less than contagious, Miranda discovered, but she followed him without protest. Christopher made no comment. They visited another class, this one more strenuous. Its students flung themselves with abandon around the padded floor of a roomy gymnasium, trading passes with mock knives.

From the gymnasium they proceeded to the armory's library. They passed a quarter of an hour there. The room was thickly carpeted; a fire burned in a raised hearth on a far wall. The library's shelves were lined with thousands of arcane volumes, presided over by a cadaverous and ancient librarian. Franz Kunkel, though, prodded from his perch behind a library table, proved an eloquent and affable host, guiding them among the books.

Next, a brightly illuminated and white-walled laboratory surprised Miranda with its stark functionalism. In its sterile quarters a team of technicians pursued refinements in tranquilizing gases to be used in riot control. The idea of such gases angered Miranda, but, as with the library and the classrooms before it, the laboratory struck her as a place of details and facts, rather than sites where she might unearth any particular truths or insights about the motivations that drove Paul Christopher. Everything she'd seen thus far would make wonderful background material for her book, and some of the details and facts could become, in her hands, quite damning. But she could always gather dry details and straight facts. Now she was beginning to resent wasting time that might have been put to better use interrogating Christopher in private. He was managing to lead her away from himself even as he revealed more of his company than any reporter had ever been allowed to see. Miranda did not intend to lose her sense of purpose. That purpose, she reminded herself firmly, was to be close to Christopher, to capture his words and thoughts. Not those of Edmund Patterson, or Angus Hill, or any other subordinate.

A moment later it seemed as though Christopher had read her mind. As they left the laboratory, Christopher stopped Patterson before the young man could continue his tour. "Edmund," Christopher said, "I believe that Miss Glenn has derived a sufficient sense of the sorts of business we do here." He looked at Miranda and she wondered if he could see the sudden renewal of interest that showed on her face. "And, of course, should Miss Glenn decide to pursue more in-depth research at this site on a later date, why, she may return here as a guest of the company." He smiled at his youthful employee. "And you may devote all of your time to her then."

"Yes, Mr. Christopher," said Edmund Patterson. His face seemed to fall a bit. "Such an in-depth tour would doubtless provide a better sense of all of the activities that go on here."

"Yes," said Miranda.

"So," Christopher continued. He looked at his watch. "It's just after two. You may return to your other duties, Edmund. It's a glorious afternoon. Miss Glenn and I will stroll about the grounds for a bit. Ian Pierce is going to give us a demonstration in about an hour."

"The tea, sir?"

"I'm afraid not, Edmund," Christopher said. "We've brought a luncheon basket from London. We'll be eating at the range."

"Very good, sir," said Edmund Patterson, drawing himself tall.

"Thank you again, Edmund," said Christopher.

"Yes," said Miranda, and offered her hand. "I look forward to returning when I have more time."

That seemed to brighten him. "Indeed," he said, almost chortling. "That would be smashing!"

Christopher interrupted. "Of course, I don't think we can expect Edmund to linger long in a position such as this. So come back quickly. Edmund is on his way *up!* Aren't you, Edmund?"

The young man simply smiled, and before he could speak, Christopher and Miranda took their leave of him.

9

THEY EMERGED FROM the house into an afternoon more suitable for May than January. Miranda stretched, raising her face to the sunlight. She became aware of Christopher's eyes upon her. She smiled at him. She wanted to say something, and began slowly. "I realize that no one's been given quite this much access before. No member of the press, that is. I appreciate it."

"We have a transaction between us," said Christopher without emotion.

"The solidus, yes," Miranda said. She bit her lip while she selected words. "And I'm grateful to you for opening . . . all of this to me. But—" She lapsed into silence as they crossed the patio and stepped onto the parking lot.

Christopher offered a finish to her thought. "But Edmund Patterson is a frightful bore!" he said, the heartiness of his laughter catching her unprepared.

"Well, yes," she admitted. Her eyes smiled. "But I wanted to thank you anyway for showing—"

Christopher cut her off. "Not at all." He smiled at her, his features outlined in the afternoon sunlight. "We have a bargain, you and I," he said. "Only I am not yet certain what your end of the bargain may be."

He looked closely at her, obviously waiting for a response.

But Miranda had none to give. She sought simply to make her position more clear. "I've had people . . . subjects, before, attempt to stonewall me," she said carefully. "To shut me out, or keep me from them. You, at least, are making some sort of effort." They left the paved lot and walked across the lawn and up a hill.

"Not feeling qualms about your method of securing an interview, are you?" Christopher asked.

Miranda shook her head. She could be honest, as well. "I'm not certain. It's not my customary approach."

"Well, perhaps we can resolve our differences," said Christopher. "To our mutual satisfaction."

"That might take some effort," said Miranda.

"Perhaps we'll be willing to make the effort," said Christopher.

She nodded.

"And, of course," he went on, "you still don't trust me completely."

"No," admitted Miranda. "How could I?" She showed him a sincere smile. "That would compromise my . . . principles." Her tone was almost flirtatious, which surprised her. She was not certain if she liked it. "I have journalistic responsibility to think of, after all."

"And I," said Christopher, although not harshly, "cannot help but feel myself—*blackmailed.*"

Miranda thought of the words she'd seen on the blackboard in the first classroom they visited. "I prefer to think that you've simply been made *willing,*" she said with a forcefulness of her own.

Christopher accepted her answer with a single nod,

and they walked across the crest of the hill toward the edge of the woods. Christopher steered them onto a neatly defined pathway that they followed at a brisk pace. Several minutes later they came upon a long, cleared meadow, more narrow than the first she'd seen. Along the meadow's far end were set up bales of hay with oversize bull's-eye targets mounted on their sides.

"We have a more clinical firing range," Christopher said as they walked down and across the meadow. "One that's more automated and accurate." He smiled at her. "But it's beneath the main house, you see, and that would mean having Patterson with us during the demonstration."

"Please," said Miranda with a grin. "This is just fine." She looked hard at him. "Demonstrating *ASP* requires a firing range?"

"Yes," said Christopher simply. Just under cover of the woods at the far end of the range three men were gathered around a large tarpaulin. Behind them stood two jeeps, one of them with a covered trailer attached. "The mysterious *ASP* will be unveiled shortly," said Christopher as they approached the men. "And there's a picnic lunch to be unbasketed as well."

Miranda could not tell what the canvas shrouded. Christopher introduced her to Ian Pierce, a sallow man with a winning smile. With the help of his assistants, Pierce was preparing *ASP* for the demonstration. He did not offer to lift the tarp for her. "About an hour or so, Mr. Christopher," Pierce said. "To get everything as you want it."

"Fine," said Christopher. He looked at the sky. "And we'll still have enough sun for the other?"

"Oh, yes sir," said Pierce, nodding. "It'll be just about right, in fact."

"Good," said Christopher before turning to Miranda. "This way," he said, prompting her with a gentle pressure to the small of her back. He led her through the woods to a clearing at the crest of a rise. Nestled in the grass was the picnic basket, deposited there by Tony Earnhardt. "We've had this clearing under special surveillance," Christopher said. "To ensure that none of our animals made off with our lunch." He bent and took the brightly checked blanket from its resting place between the wicker basket's handles. "Hungry?" Christopher said.

Miranda realized suddenly that it had been hours since the breakfast in Christopher's executive dining room. The tour of the house and the quick walk through the woods had left her ravenous. "Starved," she told Christopher.

Paul Christopher slipped off his jacket and folded it neatly before placing it on the grass. He loosened his necktie. With a deft flick of his wrists, Christopher shook the wrinkles from the blanket and it settled smoothly to cover a large patch of ground. "Shall we dine?" he asked.

Miranda seated herself beside the basket and opened it. She removed china and silver from their niches, and did the same for the condiments. In short order she and Christopher unpacked and arranged the ingredients of their picnic. It provided quite a buffet, beginning with a delicate aspic, followed by a beautifully roasted chicken and succulent cold asparagus, as well as crusty hard rolls and creamery butter. There were apples and sharp cheeses for dessert. Christopher uncorked a bottle of white wine and poured glasses for each of them. Miranda curled her fingers around the crystal stem of her glass and raised it to her lips. The afternoon sparkled around them, a perfect spring day in the middle of winter.

After they served themselves, Christopher drew his

crowded plate toward him and began to eat. Miranda approached her own food more slowly, and her portions were more modest. She was on guard against any drowsiness or failure of concentration that might follow too indulgent a meal, or too much wine. But her caution soon gave way to her appetite. Besides, the food and the wine were wonderful. It was a meal perfectly suited for the afternoon and the meadow where they ate. Miranda could not help thinking of the last real picnic she'd had. It was a meal of canned fruits eaten from paper plates a mile from heavy combat in Afghanistan. But the food had tasted wonderful then, the fruit's thick syrup the most satisfying liquid she'd ever tasted. Her companion on that picnic had been James Howard Dennis. They had been forced to abandon their meal unfinished under a hail of government small-arms fire. Now, as she stared at Paul Christopher, she wondered if that distant afternoon had really been more dangerous than this. Enemy troops were clear about their objectives, transparently so. Paul Christopher kept a curtain close about himself; yet she knew that he would soon make more clear how much he would give her. And how much besides the solidus she must pay.

"You're enjoying the tour?" Christopher asked.

Miranda swallowed a morsel of food. "Who wouldn't? It's a special place, obviously. A special environment that you've created." She took a bite of aspic.

"Whatever its purposes?" Christopher said pointedly.

"Well, it would make a fine museum," Miranda said. She sipped her wine. "To things and attitudes no longer needed," she said as she put her glass down.

"A fine sentiment," said Christopher. "Perhaps it will become a reality someday." He was several bites ahead of her. He chewed a darkly roasted leg of chicken.

"Someday soon?" Miranda asked.

Christopher put the chicken on his plate and wiped his hands on a linen napkin. "You'd permit me to recoup my investment here, first?" he asked. "It's not an inexpensive location."

"No," Miranda acknowledged cautiously. "But then, the fees you charge can certainly support it."

"True enough," agreed Christopher without hesitation. Once again he surprised her with the easy openness of his manner. "And who knows? Perhaps when it becomes a museum, I'll still be able to turn a profit from it." He happily resumed eating.

"No doubt," said Miranda. But his comment made her smile in the most pleasant way, and after a moment she did not attempt to hide it. The smile pleased Christopher, who went on to amaze her with the heroic lunch he consumed.

When their meal was finished, the china cleared away, the blanket refolded, Christopher led Miranda down the hill to Ian and the others. The tarp was still neatly secured over the mysterious *ASP,* as Christopher referred to it.

"Is it ready?" Christopher asked Ian Pierce.

"Absolutely, Mr. Christopher," said Pierce. Pride shone on his face. "She'll go through her paces for you. And don't we have a fine afternoon for it?"

"We certainly do, Ian," said Christopher. "We certainly do." He looked for a moment at the sky, then turned to Miranda. "Do you shoot skeet?"

The question took her by surprise, and a moment passed before she answered him. "Yes. I do, in fact. But—"

Christopher merely smiled. Ian Pierce rustled in the back of one of the jeeps, and produced two shotgun cases. Opening the cases, he beckoned Christopher and Miranda closer. He offered each of them a shotgun. Miranda hesitated a moment, then accepted the weapon.

It was a beautiful piece of workmanship, she realized as she hefted the shotgun. She'd fired such a fine weapon only a few times before. A Holland and Holland for which, Christopher recalled for her as she examined it, he'd waited more than four years for delivery. "Quite a wait," said Miranda.

"Worth it," said Christopher. His face grew distant for a moment, and Miranda had to strain to hear his next words. "It was the first . . . elegant gift I ever received from a client. Sir John Cedric sent me to Holland and Holland as his guest." He shook his head as though casting out a distraction.

"They never found his killers, did they?" Miranda asked. She'd heard rumors.

"No," said Christopher, examining the shotgun he held. "Anonymous cowards."

How much more does he know than he is willing to say? Miranda wondered. But Christopher stepped forward to the line, and she elected to let the subject drop. *For now.*

Ian Pierce handed them each a bag of shells. Miranda moved close to Christopher, remaining a bit to the left and behind him. His own gun was a Purdy, its side-by-side barrels no doubt as flawless as those of the Holland and Holland she would be using. "You wanted to see weapons," Christopher said to her. "It occurred to me that you just might enjoy using one." He stepped directly to the firing line and loaded his gun. He held the Purdy at the ready. From the corner of her eye Miranda could see Ian Pierce loading a clay pigeon into a complicated throwing device.

"Anytime, sir," said Ian when he was ready.

Christopher drew a breath and Miranda could see his shoulders grow tight. *"Pull!"* he called, and a clay pigeon was flung at a high angle up and across the meadow. Christopher tracked its flight smoothly, the Purdy's barrels coming up into position in a single graceful sweep. He squeezed a trigger and fired. The target disintegrated into tumbling rubble. *"Pull!"* called Christopher again, and a moment later discharged the other barrel. His aim was equally accurate. Christopher broke the Purdy's breech, and stepped back until he was even with Miranda. "Now you," he said.

Miranda stepped to the line and loaded the Holland and Holland. "What about *ASP?*" she asked before raising the shotgun to her shoulder.

"Perhaps this is part of it," Christopher said. "Anyway, let me see what kind of shot you are, first."

Miranda nodded. She braced the shotgun against her shoulder, took a couple of practice swings to accustom herself to the gun's weight. She could tell almost by instinct that the gun would be unerringly accurate. Miranda took a moment to calm her breathing, ensure the steadiness of her hands. The afternoon was quiet. *"Pull!"* she said.

The clay pigeon soared out at a less acute angle than had Christopher's first target. Miranda followed it with practiced ease, firing at the last possible moment. She grinned her triumph as the clay pigeon came apart in a puff of pieces. *"Pull!"* she said again. The next pigeon climbed high. Miranda snapped the shotgun up ahead of its ascent, fired. Pieces of target tumbled out of the sky.

"Impressive," said Christopher as he stepped back into position. "I'm surprised that you're willing to participate in this, really. Considering your hatred of guns." Before she had time to respond to him,

Christopher called, *"Pull!"* He destroyed two more clay pigeons before stepping back.

"I have no objection to sport shooting. When the fire is aimed at inanimate targets," Miranda said. She loaded the Holland and Holland. "In fact, I've shot competitively before."

"That's right," said Christopher. "You've earned your ribbons. You taught as well, did you not? At a prep school?" His face remained innocent.

Miranda broke the breech of her shotgun, stepped away from the line, and faced him. She understood all of this now. "I'd assumed from the beginning that you assembled an entire stack of information related to me." She narrowed her eyes.

"Several stacks," Christopher admitted with a nod. "I decided that you should know."

Miranda stared at him without speaking.

"Besides, it's public information."

"I'm sure you have more private data," she said. Her voice had grown harsh.

For a moment Christopher did not answer her. "You had a privileged childhood, Miranda," he said at last. "The best of everything, no?"

Miranda stared at him and did not speak.

"The best clothes, the best accommodations." For a moment Christopher studied the stock of his shotgun. "The best father."

Miranda felt a flare of anger, but managed to control it before answering him. "Yes," she said. "But I would expect you to know all about my father. After all, the files on his . . . indiscretion are part of your company now."

Christopher's expression grew gentle, almost solicitous. "I would not call it an indiscretion, Miranda. I gather he loved her very much."

She drew a deep breath to keep her voice from quivering. "Yes," she said. "I did too."

For a moment Christopher looked away from her. "What happened to your father was inexcusable. There can never be enough people of his capabilities. To ruin such a man— You're aware, of course, that I was a child myself when that happened."

Miranda's stomach felt tight, all of her muscles knotted. "But you *bought* the company that—"

He did not let her finish. "Yes," Christopher said. "I did. And if you go back and check the records you will find that I initiated certain reforms almost immediately. Any number of questionable employees were let go, a variety of practices discontinued—"

"Oh, don't defend yourself to *me!*" Miranda snapped.

"I had no intention of defending myself," Christopher said calmly. "What happened to your father was unfortunate and inexcusable. My firm does not engage in such practices. At *any* level, from security guards to our executives. My people know that I would not tolerate that sort of—"

Her harsh laughter cut him short. "Yes, well, one of your employees was more than willing to deal with *me*," she said. "And I can't imagine that you approve of *that!*"

Christopher did not respond to her anger. "Miranda," he said, his voice even, "Lee Lothrop is long dead. I purchased his company from his partner— who had nothing to do with your father's disgrace. And Jim Helmers will be retiring soon, so all of the connections with Lothrop Security are almost gone. Don't you think it's time you severed your own connections with the past?"

"Don't patronize me."

Christopher shrugged and said nothing. "I wanted you to know how I felt about what happened to your father. I think we should begin clearing the air between us. The mysteries. We each have objectives to achieve, do we not?"

"Yes," Miranda said coldly.

"There." He opened his hands to her, showing that he concealed nothing. "And you still enjoy shooting."

"I keep my hand in," Miranda said, her anger beginning to subside a bit. "I enjoy it."

"Then shall we proceed?" Christopher asked.

She took a long moment to study him, then turned back to the line, closed the breech and raised the shotgun. She called for a fast double-pull and took out both pigeons. She broke her gun open and disposed of the spent shells. "You can make me mad, Christopher," Miranda said with toughness that was more than a little feigned. "But you can't spoil my aim."

"Good," said Christopher, returning to the firing line. "I enjoy competition."

But their shooting did not become a contest, and they were both surprised by that. The afternoon air grew thick with the sharp scent of gunpowder. They took care not to overheat their guns, and for three rounds of shooting they exchanged weapons. The grass along the firing line was trampled flat as Christopher and Miranda traded and retraded places. Both Christopher and Miranda made the most of their shots. When one of them missed a target, the other offered a sensible critique. Respect grew between them.

At last Christopher broke open the Purdy and did not reload. Miranda emptied the Holland and Holland. She looked at Christopher expectantly.

"I enjoyed that," he said to her. "Very much. You're as good as I'd . . . heard."

"I don't enjoy having my privacy invaded," Miranda said firmly. "But, as you've said, we can save such talk for later. I did enjoy *this*." She gave the shotgun back to Ian Pierce. She returned her gaze to Christopher. "You're very good yourself." She stared at him speculatively.

"Perhaps we may shoot together again sometime," Christopher said.

"And *ASP?*" Miranda asked. "When do I—"

"Right now," said Christopher. "You see, the sky is getting too dim for us to be able to continue shooting with such accuracy. But our little contest was intended as a sort of prelude." He flung back the tarp. "Now it's *ASP*'s turn."

Beneath the canvas was hidden a shimmering metal cylinder, perhaps three feet tall and almost equally thick. The polished metal sparkled even in the dwindling afternoon sunlight, and in places about the body, tiny lights and gauges winked. The cylinder was mounted on overlarge bicycle tires.

"It's not a great deal to look at," said Christopher, "but I think you're going to be quite surprised by its capabilities." His smile seemed one of bemusement. "Miranda, say hello to *ASP*."

"I—" she began, but found herself interrupted by the machine itself.

"Good afternoon, Miss Glenn," the voice said. Its words were carefully formed, and there was none of the telltale hesitation, and only a trace of the tinniness that distinguished most artificial voices from human speech. "My full name is *Automated Surveillance* and *Protection*. But you may call me by my acronym: *ASP*."

Miranda stared sharply at Christopher. "A *machine?*"

Christopher laughed. "It's a . . . *device*. It's a—"

His smile grew wider. *"ASP* is something very new. It's still very experimental. This is just a prototype, a mock-up."

"What can it do?" asked Miranda.

"Come here," Christopher said, and *ASP* rolled smoothly forward, stopping less than a foot from Christopher's side. Miranda was surprised at how little noise *ASP* made as it moved. She could hear no engine noises at all. Christopher gestured for her to join him, and she did so. "Its capabilities are numerous, and if you'd like, I can provide an engineer to go over the technical information with you." He touched her arm. "Or perhaps Patterson."

Miranda gave him a fierce look. "No, thanks," she said. "But, really, what makes this so special?"

"The same as anything that's special in these days, Miranda," Christopher said. "Its level of *sophistication.* As I said, this *ASP* is only a prototype. But it's a very capable prototype."

"But what—" Miranda began to ask.

"Oh, it can beat even you at skeet shooting, for one thing," Christopher said. He ordered *ASP* forward, and nodded at Ian Pierce. A rack of clay pigeons was loaded into the throwing arm while Christopher and Miranda watched. Miranda feared that she might laugh out loud if the machine cried, *"Pull!"*

But it did not. A simple low tone was sounded. Four clay disks flew from the launcher. Miranda did not see *ASP* move, but in the space of barely three seconds the clay pigeons had disintegrated, scattering debris across the meadow. There had been no sound of gunfire, barely any sound at all. Miranda looked toward Christopher for explanation.

He shrugged. "Obviously, I'll only go so far," he said. "But it won't be long before we're going to make the public aware of the armaments system we've developed for *ASP. It's* called *WISP,* but don't ask me to decode that acronym just yet." He touched her arm again, and Miranda took a step back from him. "Perhaps you'll be granted an exclusive when we're ready for publicity," Christopher offered.

Miranda studied his features for a moment. "So what do we have?" she asked, and could not avoid following her question with sarcasm. "A robot skeet-shooting champion?"

"If you wish," said Christopher patiently. "Although we have more . . . interesting aspirations for *ASP*'s subsequent generations."

"Such as?" asked Miranda. She took a cautious step closer to the immobile *ASP*.

Christopher followed her. "Virtually any security position now held by a human can be better occupied by *ASP*," Christopher said with such nonchalance that Miranda wondered if he'd actually heard his own words.

"You must be joking!" she exclaimed.

Christopher showed no reaction. "And, perhaps more important, *ASP* is specifically suited for certain aspects of security that cannot be handled safely by humans." He stood beside her. "The protection of radioactive materials, for example. *ASP* can withstand radiation far more—"

"You must be joking!" Miranda said again.

Christopher drew a slow breath. "If you knew, Miranda, exactly how much time and money, how many resources I've committed to the development of *ASP*, you would not repeat yourself so frequently."

His face was absolutely serious. She could see no hint of mockery in his gray eyes. She had come to believe over the past two days that while Christopher would do anything to keep her from probing into his past, he would not lie to her about his business.

Miranda was aware that such a belief risked a great deal. But, somehow, she could not think otherwise of him.

Now she accepted the dictates imposed by that belief. Miranda grew serious, taking Christopher at his word. Her technical skills and the background research she'd absorbed served her well. She stepped closer, directing her attention at *ASP*. Having accepted Christopher's argument, she quickly realized that he was, indeed, telling the truth about *ASP*'s capabilities. And probably underestimating them for her. Miranda called for another demonstration of *ASP* on the skeet range where she had just finished testing herself.

Ian Pierce happily complied. *ASP* was put through its paces, and it never missed. The machine reacted with silent effortlessness, only the softest of whispers being heard before each clay pigeon exploded. For a finale, Pierce sent *ASP* rolling across the meadow at high speed, demonstrating the machine's accuracies of aim and fire. By the time *ASP* returned to the firing line, Miranda was impressed.

"But shooting's not all," she observed.

"No, of course not," said Christopher. "In fact, it's only a very small area of capability within *ASP*." He showed her a grin. "But it's the only one I'm willing to demonstrate to you today."

"How about a general description?"

"A résumé?" Christopher asked, and they both grinned.

"Please?" asked Miranda.

He nodded. "All right. What do you want? *ASP* either has it now, or is about to get it."

"Meaning?"

Christopher gave her a catalog of the machine's capabilities. "Perimeter surveillance, explosives and narcotics detection, recognition of intruders, pursuit and—"

"Execution?" interjected Miranda with some sharpness.

"Detainment," said Christopher. He summoned Ian Pierce with a wave of his right hand. "I think we'll save the rest for another day, Ian," he said.

"As you will, sir," said Ian Pierce.

"But, then, how do I know that what you're saying isn't all *talk?*" Miranda asked.

"You don't," said Christopher. "But now you know more about *ASP* than anyone outside our company. And if you do wish to know more, you may always return."

"With an exclusive?" asked Miranda.

"That will depend upon how we resolve our transaction, will it not?" asked Christopher. "But perhaps. At any rate, you may return to the armory when you wish."

"Count on that," said Miranda.

"In fact, if you prefer, you may remain here right now. The guest quarters are comfortable, the food is good. And I'm certain Ian and the other engineers would be happy to devote a couple of days to giving you a course in our *ASP*."

"No," said Miranda without hesitation. She felt sure she would want to return to CSI's elegant armory, but that could wait. At least now *ASP* was something more to her than just an enigmatic word. Now she must accomplish the same with Paul Christopher. "Thanks. But I'll take a rain check."

"We didn't need one this afternoon," Christopher said. He looked at the darkening but still clear sky. "We should be getting back to London," he said.

They walked back toward the house. Miranda may have passed on the opportunity for immediate further study of *ASP,* but that did not prevent her from posing further questions. "How intelligent is it?" she asked.

"ASP?" said Christopher with feigned distraction. He was silent for a moment. "More intelligent than any of its cousins," he said at last. "It is not a new hope, after all, to have robots accept security functions."

"Yes. But *ASP,* from what you've said, can do it all."

"We think so," said Christopher.

"And you're probably correct," said Miranda.

"Thank you," said Christopher. "And you're right. We probably are."

Miranda could detect little smugness in Christopher's answers. He spoke plainly and clearly, simply relating facts. Miranda pressed him with another question, but Christopher waved it away. "We have plenty of time to talk about *ASP,"* he said as he ushered her into the back seat of the Silver Cloud. "For now let's talk of other things."

Tony Earnhardt brought the Rolls-Royce to life. They left the parking area. "What sort of things?" Miranda asked.

"Freedom," said Paul Christopher.

"What?"

"Specifically, your freedom to join me for dinner this evening," said Christopher, his eyes meeting hers. "I'd thought we might go to Mirabelle."

Miranda hesitated a moment. But when she spoke, her words were not tentative. "Yes, Paul," she said. "I'd like that."

"Good," he said. "Shall we say ten?"

"I'll look forward to it," said Miranda.

"As will I," said Paul Christopher. The Rolls

approached the guard booth. "And what did you think of my . . . *armory?*" he asked.

Miranda searched for words. "There is no mistaking your touch throughout it," she said as they passed the guard booth. "Very elegant." She looked at him. "Very deadly."

Christopher's smile dazzled her. "What a fine description," he said. "Anything else?"

Miranda shook her head. "You can wait and read the book."

"Very well," said Christopher pleasantly. The Silver Cloud rolled toward London. After a moment Christopher snapped his fingers and said, "Damn!"

"What is it?" asked Miranda, startled.

"I forgot to show you the dungeon," said Christopher, and their laughter filled the car.

10

PAUL CHRISTOPHER CAREFULLY knotted his silk tie, then returned to his desk. He had forty-five minutes before he was due to meet Miranda in Claridge's lobby. He could accomplish a lot in three-quarters of an hour.

Before he could deal with the papers on his desk, he was interrupted by a call from Buenos Aires. He happily accepted the call. "Barbara?"

"Hello, Paul," she said. She did not waste time with small talk. "It's moving," she said. "Not fast yet, but it is moving."

"It will speed up of its own accord, Barbara," Christopher said.

"You sound like Esteban."

Did she have a note of anger in her voice? "Is everything all right, Barbara?" Christopher asked.

There was a moment of silence before she answered. Christopher listened to the slight hiss of background static behind the satellite-bounced signal. "I'm fine, Paul," Barbara said at last.

Christopher knew her too well to press her. But he also knew her too well to be unconcerned by the strange note in her voice. "Which bank finally led the move?" he asked.

"Chemical," said Barbara expressionlessly. "The others are coming in one at a time, though. Citibank's in, so's Manufacturers Hanover."

"Good," said Christopher. He had imagined the conversation so often, and each time he'd heard Barbara's voice filled with excitement, with triumph. Now she sounded simply flat. This was not the Barbara Webster he'd anticipated. "You're sure there are no problems?"

"Do you doubt me?" she asked almost angrily.

"Of course not, Barbara."

"There are no problems here, Paul," she said. "The deal is fine and will be finalized probably tomorrow."

"That's wonderful news, Barbara," he said, a flatness to his own words. He pressed his fingers against the metal desktop. "I'm very pleased."

"And London, Paul?" she asked. "Is everything well with you?"

It was Christopher's turn to pause before speaking. There had been no further progress in Hemmings's disappearance. Rita Sue remained calm, convinced that there was a logical, acceptable explanation, though she feared that it might be tragic. Christopher wished he could share her tranquillity. He and Angus grew more convinced with each hour Hemmings was not located that he had gone over.

"Paul?" Barbara said. "Are *you* all right?"

He heard concern in her voice. *She worries about me and I about her,* he thought. *It is a shame that we could not have remained—* Christopher cut the thought off. He and Barbara had known what they were doing when they began their affair all those years ago. And they knew what they were doing when they ended it. Love was the one thing they could not offer each other. Only trust. Christopher held his breath for a moment, preparing himself to question that trust.

"Is there anything else, Paul?" Barbara asked, obviously impatient.

"Yes," said Christopher, and waited.

"Well?"

"Have you . . . encountered any of the coins?" The hurt that he felt then was deeper than when he questioned Angus.

Barbara's answer was quick in coming to the point. "No, Paul," she said. "But I haven't been looking."

Christopher swiveled in his chair to stare out over London. "Of course," he said. He had been unable to read her voice. "And you would have notified me if you had."

"Yes, Paul. I would have." There was silence for a second. "Is there anything else?"

Christopher put his suspicions aside for later consideration. "For now, nothing, Barbara. I'm pleased with your news."

"I'll be in touch as things develop, Paul."

"Yes," he said softly. "I'll be looking forward to it."

"Good-bye," said Barbara Webster, and Paul Christopher was left with only the hiss of static. He felt that hiss reach deep down into his soul, chilling him. He'd held Barbara Webster in his arms once, and held her always in his highest esteem. Now he had violated that esteem, and his willingness to do so reminded him of the days when he could not afford even trust. Circumstances had led him, at twenty, to erect a wall of suspicion around himself. Christopher smiled savagely: he'd built an immense fortune providing security for other people and their holdings. Yet none of their secrets were as well-guarded as the secrets of Paul Christopher's own past, of his own heart. Had Barbara Webster betrayed him? Christopher knew now that it did not matter *who* had betrayed him. He would know soon enough. And then he would know what to do.

He found himself thinking of Miranda Glenn. The day in the country had proved far more enjoyable than he'd anticipated. His pleasure passed beyond the professional parrying between them. Christopher found her conversation to be stimulating, however antagonistic her positions. And she defended her positions well, he thought. It occurred to him that Miranda would be a resourceful and stimulating lover, as well. Christopher surprised himself by smiling at the thought. *But not now,* he reminded himself. *Not while so much hangs between us.*

Still, he could allow himself to look forward to an evening at Mirabelle with Miranda. He worked for fifteen minutes more, then drew on his Cerruti jacket and departed to pick up Miranda.

She was waiting for him in one of the carpeted drawing rooms just off Claridge's tiled entrance hall. Miranda was studying a vase of bright flowers. Christopher paused mid-stride, halting before she could see him. He moved slightly to the right, affording himself an unforgettable view of Miranda in profile. The brilliant red Scaasi dress she wore bloomed with delicate rhinestone roses that shimmered in the light. Miranda's tanned shoulders were bare, she wore no jewelry over the long perfect line of her neck. She'd tucked her hair up for the evening, and the resultant effect was nearly regal. Paul Christopher felt a surge of attraction course through him. "Miranda," he said in a voice that was almost a whisper, as though unwilling to disturb her.

She looked up, and smiled. "Hello, again," Miranda said. She caught him studying her and stepped back to pirouette. The hem of the silk dress fell just above her knees, and Christopher realized how perfect her long, muscular legs were.

"Good evening, Miranda," said Christopher. He'd missed her company since leaving her at Claridge's. They walked beside each other to the lobby, and one of the attendants there brought Miranda's matching red cape.

They left the lobby. Tony Earnhardt held the Silver Cloud's rear door open for them. Setting herself in the deep seat, Miranda drew the cape around her, clutching it almost coyly at her throat. She turned her head slightly to look at him. The cape's high collar framed her face. "Are we operating as professionals this evening, Paul? Shall I continue to be the formal journalist?"

"Hardly formal," said Christopher easily. "But our roles are at your discretion." He made a bow toward her. "Your choice, Miranda."

Miranda acknowledged with a smile. "Then, let's not. I don't think this dress would go well with technical talk."

"It goes well with you, Miranda," said Christopher.

She smiled. "Besides, we deserve a night off."

"Agreed, Miranda," said Christopher.

At Mirabelle they attracted subdued attention. Only a few patrons stared overtly at Paul Christopher and Miranda Glenn as they were ushered to their table. But Christopher was aware that many of the restaurant's patrons found excuses to cast surreptitious glances in their direction. For once, the attention bothered him only slightly. It was Miranda at whom they stared, and Christopher could find no way to fault them. Her beauty deserved a look, and for herself she seemed almost oblivious to the attention. Christopher seated himself opposite her, and moved aside the table's vase of freesias so he might view her without obstruction.

Miranda pursed her lips. "All right, Paul. I've left my press credentials outside. And you're wearing no security shield." She smiled invitingly. "What shall we talk about?"

"We have the whole world, don't we? All of history, the arts, culture. Politics—" He caught himself.

She giggled. "Probably not politics," Miranda said. She laughed again when he nodded his head in agreement.

"A wise decision," Christopher said. "We'll talk politics over brandy or chess in a book-lined room somewhere."

Miranda's eyebrows rose. "Will we? It sounds wonderful."

"It will be a pleasure to correct your political thinking," said Christopher. He creased his features with a grin before she could take offense.

"Oh, I'm sure my research will stand up to the . . . security with which you hold the wrong opinions," Miranda said.

Christopher held up his hands in mock surrender. "No politics," he said. In his mind's eye he caught a sudden unexpected glimpse of Miranda, wrapped in a bulky sweater, her head bowed in concentration over a chess problem. Through tall windows behind her, Christopher imagined he could see great waves breaking on tall rocks. For just a moment the image was as vivid as the reality of the restaurant around him. A shiver danced up Christopher's back. He blinked twice. The cozy vision dissolved, and Christopher was returned to Mirabelle and the real Miranda. She was staring quizzically at him, and Christopher sought to improvise words to fill the silence. "I was thinking of the rules of order a debate might impose upon us," he said.

"And whether or not you would be willing to follow them?" asked Miranda.

"Oh, you should know that I pay careful attention to the rules," said Christopher. He was no longer distracted; he gave her his complete concentration. "Once I understand exactly what the rules are."

Miranda did not wilt before his gaze. She raised her head slightly and he could see the strong pulse in her neck. A deep breath rustled the dress. Christopher looked into her eyes as she spoke. "You would insist, Paul, upon making the rules yourself? As you go along?"

"Not at all," said Christopher. "I can negotiate. And I have been known to compromise. Believe it or not." He summoned the sommelier. "Permit me to select the wine," he said to Miranda. "I feel as though exuberance is in order."

"Oh, yes," said Miranda. Eyes sparkling, she leaned forward. "Splurge!" she said, and giggled again.

Christopher ordered a Château Latour 1920, and he and Miranda studied their menus with the wine selection in mind. They laughed when they chose identical meals.

Christopher waited until the truffled eggs they'd ordered as first course arrived. "We'll be leaving early in the morning," he said.

"Back to the armory?" Miranda asked.

Christopher shook his head. "Leaving the country." He popped a bite of truffle into his mouth and savored its taste. "I hope that won't cause any inconvenience."

Miranda grinned at him. "You must be kidding. I've packed on shorter notice than this. But where are we going?"

"Oslo," said Christopher. "So dress warmly. And this time we'll be flying by private jet. If your integrity doesn't object."

"No," said Miranda. "I suppose not." She mused for a long moment. "Oslo. Your software team."

Christopher raised his hands and brought them together slowly in silent applause. "Again, your research was quite thorough," he said.

"I told you so," teased Miranda. "Why Oslo?"

Christopher watched her for a moment. "Before we're through, you will have visited each of our European offices. But I've no set itinerary. I picked Oslo this afternoon."

"What made up your mind?" Miranda asked. She leaned forward eagerly. "Some grand intrigue? Something with international consequences and global ramifications? An emergency of—"

Laughing, Christopher interrupted her. "Nothing so melodramatic," he said.

"Then what?" asked Miranda.

"I wanted to show you Oslo," he said. "I want you to see what CSI is doing there."

Miranda took a bite of egg. "No set itinerary," she said. "I thought you were the programmed man. The man of schedule by the second, and precision—"

"You've been reading too much journalism," said Christopher with a wide smile.

The main course was superb. After only a few bites, Paul and Miranda agreed that *medallion de boeuf Mirabelle* was one of London's true treasures. The wine was equally fine, and as the evening progressed their conversation grew more and more relaxed. They told funny stories, and each was delighted when the other laughed at precisely the right moment. By the time their coffee had arrived they were speaking as warmly as old friends. *Or new ones,* Christopher observed.

"I'm looking forward to Oslo," Miranda said. She sipped her coffee. "But leaving at six! Are you sure you're not trying to simply cloud my judgment by denying me sleep?"

"I doubt that I could cloud your judgment, Miranda," Christopher said. "But, seriously, I make my schedules in such a way as to give me a full day's work at my destination."

"Right off the plane," Miranda said.

"And right to the office," said Christopher. "I trust that the pace will not distress you."

"Don't worry about me, Paul," said Miranda. "I *like* this pace."

Christopher thought of all the women who did not. "That makes you unusual," he said.

"I never claimed to be otherwise."

Christopher stared at her for a moment, and saw color grow deeper in Miranda's cheeks. Her eyes were wide, but their gaze was distant. Christopher understood what was happening. *She's imagining me, just as I was her,* he thought. *She feels the attraction as well.* He stared at her for a moment. He knew what he wanted, but also the reasons he could not have it. *And so we become more dangerous to each other, even as we become more attractive.*

Miranda's distraction lasted no longer than Christopher's had. When she gave a shiver and her eyes suddenly focused, he did not press her. Miranda finished her coffee before speaking. "You never know when a story's going to just come *alive,"* she said. "When it's just going to take off with a life of its own. And when that happens, all you can do is follow it."

"And if my story never comes alive for you?" Christopher said. "How long do you follow?"

She answered immediately. "Oh, Paul, there's no question that you're worth following. That your story is worth following."

"And what do you know of me?" asked Christopher. "Other than that I have an interest in ancient coins."

Miranda grew flirtatious. "Oh, I know a few things," she said. "Enough to keep me interested."

"Well, I am glad of that," said Christopher. "I would not wish to lose your interest."

"Wouldn't you?" asked Miranda. "I'd thought you would be happy to be rid of a meddlesome journalist."

"No," said Christopher. "Not now. I've grown too curious."

"About what?"

"About the results of your work. The book or stories you will eventually produce. I want to see how I turn out after my turn under the light of your investigation."

Miranda studied him closely. She spoke little as they left the table, collected her wrap, and returned to the rear seat of the Silver Cloud. "There's something more you want, Paul," she said.

Christopher faced her. "Tell me what that is."

"You want to know who sold me the coin."

Christopher stared hard at her. "I thought you understood by now. I will know who provided you with the solidus, Miranda. Whether that information comes from you or not is wholly your decision."

"And when you know?"

Christopher shrugged. "That is one of your questions that I choose not to answer," he said.

"As is your prerogative," said Miranda. "Of course. But—"

"Yes?"

"Thank you for a lovely evening, Paul," she said unexpectedly. "I enjoyed myself even more than I expected."

"No more than did I, Miranda," said Christopher. The Rolls-Royce neared Claridge's.

Miranda turned away from Christopher for a moment, staring out at the city lights. Without facing him, she spoke softly. "Back to work in the morning."

"Yes," said Christopher.

"It's almost a shame," Miranda said.

Christopher sighed. "It would be too much to ask, I suppose, that you surrender your story."

Her laugh was harsh, although her voice remained soft. "You know it would, Paul."

Christopher chose to make it easier for them. He spoke brightly. "A nightcap would not be too much to ask, would it? At the hotel?"

Miranda turned back to him. "That's a fine idea. It's too early to call it a night just yet."

At Claridge's they walked past the crackling fire in the lobby fireplace. A great wrought-iron staircase loomed over the entrance hall. Paul Christopher and Miranda Glenn seated themselves in comfortable chairs in a drawing-room lounge off the lobby. They ordered brandy, and they did not speak until snifters were in their hands.

Christopher raised his glass and studied the liquid it held. "May we have more such pleasant days," he said, not quite toasting her.

"Yes," said Miranda. "Freed from our professional roles. I'd like that."

Christopher hesitated a moment before speaking. He knew that Miranda had left things unsaid in the car. "There is no reason, you know, for us to return unchanged to those roles," he said at last. "Mine is, as you said, an *evolving* story."

Miranda wafted her snifter beneath her nose. "No," she said. "No reason other than the dictates of our own natures."

"Meaning?"

She shrugged her strong bare shoulders. "We're alike, Paul. I've spent my life putting professionalism ahead of all else. And my professionalism rests upon suspicion. That's my *job*. It's any reporter's job. To be suspicious, to refuse to believe until we've *seen* or *touched* the truth."

"You still don't trust me," Christopher said.

"Oh, Paul," said Miranda with a soft laugh. "In many ways I would imagine you are the most trust-worthy person I've ever met. Certainly your clients hold high opinions of you." She sipped her brandy, holding it for a long moment in her mouth before swallowing. "I just don't know what it would mean to me. To . . . alter my sense of myself in such a way. To become too close to a subject of whom I may have to write harsh things."

Christopher watched her. Her face reflected the difficulty of the decision she was trying to make. "Miranda," he said.

"Yes, Paul?"

"There are many things between us. There are questions that each of us holds. And those questions must be answered. You wish to know about my past. I wish to know how you came by the coin that you sent to me." He took a sip of brandy, and savored its richness for a moment. "Yet we have found that we have many things in common. That we . . . respond to each other well." He waited a moment.

"I know, Paul," said Miranda. "Tonight, at Mirabelle . . ." She trailed off.

Christopher said nothing.

"So what do we do?"

Christopher wanted to say to her that she should come into his arms and be smothered beneath his kisses. *But no: however appealing the prospect, we must play out our roles until our questions are answered,* he thought. *Or at least my questions. To do less would be to commit my own betrayal of those who believe in my company.*

He made his face cheerful. "We continue as we are," Christopher said in a bright voice. He was bold enough to reach over and give her hand a squeeze, and was pleased that her fingers closed quickly around his. For a brief moment, they held hands. "And after our questions are settled," Christopher said. "When we each know what we must—"

"Then what?" asked Miranda.

"We establish the rules for our debate," said Christopher. They relaxed into their chairs and finished their brandy. "May I escort you to your room?" Christopher asked as they rose.

Miranda gave a mock curtsy. "That would make me feel very . . . *secure,* Mr. Christopher," she said.

They stood close together in the elevator. Once, their hands brushed, but their fingers did not entwine. *I would hold her hand,* Christopher found himself thinking. *I would hold it whenever she asked, were there not a betrayal between us. I must settle that, and Miranda must settle her own mind before we can permit ourselves to go farther.*

At her door they paused. Miranda stared at Christopher, as though searching his face for a clue to their future. "Today was very special, Paul," she said.

"For me as well," said Christopher.

Miranda nodded solemnly. "But—"

Christopher touched a finger to her lips. His other hand found her shoulder and rested there for a moment. Christopher stroked Miranda's cheek. They came closer, their lips approaching, but at the last moment they stopped. Each realized that the next step would be one step too far.

"But only for now," said Christopher to Miranda.

"We can hope so," she said, and turned and entered her room.

11

AFTER A SHOWER, Miranda made quick work of her packing. She had only a few hours before Christopher would pick her up. Miranda called room service and ordered a pot of cocoa. When it arrived she settled herself into one of the plushly upholstered armchairs to enjoy a steaming cup of the rich chocolate.

Miranda doubted if the chocolate would make her sleepy. She was too keyed up. She had too much to think about. And all of her thoughts revolved around Paul Christopher.

Was that his intention? Miranda wondered. She curled her long legs underneath her, and took a sip of the cocoa. Its warmth flowed luxuriantly through her. She shivered deliciously, thinking of how things would have been changed had she invited Paul Christopher into her room. Into her bed.

But the possibility that Paul Christopher was deliberately manipulating her emotions would not go away. She'd had absolutely no trouble picturing Christopher as dark and manipulative before she met him. But their conversations, the long day and delightful evening they'd just passed, were working to change her mind. She was powerfully attracted to him. It was no easier than before for Miranda to approve of Christopher's business dealings. And the

ASP he'd shown her was a heavily armed abomination. *But he is not,* Miranda made herself admit. She closed her hands tightly around the Wedgwood cup.

She felt torn. Paul Christopher was quickly becoming more interesting to her than any man she'd encountered in— Miranda grinned wryly. She realized that Christopher was more interesting to her than any man she'd ever met. But at the same time, his story, the story of his financial empire and the violence upon which it was built, grew more appealing by the day. It would make a terrific book. She could not have conceived of better background locales than those offered by CSI. Its armory would make half a dozen chapters come alive! And the tendrils of his operation reached into many of the boardrooms and government offices that controlled much of the free world's wealth and power. Miranda knew that she could write a book about Paul Christopher that would *last. But what would that do to Paul?* she wondered.

Miranda finished her cocoa and drew the drapes against the deep London night. She climbed into the large, firm bed and switched out the room's lights. She lay in the dark room alone, and knew that she was alone by choice. From his eyes, from the way he spoke and carried himself, Miranda Glenn was sure that Paul would be a marvelous lover. She'd shuddered with pleasure when he touched her shoulder, and wondered now if he had noticed.

But for all the promise that a romance with Christopher offered, Miranda was aware that something must be surrendered. Her journalistic sixth sense had not stopped tingling for all of the diversions Christopher offered. There was a story brewing around Miranda. Would she compromise it? Would she allow herself to be distracted from it by Paul Christopher's formidable charms? Or would her pursuit of the story jeopardize a relationship that might become the most fulfilling of her life?

It took Miranda nearly an hour to fall asleep, and when she did, her dreams were of Paul Christopher.

In his London office, Christopher met with Angus Hill. There was still no sign of Nigel Hemmings. Searchers were pushing deeper into the country where Hemmings had hiked, but their prospects were growing bleak.

"And you could not have asked for a finer day for a search than this one was, Paul," Angus said with a shake of his head. "And we've still found nothing."

Christopher stared out over nighttime London. It was past one, but he was scarcely sleepy. "How long since you've spoken with Lady Cedric?" he asked.

"Late this evening, Paul," Angus replied. "She's worried about Hemmings's safety, still. Less so about whether or not he's turned traitor against Cedri-Chem." He chuckled. "She's leaving for France in the morning, you know. She has a conference there this weekend, and is traveling by automobile."

Christopher smiled at Rita Sue's calm. "She could still be correct, you know," he said.

"I'm hoping so harder every hour, Paul."

"And every hour it gets harder to believe."

"Aye," said Angus.

Christopher seated himself behind his desk. He quickly scanned the latest electronic memos his terminal contained. "Barbara says tomorrow afternoon, her time, for the final transfer," Christopher related to Angus. "And then you'll be taking over your new position."

"Always assuming CedriChem doesn't blow up in our faces!" Angus exclaimed.

"Don't be so pessimistic, Angus." Christopher flashed a grin. "We've been through rough spots before. This will work out as well. I'm positive of it."

"Aye, you're always positive," Angus said. "And, I must admit, you came back from the country in a fine mood this afternoon."

"We shot skeet," Christopher said. "And shared a picnic." He grew warm at the memory.

"You and Miranda Glenn," said Angus with a cluck of his tongue.

"You disapprove?" asked Christopher.

"I suppose not," said Angus. "Not after meeting her. But how such a beautiful woman can write such wrongheaded pieces—"

"Idealism, Angus. That's all. An unstoppable idealism."

"Aye, well . . . what did she make of *ASP?*"

"Oh, she was impressed. It made her angry. But she *was* impressed."

"Do you trust her, Paul?"

Christopher took a long moment to consider his answer. "Yes," he said finally. "Not her opinions. But her integrity, her character? Yes, Angus, I trust those." He waited for Angus's response.

"Even after she procured the—" The Scot paused mid-phrase. "Which one was it?"

"A Byzantine solidus," said Christopher.

"Even after that, lad?"

"Yes," said Christopher. He'd given the matter a great deal of thought. "How could I not, Angus? She did not betray me, someone within my own organization did. And, Angus, how many times have we resorted to . . . unorthodox methods of obtaining the information we wanted?"

"But we were doing our job, Paul."

"So is Miranda. She just doesn't fully understand our function yet." Christopher sighed heavily. "She will."

"I hope so," said Angus. "And what next?"

Christopher did not answer for a moment. "I am going to call Barbara Webster," he said. "She should be made aware of the Hemmings situation. Should anything go wrong, she'll feel the first wave break. I want her to be prepared."

"And if she—" Angus said no more.

Christopher looked at the Scot. He smiled bitterly. "It's one of you, Angus. If it's Barbara, then I'm taking a big risk." He ran his fingers along the smooth edge of the desk. "But it's not Barbara."

"No," said Angus.

"And I'm off to Oslo in the morning with Miranda."

Angus beamed at the news. "Give Olaf my very best," he said. Then a frown as suddenly clouded his features. "I don't like this, Paul. Not knowing who. Thinking such thoughts about people who have been friends for years."

"I know what you mean, Angus," Paul Christopher said firmly. "And I don't intend for it to go on much longer." He waited until the Scot had left the room before calling Buenos Aires.

Three hours later Barbara Webster sat beside Esteban Rojas as he guided the big Cadillac along the highway leading out of Buenos Aires. It was a balmy evening, the car's top down, a warm breeze toying with Barbara's hair. She watched Esteban as he drove. Esteban kept his eyes on the road.

He'd not seemed surprised when she asked him to take her for a nighttime drive. The evening was too lovely to be wasted indoors. Barbara had not yet said to him the things she felt must be said. The Argentine banker had every right to know what Christopher had told her during their telephone conversation.

Barbara was glad the call had come. It put things into perspective for her. The creation of Christopher Defensive Systems was nearly complete: Esteban expected final transfer and initialing of documents to be accomplished by midday tomorrow. Paul Christopher had seemed calm as he spoke to Barbara, and she admitted to herself that there was little chance the Alphasome situation would explode before the deal was consummated. Yet no matter when the explosion came—if Hemmings had carried the secrets of the Alphasome lymphokine to a competitor or, worse yet, to an unfriendly nation—its ramifications could rock CSI. Badly enough, in a worst-case scenario, to cause Christopher Defensive Systems to collapse before it was well begun.

Esteban left the main highway some distance from Buenos Aires. He drove rapidly down a well-maintained secondary road until he reached a hilltop shaded by tall trees, gleaming in the moonlight. Esteban parked the Cadillac and turned in his seat to face Barbara Webster. "You said we must speak in confidence," he said. "I assure you, there is no one here to listen, except myself."

Barbara measured her words carefully. "There may be a problem at CSI," she said slowly, and told him of Hemmings's disappearance. She did not mention Miranda Glenn's name, nor the coin by which the journalist had purchased her way into Paul Christopher's life. Those items must remain confidential, although as Christopher had pointed out, hopes of confidentiality in the presence of such a famous journalist were probably foolish. The trick, he'd explained, would be to discover the source of the solidus without Miranda's help. Barbara had been surprised to hear Christopher call the journalist by her first name. She finished relating the story of Hemmings's disappearance.

"I appreciate your honesty with me, Barbara," Esteban said when she was done. "And I share your concern. You don't think that Paul will wish to cool the deal, do you?" he asked. "To slow it down until there is a resolution?"

"You don't know Paul Christopher!" Barbara exclaimed.

"Yes, I do, Barbara," said Esteban with a bright smile in the moonlight. "But I felt that I must ask. Paul is correct: we must proceed as though nothing is wrong, we must give no suspicions to the banks or the government."

Barbara relaxed against the Cadillac's seat. She stared up at the starry sky. All of the feelings that flowed through her in Esteban's presence returned to her then. And this time she decided that she must act upon them. The possibility of disaster, of the collapse of everything she and Paul and Esteban had worked for, served as a spur to her. "Esteban," she said softly.

"Yes, Barbara?"

"If things do go badly, what will you do?"

"Bounce back quickly," said Esteban with a laugh. "I am—how do you say it?—resilient."

Barbara shook her head. "Seriously, Esteban. How badly will you be hurt?"

He shrugged. "No more or less than I have been before. It is all a matter of degree in this life, Barbara. You know that."

"Yes," she said. "I do."

"When I was a boy I loaned a few pesos to a friend. He would repay me double, he promised. I never saw the money again. And I fretted and worried over it for days. Until I realized something."

"What was that, Esteban?"

"I realized that the time I spent worrying could be better spent making more money. From that it was an easy jump never to worry about my losses. I seek to minimize them, of course. But a disaster is only as bad as you allow it to be."

"You *do* sound like Paul," she said.

"And, besides," Esteban added, "business is simply business. If it all fell into rubble tomorrow, I would still have the pleasure of the work we have done together. The joy of watching you perform your wonders more smoothly than any banker, any businessman I've ever witnessed."

"You mean that, don't you, Esteban?" she said.

"I would not lie to you, Barbara," the banker said.

"But have you not wished we could . . . share something more than a purely business relationship?" Barbara asked. She looked away from him.

"I thought we did," said Esteban.

Barbara looked back at him. "What do you mean?"

"Our time together," he said in explanation. "You would not deny that lately we have enjoyed more than simply business between us."

"No," she said, confused. "But, Esteban—"

"Our evening in La Boca, our long dinners. Surely that was not simply . . . work to you?"

"No, Esteban. Of course not." Barbara feared she would stammer. But her questions still remained. She shared them with Esteban at last. "Why, then? Why haven't you been more open about your feelings?"

Esteban smiled at her, but did not speak.

Barbara could not stop herself. The words came out quickly, as though a torrent unleashed. "You always stopped," she said to him. "Each time I expected you to take me into your arms, to kiss me, and make love to me—you stopped. You left."

"Yes," said Esteban. "Everything you say is true."

"But, Esteban, *why?*"

His laughter echoed through the night, enveloping her. "Because it is *you*, my love, who possesses the reputation for being the great master of negotiation. Of the stalk and the wait. I promised myself that I could outwait you." He reached and caressed her cheek. His fingers found their way to the back of her neck, but he did not yet pull her to him. Their eyes met. "I do hope I have caused you no anguish," he said warmly. "You should know that it was not easy to walk away from you."

"And now?" she said in a hushed voice.

"I'd not intended to let you leave Argentina without making my desires known," Esteban said. He seemed amused, and Barbara found herself becoming more amused by his wiles. "But I had hoped to wait until the deal was completed."

"Now—" she said again.

"Now it all may collapse around us," Esteban said. "Why wait?"

"Why indeed?" answered Barbara, a wicked smile crossing her lips.

"No more negotiation?" asked Esteban.

"None. You win. Have your way with me."

"Have our ways with each other," said Esteban.

Their lips met and Barbara surrendered herself to Esteban's embrace. His strong hands stroked her back firmly, bringing her even closer to him. Their bodies pressed together and the kiss deepened until there could be no doubt as to its consequences.

At last Esteban drew back a bit. "Of course the location of a successful negotiation is important," he said. His breath was sweet and warm against her face.

"You suggest . . . ?" she said.

"Here, Barbara," said Esteban. "Now."

Barbara kissed him again. "Yes," she said. "Please."

Esteban stepped silently from the car and fetched a large brightly colored quilt from the trunk. He spread the quilt upon the ground and then returned to the passenger door. When Barbara climbed out of the Cadillac, Esteban pulled her to him, and kept his arm tight around her waist as they walked to the edge of the quilt he'd arranged. Their mouths met once more as they stood beneath the moonlight, and when the kiss broke, Barbara and Esteban began slowly to undress one another. Barbara unknotted Esteban's necktie and unbuttoned his shirt. She stood straight and tall as he unbuttoned her blouse and slipped it from her shoulders.

A long, deep shudder shook her when Esteban filled his hands with her breasts. She arched her back, a soft cry escaping her lips. Barbara's fingers busied themselves at Esteban's belt, and then his trousers. She took a step back at his urging, and then sank slowly to her knees. Barbara pulled Esteban's trousers down and cast them away. His legs were thick with corded muscles. His firmness brushed against her face, and she turned to fill her mouth with him.

But Esteban would not allow her. His warm hands closed about her shoulders and he pulled her erect. He smothered his face in her hair, kissed her neck. Then he fell before her and tugged at her skirt until she was fully revealed to him. Esteban buried himself in her with the ferocity of an animal. Barbara cried out his name. When at last he brought her gently down to the quilt and rose over her, she cried out his name again, then met his thrusts until all else faded before her ecstasy.

Afterward he held her beneath starlight. Barbara curled against Esteban until her face rested against his throat. She licked salt from his warm flesh. The night air was like a gentle cloak over them, and Barbara drifted in and out of a dazed somnolence. She thought of Paul Christopher, of the things he had told her. And of how those revelations had led to this mad hour with Esteban. Soon they must return to Buenos Aires and face the final hours of the takeover. Assuming there was no interruption of the process. She found that she could think more clearly now that she and Esteban had made wonderfully clear their feelings. She draped her thigh across his bare legs.

Even as her senses reveled in the afterglow of lovemaking, Barbara found herself seeing as though for the first time the truth about Paul Christopher's predicament. *He suspected me of sending her the coin,* Barbara thought. *He suspected all of us. He had no choice.* But it was not Christopher's suspicion that concerned her. Barbara knew too well the havoc she could have wreaked, had she wished to harm Christopher Security International. None of the others were responsible for so large a concentration of CSI's financial resources and obligations as Barbara. *But each holds enough power to cripple the company,* she realized. *Who among us would dare betray Paul?*

Esteban sensed something. "Barbara," he said. "You look too serious. Come here."

She kissed him tenderly. "Take me back to Buenos Aires, Esteban," Barbara Webster said.

"And there?" asked Esteban.

Barbara looked at Esteban for a long time. "It does matter, you know," she said gravely.

"Of course it does," said Esteban. "Perspective, you see."

"Yes."

"Before we made love, Barbara, all else seemed . . . an intrusion. We waited until precisely the correct moment. When all that existed for us was ourselves."

"Yes," she said again, and lowered her face to nuzzle his neck.

"Now our business returns."

"Dangerous stakes, Esteban."

"We knew that from the beginning, Barbara."

"But—" She thought of the things Esteban did not know, and for a moment considered telling him. But she kept her silence. "What will happen if something should go wrong?"

"Do not be so serious, my love," Esteban said.

Barbara felt herself filled with sudden deep love for the Argentine. She stroked his face.

"Barbara, don't underestimate your employer's ability to handle himself."

"Oh, no," said Barbara. "It's you I'm thinking of."

Esteban laughed, and tickled her until she laughed with him. "There! That's better, my love. Don't be so gloomy! This is Argentina! Another hundred million dollars' debt—who would notice?"

"Can you be serious?" she asked.

Esteban kissed her until he smiled. "All right," he said. "Yes, I will be serious. Nothing will go wrong. Nothing can go wrong. Everything will go exactly as planned."

"But—"

"You see, Barbara, it must. There is no alternative. And do you know why?"

"Tell me," she said.

"Because this is a *good* loan. The whole venture is as sound as can be. As I have said so many times before, Barbara—this is good for my country. Nothing will interfere with that."

They stood and dressed, returned to the Cadillac. Barbara sat close beside Esteban as they returned to Buenos Aires. They did not speak until they were near the city. "You still have not told me what you wish when we return to the hotel," Esteban said.

Barbara rested her head upon his shoulder as she spoke. "Stay the night with me, Esteban. Make love to me again." She thought of Paul Christopher, and silently wished him well. "Hold me," she said to Esteban Rojas.

12

OSLO WAS DUSTED with a light covering of snow. It looked lovely to Miranda as she followed Paul Christopher and Olaf Nyquist on a tour of CSI's software development facility. Miranda wished she were out in the snow. She wanted to walk through winter whiteness, she wanted to be embraced by the cold. She could not take her eyes from the snow. She wanted to lose herself in it, to walk far enough into the snowfields that all became white and featureless.

The story had appeared in the early *Times* she carried onto the plane. The paper had remained folded beside her through much of the flight. Miranda's attention had been focused upon Paul Christopher, but to little effect. There had been something unspoken between them from the moment he came to Claridge's to pick her up. During their conversations in the car and on board Christopher's sleek Lear jet they often fell into long silences. Miranda wondered throughout the flight if she'd surrendered too much of herself the night before. Had they been too honest? She knew that the same thoughts troubled Paul Christopher. At last, when one silence seemed impenetrable, Miranda turned in frustration to the newspaper.

The scantness of the story's details was a result of its late arrival. This is *breaking* news, thought Miranda bitterly when she fully comprehended the information the piece contained. JOURNALIST KILLED, the headline read. FILES, FILM STOLEN. James Howard Dennis had died in the New York apartment he'd leased for his stay in the city. The apartment had been ransacked, but only James Howard's files and film were missing. According to the story, he'd only that afternoon contracted with *Life* magazine for a long piece on Middle Eastern terrorism. Knowing James Howard, Miranda could imagine devastating photographs accompanied by heartbreaking copy.

Her own heart broke and a gale of grief stormed through her. She showed Christopher nothing of her emotions, and drew rhythmic breaths until her composure was complete. Miranda read the article several more times, until she had it virtually memorized. More than once she caught memories of James Howard, of the recent time they spent together, and of earlier times they'd shared, rising into her mind's eye. *Not now,* she told herself, and repeated the phrase until she believed it. Almost.

Christopher was all business once they arrived in Oslo. And, through all the ache of emotion, the journalist in Miranda could agree that what he showed her was important. The software research group that Christopher had assembled in Norway comprised some of the most acute minds in the computer and security industries. Their attention and talents were focused upon the development of indecipherable access codes and tamper-proof software to help guard, among other things, banking and credit data from unauthorized electronic intruders. "More than that, though," Christopher said. "It seems to us that it should be possible to protect data files from improper *use* of the information they contain—even by authorized users."

"You're talking about giving judgment to machines again," Miranda said to Christopher and Olaf Nyquist.

The tall, balding Norwegian agreed with her. *"Ja,* we are," he said. "But it's *our* judgment, *our* rules. The machines will use them to defend *our* rights."

Miranda would have none of it. "Just words," she said to the two men.

"Words are *your* chosen weapon, Miranda," said Christopher. He did not smile.

"Fair enough," admitted Miranda impatiently. "But better still to have no use for such things as this at all."

"You would return us to the Dark Ages, miss?" asked Nyquist, not unpleasantly. "We're simply dealing with things as they are."

Miranda nodded at him. "Yes," she said. Her voice was harsh. "You just respond to the needs of the world, isn't that it? I've heard that before, too," she said almost wearily. She took a step to the window and for a moment stared out at the gently falling snow. An enormous sadness filled her. She would never see James Howard's rugged smile again, she realized. There were so many things about him she would miss. He had taught Miranda a great deal over the years, about herself and her profession. She'd loved his work as much as she loved him. *And anonymous bastards stole his work as well as his life.* She was afraid to seek words to convey the retribution she would wreak upon James Howard's killers, if she could. In a way, she did not wish to know that such savagery dwelt within her. But it did, and as the morning with Christopher wore on, her mood grew increasingly bleak. "But what, gentlemen," she said angrily to Christopher and Nyquist, *"what* do you do to make the world better?"

The office was silent for a moment, and Miranda studied the snowflakes that clung briefly to the window before melting. "Everything we do is directed toward that end, Miranda," Christopher said in a low voice. "Don't you know that by now?"

"Well, it doesn't do a hell of a lot of good, does it?" she said sharply as she spun to face him.

Christopher stared at her for a long while, his face impassive. When he spoke, it was to Olaf Nyquist. "I think that's enough for today, Olaf," he said.

Miranda began to speak. "Now—"

Christopher shook his head, and she fell silent. Olaf bade them good-bye and left the room. "Miranda . . ." Christopher said.

She made a mask of her features. "Why did you do that?"

Christopher stepped close to her. "Because I've had enough for today. Enough of this." His eyes were fierce, penetrating. "You lost someone you cared about," he said gently.

Miranda stiffened. "What do you—"

Christopher did not permit her to finish. "I've told you. I won't lie to you, Miranda. I know things, I am aware of—"

"All right," said Miranda. "I understand." She showed him nothing but coldness.

"I would like to talk with you about it. If I may," he said.

"Why?" she asked, wary of him.

Christopher moved even closer, took her by the shoulders. He looked deep into her eyes. "Miranda, don't," he said. "Don't do this."

She pulled against his grip, but could not break free. "Paul," she said sharply.

"No," he said. "No, don't. Miranda, I know what

you are feeling. I've lost friends to mindlessness as well. I know how it can hurt, what it can do."

"How?" she asked. He still would not let her go, and Miranda ceased straining against his grip. "How can you know?"

"John Cedric," said Christopher. "For one. My dear friend John. And employees of mine."

"Your *business*," said Miranda, making the word ugly.

"I have personal feelings as well," said Christopher. His fingers tightened on her shoulders. "Or have you forgotten last night?"

"Last night James Howard was still alive," Miranda said. "I—"

"You could afford to cling blindly to your idealism!" Christopher said, almost shaking her. He seemed suddenly to realize what he was doing, and took his hands from her shoulders, stepped back from her. "I'm sorry," he said.

Miranda crossed her arms and stared at him. She saw pain in his eyes and her mood softened a bit. "More than those you mentioned?" she said.

"Yes," said Christopher.

She took a long time before she spoke again. "Tell me," she said at last.

Christopher spoke softly and slowly. "Her name was Maria," he said. "We were students together. We were going to be married."

"How old were you?" Miranda asked. "And where—"

But Christopher shook his head. "We must remain guarded, you and I," he said with a hint of a smile. "There are some questions I will not answer yet."

"All right," said Miranda.

"She was in her own way as beautiful as you,"

207

Christopher said. His eyes grew distant, yet Miranda did not look away from him. "And as bright. She was an exceptional girl, full of the promise of becoming a vital woman."

When Christopher was silent for a moment, Miranda spoke. "What happened to her?"

Paul Christopher gave a slight shrug. "Those were troubled times in my homeland," he said. "Dangerous times for people filled with silly ideas such as freedom. Maria was alive with such ideas, and then she was dead by the hands of those who oppose freedom." His voice was hollow and empty.

"And you?"

Christopher's smile almost frightened her. "I did not die," he said. Then sighed, and his demeanor softened. "Maria and I walked through open fields," he said. "There are divisions encamped there now."

Miranda watched as Christopher took his turn at the window. "I'm sorry, Paul," she said.

He shook his head. "I share your grief over the loss of James Howard Dennis. I admired his work."

"Did you?" Miranda asked accusingly.

"As a matter of fact, I did."

Miranda averted her eyes. "I'm sorry, Paul."

"No," said Christopher gently. "I do understand."

She looked up at him. Her eyes glistened, and she fought against a catch in her throat. "And I do believe you, Paul," Miranda said. She blinked against tears, but could not hold them back. "Oh, Paul—" she cried, and came into his arms.

Miranda wept against Paul Christopher's chest, and took comfort in the strength of his arms around her. Christopher stroked her back gently, and whispered against her hair. "It's all right, Miranda. You cry now." Miranda shuddered violently against him.

Then, slowly, she felt her own strengths beginning to regather. Her breathing settled, her tears ceased to flow. Her face grew flushed and hot. Miranda's awareness of Christopher's hands playing upon her spine and neck was transformed. From comfort offered a weeping woman, Christopher's touch gradually became more sensual, a caress. An ache of longing, a desire to hold and to be held swept through her, and she was taken by another shudder. Her eyes would not focus. She felt as though she were in a dream, the air warm and moist around her. She turned her face up to Christopher, seeking him.

But he slowly drew back from her. His eyes were sharp, and in their focus Miranda found her own. She shivered again, then stood tall. Paul Christopher's gaze was solemn, but his eyes were warm and caring. Miranda showed him a small, brave smile. After a moment Christopher released her from his embrace and stepped back.

Miranda waited a long moment before saying, "Thank you, Paul."

"Unnecessary," said Christopher with great gentleness. "As I said, I *do* understand."

Miranda blushed at the thought of the fever which had swept her. She looked gratefully at Christopher. "You could have—"

"No," he said. "I could not. Not in your grief. Not without . . . establishing the rules."

She was surprised at how easily she smiled. A last fleeting glimpse of James Howard Dennis's craggy features darted through her memory. Then Miranda put those memories away. She would mourn properly for her friend later. For now there was work to be done. "Paul?"

"Yes, Miranda?"

"What chance do the police have of finding the men who killed James Howard?"

"Men *and* women, likely," said Christopher. "Women can be terrorists too."

"You didn't answer me."

"No," said Christopher. "I did not."

"*No* chance," said Miranda sharply. "Is that what you're saying? What you don't want to tell me?"

Christopher spread his hands wide. "They could get lucky," he said. "But—if it's a group ambitious enough to go after a journalist instead of a schoolbus full of children . . ." He smiled bitterly. "They're away clear, Miranda. I'm sorry. The police would stand very little chance—"

"Would you?"

Christopher did not answer her.

"They never found Sir John Cedric's killers either. Did they, Paul?"

"No," said Christopher. "They never did."

"Did you?"

"Are you asking me to find James Howard's killers, Miranda?"

"I'm asking questions as a journalist. Nothing more," she said.

"Then I choose not to answer you."

Miranda did not press him. He'd been too kind. She stepped to the window and stared out at the snow. After a moment she said, "It's the work."

"What is, Miranda?" Christopher asked.

"The work they stole." The laugh she gave was bitter. "Poor James Howard. I knew him—he'd never rest until a story was filed. Now this one won't be."

Miranda spun toward him, and made her face bright. "Let's get back to work," she said. "I'll raise a glass to James Howard tonight."

"You're sure?" Christopher asked.

"Positive," Miranda said. "I'm all right. But, Paul . . ."

"Yes?"

"You've made me curious. Without treading on . . . forbidden ground, could CSI find terrorists who strike anonymously? Could you do that where the governments and police forces fail?"

Before Christopher could answer her, he was interrupted by a chime from his communications console. He stepped to his desk and spoke softly. When he looked up he was apologetic. "May I ask you to excuse me for a moment?" Christopher asked. "I must attend to something elsewhere."

"Of course," said Miranda.

But Christopher did not leave right away. "Are you all right, Miranda?" he asked. She could hear the concern in his voice.

"I'm *fine,* Paul," she said. "Really. He was a dear friend, and I will miss him. But he understood, as do I, the risks you take when you cover some stories." She slapped a fist into a palm. "Damn them for stealing his work," she said fiercely. "Almost as much as for stealing his life." Composure returned, and she laughed. "Thank you, Paul. I'm all right."

Christopher took a step toward the door. "I won't be long," he said. "Should you wish to prepare more questions."

"I'll work on some you'll feel free to answer," said Miranda.

"And perhaps I shall answer those you asked earlier," Christopher said. "Assuming you are still interested. And know what you are asking for."

Miranda stood at her full height and spoke evenly. "I know, Paul," she said. "I do know what I am asking for."

Christopher nodded, then turned and left the office. Miranda looked after him for a moment, then prowled around his office, glancing at objects, studying the few paintings. At last she returned to the window and lost herself once more in the whiteness of the snow.

13

ANGUS HILL COULD barely control his impatience as he waited for Paul Christopher to reach the telephone. There was half a tumbler of Glenlivet before him, and Angus tossed off another gulp. The Scotch seared his throat and a tear rose in his left eye. Chuckling, Angus brushed the tear away and began to whistle. If he'd had his bagpipes handy, he'd have played triumphantly upon them. Angus was raising his glass once more to his lips when Paul Christopher came on the line. "Angus?"

"Paul!" the Scot exclaimed, and banged his glass down. Scotch splattered across his leather blotter, but Angus did not mind. "We found the bugger!" he said, almost laughing once more. "Paul, we found Nigel Hemmings!"

"Where?" Christopher asked. "And on whose side?" Christopher's voice was calm, and Angus grinned. He might have known that not even this news would rattle Christopher.

"On our side, lad, on ours," said Angus.

"What happened?"

"It's a wonderful story," said Angus exultantly. "It'll make you weep."

"Angus," said Christopher firmly. "Control the

poetry. And I can't weep until I know the facts. Where did they find Hemmings?"

"Not fifteen kilometers from Hadrian's Wall. Within five kilometers of a small resort."

"What had detained him?" Christopher asked.

"As well-broken a leg as you'd ever care to see, Paul. And for all that, he'd thrown himself together some shelter, and was curled up in it spouting Wordsworth at the top of his lungs when we found him."

"His health?"

"Oh, he's lost a few pounds, lad. But he knew what he was doing. Took as good care of himself as he could. Better than most would have done under the circumstances. He'll be fine."

"Wonderful," said Christopher. "Knowing how well you do your job, Angus, I'm sure you called Lady Cedric before you called me."

"Aye, Paul."

"And?"

"She said to send you an enormous I-told-you-so," Angus said with a hearty laugh.

"Tell her I accept it most graciously," said Christopher.

"And she's motoring toward Paris now. *Happily* on her way, she said." Angus combed his beard with his thick fingers. "She also said to tell you thanks."

"Unnecessary," said Christopher. "But she knows that."

"Aye."

"All right, then," said Christopher. "A fine way to begin the morning. Very good news, Angus!"

"I'm more than a wee mite pleased, myself," said the Scot.

"What have we heard from Barbara Webster?" Christopher asked.

"Her reports remain the same," said Angus. "Progress not quite hourly, but it's there."

"Good, Angus."

"Aye. I cannot wait." Angus sipped a bit more celebratory Scotch. "How is Miranda?" he asked.

Christopher did not answer for a moment. "She has great reserves of strength," he said at last. "She's fine."

"Give her my best, Paul."

"Yes," said Christopher. "Now, Angus, there's something I want you to take care of."

"Go ahead," said Angus. He pushed aside his whiskey, took up a pen, and made notes while Paul Christopher delivered careful instructions.

Miranda Glenn was standing at a far window when Paul Christopher returned to his office. Once again he was all but stopped in his steps as he approached her. The snowy backdrop only heightened her beauty. "It's a lovely city," said Christopher.

Miranda turned and looked at him. "Yes," she said. "It's my first visit."

"I didn't know that," said Christopher with mock alarm. "We can't have you spending your first visit to Oslo cooped up in a stuffy office! It's not right." Christopher took a step closer to her. "Allow me, then, to make a suggestion."

"Yes?"

"Let's play hooky," Christopher said lightly. "Let's get away from all of this." He looked warmly at her, his eyes offering invitation as well as his words. "Let me take you for a walk in the snow."

"What?" Miranda said with some surprise.

Christopher grinned back at her. "Let's leave our work here, Miranda. Where it belongs." He gestured at the snowy scene seen through the window. "That's where we belong."

"But we can't—"

Christopher quickly hushed her objections. "Of course we can. We've put our work aside before. And I know that I enjoyed last evening far more than I had any right to expect." He held out a hand to her. "Let me show you this city, Miranda. Take a walk with me."

"A walk in the snow," Miranda said softly in a distracted and almost girlish voice. "But we'll never get any work done."

Christopher waved a hand, dismissing her objections.

"All right," Miranda said suddenly. "Yes! Let's go." She turned swiftly and took a step toward the door.

"Not quite that quickly," Christopher said. He studied her for a moment. Her thick Shetland sweater complemented a heavy wool skirt. Dark Ferragamo boots climbed toward her knees; her legs were sheathed in navy tights. "You're dressed for an afternoon outdoors." He plucked at the lapels of his Perry Ellis suit. "Give me a moment to make myself more casual, and we're off." Christopher changed quickly, drawing on a bright flannel L. L. Bean shirt, sturdy corduroy trousers. He laced his hiking boots high above his ankles, then drew on a shearling-lined leather jacket. By the time he returned to his office, Miranda had collected her down-filled parka.

"You look like you're ready for a long walk," she said to him.

"I enjoy walking," said Christopher as they stepped from his office. An elevator whisked them down toward street level.

"I love to explore new cities on foot," said Miranda.

"Another enthusiasm we share," Christopher said as the elevator doors opened. "Shall we?"

The air outside was bracing, but not bitter. Christopher and Miranda drew in great drafts of air as they walked, color rising to their cheeks. He led her at a quick pace along Karl Johansgate, Oslo's main avenue. Snowflakes danced against them as they walked easily up a gentle incline, approaching the Royal Palace. Christopher stopped before they entered Slotts Parken, the pastoral setting over which the palace presided. He ushered Miranda onto a large raised terrace. "Kongeterrassen," Christopher said to her. "Where the people congregate." With his hands he made an encompassing gesture. "Come and see the statue." Christopher hurried ahead of her, and Miranda scurried through the snow to catch up with him.

"King Haakon the Seventh," Christopher said to her as they stood beneath the statue of the monarch who guided his country so valiantly against the Nazi invaders. "A great man," Christopher said somberly. "A man of principles and honor. Who cared only for order, for peace, for his people."

Christopher was aware of Miranda studying him closely. *Does she understand yet that those are my concerns as well?* he wondered. For a moment longer they stared at the statue of caped King Haakon, then Christopher clapped his hands together. "Come!" he said. "We'll see the palace tomorrow."

"Where now?" Miranda asked as they turned and made their way from the terrace.

"In Norway," Christopher said, "one is not considered fully alive until one has gone to sea. Let us do the same."

Miranda followed Christopher several blocks until they reached Oslo's docks. "In summer, we could take a ferry, but I'm afraid today you must settle for my own launch," Christopher said.

"To where?" asked Miranda again.

Christopher pointed to the far peninsula. "Bygdøy. There are some things there that I think you will appreciate." They walked a short distance farther, until they reached the pier at which Christopher's launch was tied. He helped Miranda down into the sleek boat. "Will you cast us off?" he asked her.

"Aye, aye, skipper." Miranda grinned. She offered a jaunty salute before attending to the lines.

The launch's engines came to smooth life, and Miranda joined Christopher at the controls. "When I was a boy I dreamed of going to sea," said Christopher as they left the dock.

Miranda turned to watch the main city recede. "You wanted to be an admiral, I'd bet," she said. Snowflakes and spray pelted them as they crossed the harbor.

"You would be wrong," said Christopher. "I wanted to be an explorer in search of new lands."

"A difficult profession for the twentieth century," Miranda observed.

"Indeed," said Christopher, and laughed. But he grew more serious. "But when I was a boy I didn't care much about this century. My mind was elsewhere, in the past, lost in books and ideas." His breath frosted as he spoke. "My teacher—" Christopher fell silent.

Miranda waited a moment before prodding him gently. "Yes?"

"My teacher would recommend books for me to read, would buy me books as gifts. He knew what I was interested in, and he encouraged my interests. As

218

I grew older, he began shaping my concerns in such a way as to suit me for this century."

"What do you mean?" Miranda asked.

Christopher shrugged. "Oh, perhaps there are no distant lands to explore any longer. But he showed me that there were still challenges to face, discoveries to be made." Christopher laughed again, but there was a harshness to it. "I was many things then, all in my mind. I thought of becoming a biologist. For a time politics appealed to me—but I got over that quickly, I must assure you," he said.

"What else?" asked Miranda.

For a moment Christopher watched the way the snowflakes brushed against her skin, caught in her hair. "An attorney, a teacher. A priest."

"A priest?" she said, seemingly genuinely surprised.

"Oh, not because I was in any way particularly holy. I made as much mischief as any youngster." Christopher drew a deep breath. "But it was not an uncommon choice of life for young men . . . where I come from, at any rate."

"And where is that?" Miranda asked, almost offhandedly.

Christopher did not answer her. "My teacher, whom I admired intensely, was a priest in the town where I was born. Nor was I the only one to admire him with such a passion. We thought him a great man." Christopher was willing to say no more. The launch approached the docks at Bygdøy, and Christopher and Miranda worked together as though they'd been a team for years.

When they stood on the docks, their lines well-secured, Miranda's attention was captured by a tall, tentlike roof that rose high not far from them. "What is that?" she asked.

But Christopher guided her inland, away from the museums that stood at water's edge. "We'll save these for last," he said. "We can get quite a good meal here, as well. And we'll be hungry by the time we return."

"Where are we going, then?" Miranda asked.

"To see history," said Christopher, quickening his pace. Miranda kept up at his side.

They came at last to Oslo's sprawling Folk Museum. Its reconstructed timber-and-log buildings numbered more than one hundred, each an accurate recreation of past life in Norway. Christopher and Miranda made a brisk tour of the museum. They saw Henrik Ibsen's workroom, they paused to admire colorful tapestries and beautiful woodwork, clothing and utensils from the distant past. They reached at last the Gol Stave Church, a proud wooden edifice perfectly preserved from the twelfth century. "It's wonderful," said Miranda.

"It's a wonderful country," said Christopher. "It has surrendered none of its freedoms. I admire its people enormously."

Miranda was staring at the thick staves and timbers of which the church was constructed. The snow was falling steadily, muffling the sounds of early afternoon. They'd seen as they walked only a few tourists wandering among the wooden buildings. The snowfall concealed any traces of the modern world. It struck Christopher that he and Miranda might have stepped into the distant past, rather than just its representation. He looked at her.

"It would have been a good life," she said to him. She moved closer.

Christopher stared at her, drinking in her beauty. "You would have done well, Miranda," he said. "In any age."

She cocked her head at him. "And you, Paul?"

"Well, I would have done well had I you beside me," said Christopher with odd formality. He reached out to brush a snowflake from her cheek, and he could not resist caressing her face for a moment. "It would not have been an easy life, Miranda."

She pressed her face against his touch, nuzzling his gloved hand. "I never wanted an easy life," she said. "And no matter how hard, it would not have borne the . . . complication that we face today."

At last Christopher withdrew his hand. For a long time their eyes remained fixed upon each other. Christopher caught a glimpse of great sadness in her gaze, and wondered what she found in his own. "Ah, Miranda," he said, speaking as softly as a sigh. "Wouldn't it have been something? To face the challenges these people lived with daily. To have a world to bring order and justice to."

She nearly smiled. "But then you'd have been out of a job," she said cheerfully. "What global security needs did these people have?"

"On the contrary," said Christopher, any darkness lifting from his thoughts. "I'd have been free to pursue my career of first choice. I could have sailed ships." He took her hand for a moment. "Let's see some."

They left the grounds of the Folk Museum, walking at an easy pace through the snow. "The Viking Ship Museum," he said as they approached a more modern structure not far from the wooden village where they had walked. Inside the museum their breath was taken by the three magnificent ships the structure held.

"They look as though they could put to sea immediately," Miranda said as she stared at the high-prowed longship before her.

"And wouldn't that be an adventure?" Paul Christopher mused aloud. "To raise sails for distant seas for the first time."

"Not to mention all of the raping and pillaging that go with it," said Miranda with a wry chuckle. "All of those women. And leave your own women at home."

Christopher shook his head. "I would not be concerned if I were you. I cannot imagine even the most restless rover ever being willing to depart from one such as you, Miranda." For a moment she looked as though she expected him to kiss her, and for a moment Christopher was tempted. Before the temptation could grow too strong, he forced his attention away from her, and they resumed their tour. They walked slowly through the spacious museum, taking in the Tune ship, and the Gokstad longship, and passing several moments in awe of the restored beauty of the Oseberg ship, as immaculate as it must have been when first built, in the ninth century. "To have sailed in that . . ." said Christopher, feeling for just a moment completely out of place in his own world.

Miranda came close. She touched his arm. Her eyes smiled brilliantly at him. "Oh, Paul," she said, "I think that you find enough adventure here and now. I really do." She waited until Christopher smiled with her, and Christopher found the invitation too difficult to resist. He was at that moment freed from all of his concerns. Unexpectedly the image of Nigel Hemmings, broken-legged but able to quote poetry in the winter wilderness, came to Christopher. He began to laugh.

"I do," he said to her. "More than enough adventure." They walked toward the doors. When they stepped outside, the snowfall had slowed. "This way," said Christopher, leading Miranda back toward the docks. "Hungry?"

"Starved," said Miranda.

Christopher nodded. "We'll eat at Najaden in the Maritime Museum." His grin was contagious. "And look at more ships."

Najaden was not crowded, and Christopher and Miranda took a table at a window overlooking the harbor. Even in winter the water was busy with modern ships. Soon Christopher and Miranda's attention was distracted from the ships by the enormous platters of food and tall steins of dark beer that were placed before them. With mutual enthusiasm, the two attacked thick slices of ham and roast beef spread with rich mustard. Potato salads, crisp vegetables, crusty breads, perfectly smoked fish disappeared before them. Christopher was delighted to watch as Miranda's appetite kept pace with his own. They grinned at each other over forkfuls, unwilling to interrupt the meal for conversation. She matched Christopher beer for beer as well, and a whimsical glow came over their table.

At last, after nearly an hour, they sat back. "One last beer," Christopher said, signaling to their waiter.

"To protect us from the cold?" asked Miranda. She laughed.

"Indeed," said Christopher. He raised his eyebrows. "We do have to keep our strength up."

"If not our guard?" asked Miranda seriously.

Christopher said nothing as the waiter delivered their steins. He raised his above the table, holding it steady as Miranda touched hers to it in toast. "To lowered guards," he said.

Miranda hesitated for a moment before drinking deeply. "An unusual toast, coming from a member of your profession," said Miranda when they'd set down their steins.

"Is it?" asked Christopher innocently. He sipped some more beer. "That sounded like a professional comment itself," he said to Miranda. "I thought we'd left our jobs at my office."

"You must admit, Paul, that lowered guards are not what your company sells."

"No," said Christopher. "But perhaps I was speaking personally."

"That would change things," said Miranda.

"How?"

"Oh, I *loathe* the profession," said Miranda. "But I do like the man behind it. I like him very much."

"But we are one and the same, Miranda," Christopher said. "You must understand that. My business and I are one." He spoke quietly but firmly. His gaze hardened and he kept it on her. Wistfully, Christopher realized how little Miranda truly knew of him. And he realized as well that before he could grow more involved with her there were matters that must be put straight. He narrowed his eyes.

Miranda gave a slight nod. "'Loathe' was perhaps too strong a word, Paul," she said after a moment. "Or inaccurate. Would you accept . . . *dissent?*"

Christopher's smile returned in an instant, ignited by her quickness and her choice of words. Perhaps they could find a way through the difficulties that lay between them. "Dissent is something I always welcome," said Christopher. "As well as a right my company helps defend. It provides opportunity for debate, which I always enjoy."

"I know *that,*" said Miranda with a chuckle.

Christopher drank from his stein. "You know, I won ribbons for my debating when I was young," he said almost shyly.

"Coached, no doubt, by your mentor," Miranda said. "The priest. What was his name?"

For a moment, Christopher did not answer her.

"Josef," he said. "Father Josef. I will tell you that much."

"You admired him."

"A great deal. We all did."

"He taught you to love reading and debating," Miranda said.

"Oh, he taught me many things," said Christopher. They finished their beer. Christopher held Miranda's chair for her as they left the table, and helped her on with her jacket. As she slipped her arms into the sleeves, Christopher stood behind her, for a moment wishing he could take her into his arms. But he made no move, and they left Najaden to walk to the *Kon-Tiki* museum. "Now, *that* was a book," Christopher said to Miranda as they stood before the frail-looking craft on which Thor Heyerdahl had made his epic voyage.

"It's a wonderful book," agreed Miranda.

They circled the boat twice, then Christopher ushered Miranda back outside. Afternoon shadows were beginning to gather. The snowfall was growing heavy once more. Christopher glanced at his watch, and a fat snowflake settled onto the gold coin that Corum's craftsmen had transformed into an elegant timepiece. "One more museum," he said to Miranda. "And then we'll take the launch back to the city."

"That one?" Miranda asked, pointing at the high, tentlike roof that had first caught her eye.

"Yes," said Christopher. *"Fram."*

Inside the museum they found the vessel that had carried Fridtjof Nansen farther north and Roald Amundsen farther south than any explorer before them had ever fared. "What I would have given to have covered those stories," said Miranda. "To have been with the first at the South Pole."

"But you would have found few corporate controversies on such assignments," said Christopher as they circled the *Fram*. "No government malfeasances, no—"

"I wouldn't have been looking for them, Paul," she said. "Not given the chance to share an adventure." Once more her hand found his.

Christopher said nothing. *Does she know what she is saying?* he wondered. *What is she telling me?* With his thumb he stroked her knuckles for a moment. "We'd best be getting back to the city," he said. "It's getting late to be on the water."

They returned to the docks and boarded Christopher's launch. As he piloted the craft across the harbor, Christopher found himself unable to forget Miranda's words. He could share his adventure with her, he thought. Once he discovered who had provided her with the solidus. Once he knew who it was among his trusted who had betrayed him and the things Christopher and his company stood for. He turned to watch Miranda.

Her face was uplifted to the spray and the snow, her cheeks glistened. Before too many days had passed, they would be in Rome, his advisers assembled before them. Christopher would know by then who had betrayed him; he knew already the measures he would take. Beyond that, he could see himself and Miranda, the two of them together, their life's adventures shared. At that moment, all that mattered was the delight he found in her presence. The rest receded. As Christopher stared at Miranda, he realized that he had not felt such emotion in years. A soaring surged through him and he caught his breath. What he felt now had been gone for so long that he had forgotten himself capable of such feeling. He steadied the wheel of the launch, preparing himself to take Miranda into his arms.

But all evaporated when for a moment he saw not Miranda's face before him, but Maria's. That face whose innocence and joy had filled his universe. That face he had kissed so often. That face whose beauty he'd seen ruined by a soldier's rifle butt. Those eyes he had closed after the spark of life within Maria had died.

Christopher tightened his grip on the wheel and kept his eyes forward.

"I enjoyed our afternoon, Paul," Miranda said. "I enjoyed it very much."

"Yes," said Christopher curtly. He gave the wheel a turn, and brought the launch to the dock. Miranda bounded up and made fast the lines. Together, wordlessly, they drew down and secured the boat covers. They stood beside each other on the docks.

"What now?" Miranda asked enthusiastically.

Christopher's face was stern. "Perhaps we should return to work," he said in businesslike tones. "Perhaps it might be best for us to resume our professional roles."

Miranda's smile vanished. She chewed her lower lip. "Did I say something?" she asked. "Did I—"

Christopher shook his head. "I simply think that we may have been ignoring certain . . . facts that have a bearing on what we may and may not do." He spread his hands. "The afternoon was my suggestion. I accept the responsibility."

"For what?" asked Miranda angrily. "For a wonderful few hours? For the chance to get to know each other better?"

"For refusing to accept our differences," said Christopher. He walked away from her, striding quickly through the snow and back toward the heart of Oslo. After a moment Miranda followed him, but made no attempt to catch up.

Christopher clenched and unclenched his fists as he walked. He had made his peace years before with Maria's death, and he had spent the years since then erecting barriers around the emotions that had seized him when she died in his arms. *Now I could fall in love with Miranda,* he thought. *And what? Lose her when my traitor is uncovered? Lose her because she cannot know the truth about my past? Or lose her because she does?* He clenched his fists, his thoughts seething, and was taken completely by surprise when a snowball burst against the back of his head.

He spun, dropping into a low, instinctive crouch, one hand darting into his jacket out of reflex. Christopher checked his motions as he saw Miranda Glenn, standing hands on hips, staring at him with laughter in her eyes.

It was not long before the laughter came from her lips as well. "Oh, Paul," she said. "I couldn't resist. You just looked so serious as you stalked along the streets."

Christopher drew himself erect and brushed the snow from his shoulders. "Your aim was quite good," he said when Miranda had joined him. He turned and they walked back in the direction of the building where he maintained his offices. Miranda sought to link her arm with his, but Christopher drew away from her. "No, Miranda," he said. "I don't think that would be wise."

"If that is the way you want it, Paul," she said coldly.

"It is the way it must be," he said. "If you have any questions, you may ask them of me."

"All right," said Miranda as they walked through

the lengthening shadows. "What is it you're afraid of?"

Christopher ignored the question, and Miranda posed it again. He stopped at a street corner.

"What is it, then?" she demanded. "Why did you change so abruptly?" She held out her hands to him. "We can resolve—"

"Fine," said Christopher. "Let's make our resolution *now*."

Miranda said nothing.

"Who sent you the coin?" Christopher asked her harshly.

"Why does it mean so much to *you?*" Miranda responded.

A silence hung between them. "You see?" said Christopher with some calm.

"You toasted lower guards," said Miranda.

"An error in judgment," said Christopher.

He could see that he had hurt her, and for a moment he was filled with regret. But the moment passed.

Miranda shook her head. "Oh, Paul," she said wistfully. "I thought—"

"No, Miranda," Christopher said. "We cannot allow ourselves." They crossed the street and once more he set a quick pace, pulling ahead of her. The second snowball missed his shoulder, and when Christopher spun to demand that Miranda grow more serious, she flung another snowball, and caught him squarely on the nose. Her laughter filled the afternoon as she danced past him, running ahead and gathering snow in her hands to make another missile. Christopher dodged it, and set out in pursuit of Miranda.

She laughingly pelted him with snowballs each time he came close to her, and before they'd traveled another block Christopher found himself fighting against the impulse to smile. But the smile gathered force within him, and spread across his face. He reached to gather snow of his own, and when Miranda turned to throw another snowball at him, he was prepared. Christopher sidestepped Miranda's projectile. His own found its target, snow exploding on her left shoulder. Christopher began to laugh, and Miranda joined him.

"You see, Paul," she said. "We can laugh together. We can—"

"We can be cordial," Christopher said, unwilling to offer more. "We can be friends, and professionals. But no more."

"I thought you wanted adventure," she said.

"I want order," Christopher said. They resumed walking. "Now, ask your questions."

Miranda drew a deep breath. Her cheeks were red from the running snowball fight. "Just one."

"Yes?"

Miranda patted her stomach. "It felt good to run after such a huge lunch," she said. "And Mirabelle last night." She looked gravely at Christopher. "How *do* you keep in shape, Paul?" she asked. A smile blossomed. "Call it a human-interest question."

"A simple question, easily answered," Christopher said as they rounded a snowy corner. "I maintain an exercise room, a gymnasium, at each of my offices. A workout helps me escape any tensions."

"I'd say you need that now," Miranda said. "I know I do."

"You're welcome to use the gym and sauna," said Christopher. "In fact, you should have them to yourself."

"Won't you join me?" said Miranda. "We could

talk as we exercise. We could get some . . . *work* done."

Christopher said nothing for a moment. "All right," he said. "If you like."

"Yes," said Miranda. "I think it would do both of us good. Our waistlines, if nothing else." She spied a boutique a short distance ahead. "Just let me duck in here and get myself outfitted," she said. She darted into the store.

Christopher waited outside in the cold. His thoughts were cold, for all the laughter the snowball battle had provoked. He could not recall wanting a woman as intensely as he desired Miranda Glenn. Nor could he recall any woman who seemed so perfectly suited to him, with whom he shared so many things. His discipline took hold, though, restraining such thoughts. Gradually he made his mind blank, and waited in the snow for Miranda.

14

CHRISTOPHER PROWLED AMONG the gleaming exercise equipment that filled the mirrored gym. Miranda was changing in the adjoining sauna. Christopher was already clad in thigh-length exercise shorts, a light shirt, sneakers.

The walk back to the office building, and the elevator ride to this floor, had passed in relative silence. Miranda carried a large shopping bag that rustled as they walked. What few words there had been came from her, little jokes and comments to which he chose not to respond.

The telephone mounted on the far wall gave a chime, and Christopher stepped to it. "Yes?"

"Barbara Webster from Buenos Aires," he was told.

"Put her on," said Christopher. "Hello, Barbara?"

"Hi, Paul," she said. He could hear the happiness. *"Mañana,"* she said, giving a thick Spanish roll to the word.

"Tomorrow?" said Christopher. "You're certain?"

"More or less. Enough to make the call. We have a classic bit of lead-lender manipulation going on right now, but I don't think they know who they're trying to manipulate."

"Details?"

Barbara sighed. "Chemical wants another half point. It's a nice try, actually, pretty well-thought-out."

"And our response?" asked Christopher, although he already knew the answer.

"Oh, I'll offer a quarter point in the morning."

Again he knew her answer before asking his question. "And if we find our offer refused?"

"Then we walk happily away," said Barbara, who began to laugh. "The choking sound you hear is Esteban Rojas," she explained. "He's turning purple at every word I speak."

"The color should suit him," Paul Christopher said with a chuckle of his own.

"I don't think we'll have to walk very far," said Barbara.

"I'm sure you're right, Barbara."

"Congratulations, by the way, on settling the Cedri-Chem problem," Barbara said. "I had a long conversation with Angus."

"The congratulations rightly belong to him," Christopher said. "Or to Nigel Hemmings himself for simply staying alive."

"Whatever," said Barbara, "it's nice to have it behind us. Angus is practicing his Spanish. You wouldn't *believe* his accent!"

"*You* sound wonderful, Barbara," Christopher said. Gone was any hint of the darkness that had clouded their earlier conversation.

"I *feel* wonderful!" Barbara said.

"You should. Everything seems to be coming together for us."

"Yes, Paul, it is."

"I can't help but wonder, though," Christopher said. "What part does Esteban play in your happiness?"

Barbara was silent for a moment. "You always were smart, Paul."

"Shall I take that as your answer?"

"Let me put it this way, my old friend." Her voice grew warm. "Maria's wedding may not be the only one you attend soon."

"Are you serious?" Christopher asked, delighted.

"That choking sound your hear is Esteban once more," Barbara joked. "I don't quite have him persuaded."

Before Christopher could speak, he heard another voice, then Esteban Rojas came on the line. "Don't believe this woman, Paul," the Argentine banker said. "I am trying to make an honest woman of her and—"

"And she's *negotiating* with you!" Christopher interrupted. He felt more relaxed than he had since early afternoon. Since he thought of Maria. His grip tightened on the telephone receiver.

"You are exactly right, Paul," said Esteban. "And she is a difficult negotiator. She expects me to give her—"

"Esteban," said Christopher. "Give her anything she wants. You will never regret it."

"You know, Paul," said Esteban, "I do believe that you are absolutely correct. Here's Barbara."

"Well, Paul?" she asked.

"I can't tell you how happy I am for you, my old love," Christopher said. "Unless, of course, this affects your position with CSI." He laughed to assure her that he was joking.

"Oh, we might have to do some renegotiating, Paul."

"Anything you want, Barbara. I'll make it a wedding present."

"Thank you, Paul," Barbara said softly. "For everything."

"It is a pleasure," he said. "As it will be to see you soon. Will Esteban be coming to Rome?"

"I have no intention of letting him out of my sight."

"Then we must celebrate," said Christopher. "I will toast your happiness."

"And what of yours, Paul?" Barbara asked. "How do things progress on the . . . journalistic front?"

Christopher answered only after glancing toward the sauna door. What was keeping her? "As far as the source of the solidus, nothing yet," he told Barbara. "As far as what she will write, I can only say that I find Ms. Glenn to be eminently professional."

"*Ms*. Glenn?" asked Barbara. "That's not what Angus calls her. He's still talking about *Miranda* and how—"

"Professional cordiality," said Christopher. "Nothing more."

"Oh, Paul," said Barbara with a happy laugh. "What you have in store for you."

"What do you mean, Barbara?" Christopher asked.

"Never mind." She chuckled deep in her throat. "It's just love talking. I'll call tomorrow and let you know Chemical's reaction."

"I'll look forward to it," said Christopher. After he hung up he began going through his stretching routine, clenching and unclenching his muscles, making himself limber for exercise. He began to grow impatient at the length of time Miranda was taking. When the sauna door opened, he did not break his rhythm immediately, but took a moment to complete the exercise before looking up.

Miranda was radiant. Christopher did not look away from her as she walked slowly across the gymnasium. Fully clothed, her figure was lush. Clad now in a forest-green skintight Danskin, her full breasts swayed gently as she made her way to him, their round swell broken only by the poke of nipples against fabric. The smooth curve of Miranda's hips was exposed by the leotard's cut. Between taut thighs, a firm mound burgeoned against cloth. Miranda's long legs were bare.

Their eyes met. "Well?" asked Miranda, a hint of defiance in her tone. "Shall we begin?"

"Of course," said Christopher. Putting a few feet between them, he resumed his stretching. After a moment Miranda followed suit. Their pace grew gradually more strenuous. They moved from simple stretches into more vigorous competition.

"No music?" Miranda asked with a haughty laugh as she began putting herself through aerobic paces.

Christopher stepped to a suspended speed bag. He drew on four-ounce gloves and tied them tight. Circling the bag, he began peppering it with punches. "I make my own," he grunted as he skipped from position to position around the bag.

Miranda increased the pace of her dance.

Christopher said nothing. He had nothing to say to her. He worked his left jab hard. The speed bag's steady clatter echoed around him as he shifted among combination punches. He kept his concentration upon the bag and his fists, only occasionally allowing himself to notice the fevered gyrations through which Miranda was putting herself. When she reclined upon an exercise mat, he did not look at her at all.

After ten minutes, Miranda began gradually slowing her dance. She wound down carefully, giving each muscle attention as she stretched herself once more. A sheen of perspiration glistened on her bare shoulders. Wetness darkened the Danskin in places. She walked at last to the wall-mounted towel. Miranda mopped her face and arms, catching her breath before moving to the first of the series of Nautilus machines whose chrome ranks lined one of the walls of the gym. Christopher continued punching as Miranda adjusted the machine's balancing weights. Only after Miranda had settled into a series of ankle and calf exercises did Christopher step away from the speed bag and remove his boxing gloves. He stared at her for a long minute. She worked the weight well, her nostrils flaring with exertion, breasts lifting high as she strained and tested her muscles against the tug of gravity. Miranda's mouth was drawn into a tight line, and tiny creases gathered at the corners of her eyes. Christopher looked at the amount of weight she was carrying. "Don't strain," he cautioned.

Miranda let the weights fall. She drew a deep breath before speaking. "I might say the same to you. I thought you were going to demolish that bag."

Christopher shrugged. His shirt was wringing wet. Staring at her, he pulled it off. Thick muscles corded across his shoulders, dark hair only beginning to be fleckcd with gray made a thatch upon his chest. Christopher took a towel from the rack and ran it roughly over his shoulders and down his arms. Miranda followed him with her eyes. He said nothing.

Still without speaking, Christopher took up a position before the Nautilus. Miranda did not move, but stared with obvious speculation at him. "Do you want me to move?" she asked archly.

Christopher ignored her as complctely as he did the urge to pull her from the machine and take her to the mat beside it. "I can wait," he said as he stared at her.

For another moment Miranda remained motionless, then glided effortlessly to her feet and stepped aside for him. "I wouldn't make you wait, Paul," she said.

"But I would," said Christopher. He increased the weight, then settled himself into the Nautilus and began his first series. Miranda moved on to the next machine. Each time he completed his work and approached the next Nautilus, Miranda lingered before him for a moment, holding her position in the machine. At last he reached the final piece of equipment, and she yielded her position quickly. As Christopher labored his way through neck and shoulder exercises, Miranda studied him.

"You *would* wait, wouldn't you, Paul?" she said to him softly. "I believe that."

Christopher spoke between clenched teeth as he pushed against the weights. "You should know me by now," he said.

"Yes," said Miranda. She caught her lower lip between her teeth for a second, and appeared in deep concentration. Christopher finished his exercise and sprang up from the machine. After he had toweled himself he faced her. "Paul," she said.

"Yes?" Christopher's breathing settled. He moved no closer to Miranda.

"You held my hand this afternoon."

"Yes," said Christopher. "I did."

"And last night."

"Yes."

"But not me." She shook her head and a curl spilled free. She brushed it back. "You haven't held me."

"I cannot," said Christopher curtly. "It is something I cannot allow."

"But why?" she asked, and Christopher could see the bafflement and hurt that shone clearly in her eyes.

He was not unmoved, but he held himself in check. He could not respond to her. "Paul, *why?*" she implored him. "Don't I have a right to know that?"

Christopher laughed almost cruelly. "A *right?*" he said. "Miranda, to speak of *rights—*"

"No!" For a moment he thought she would strike him. "No more noble *words!* Tell me *why—*"

Christopher narrowed his eyes. Miranda's were wide, dilated. He did not speak until she had grown calm once more. "Because of what you sent me," he said. "Because of—"

"Because of what I *am,* you mean," Miranda said. "Because of my profession, and your contempt, your distrust—"

"No." Christopher nearly seized her shoulders, but still refused to touch her. He stepped back. "You misunderstand. What you are, Miranda," he said, speaking her name with great gentleness, "is a wonder. A delight, a joy." Christopher watched as Miranda's anger gave way to a softer expression at his unexpected words. "To say less to you would be a lie. And you do have the right to the truth from me."

"Then *why?*" she asked once more.

"Because of the solidus that you obtained, I am faced by a violation of the highest trusts I have permitted myself," Christopher said. "You understand that?"

"Yes, Paul, I do. Of course I do." She tossed her head violently, as though in frustration. "But—"

He spoke tenderly. "Miranda, please do not put yourself through this. If you seek reassurance, be assured that I find you the freshest breath of air my recent life has known—more than that. I could not tell you what you mean to me."

A tear trickled from her left eye. "Tell me, Paul," she said. "Please—"

"No." He reached out and brushed the tear away. "I cannot. Perhaps soon, when this has reached its resolution . . ." His voice trailed off. "Forgive me. To pretend that would be unfair. I am sorry, Miranda, and you may believe that." He turned away from her. "If you will excuse me, I am going to the sauna. Join me, if you like." He walked away from her with deliberate steps. At the sauna's door he removed his shoes.

The sauna filled with steam, and Christopher activated the jets that churned the water in the small pool into whiteness. He drank steam into his lungs, and stretched a few times to work the last kinks out of his muscles. Alone, he gave free rein to his thoughts, and they did not surprise him. *I have come to love her,* he thought. Perspiration beaded on his well-muscled body as the room grew hotter. Christopher stood tall against the swelter, letting the heat penetrate, hoping that it might scald away his longing for Miranda. But when he heard the sauna door open and close softly, he was not surprised that his heart soared. He turned to face Miranda.

15

Miranda's eyes were red, as though she'd been crying, but her gaze was clear and steady. Christopher swallowed hard against the knot in his throat. He took a single step toward her, then found himself hesitating —but only for a second. And then everything beyond the room, beyond Miranda, evaporated. Hoarsely Christopher said her name.

"You were right, Paul," she said. Steam swirled around her. "I *do* know you. And knowing you . . . I love you, Paul." She shook her head and without warning a wry grin appeared. "It would have made one hell of a book. But there are lots of books." Miranda's perfect features grew solemn. "I would rather make a love."

"Miranda—" Christopher said. She pursed her lips and he fell silent. A long look passed between them. Then Miranda tugged at her Danskin, slipping it from her shoulders and drawing it slowly down. Her breasts came free, their firmness almost haughtily high upon her chest. When she had revealed herself to the waist, Miranda hesitated, then pulled the leotard down, stepped out of it and stood before him. Christopher reached for the waist of the brief shorts he wore, but Miranda shook her head and stepped to him. Her fingers danced against his skin, and her lips pressed against his throat. She bent at the knees and pulled his clothing away. Christopher's blood raced and he swelled at her touch. He placed his hands upon her shoulders and pulled her up to him. Their mouths met.

"Paul," she whispered when their kiss broke. Miranda's sweet breath was hot on Christopher's face. "Oh, Paul, yes," said Miranda Glenn.

Christopher filled his hands with her breasts. Her nipples grew stiff against his thumbs, and Miranda arched her back. Her fingers circled around him and squeezed tight. Christopher's fingers raked the fields of her breasts, and Miranda's hands reached lower to cup him and tease him. Christopher buried his face in her hair. Miranda called his name again and again. They found their way to the padded floor that surrounded a small, frothing pool.

Miranda once more arched her back to Christopher. He showered kisses and bites upon the pulse of her throat, the tautness of her shoulders, the tips of her breasts. She opened herself to him and Christopher moved between her legs. Miranda's tongue circled her lips again and again, as though she could not slake their dryness. Christopher kissed her. He reached down to guide himself, and found Miranda wet, scalding, overflowing. As they came together, their bodies melting into one, Miranda tore her mouth from Christopher's and cried his name. Christopher filled her.

For a moment he did not move, and when he did it was slowly, with great gentleness and care. Miranda wept beneath him, her hips following his lead in a long, slow roll. "My love," she said. She rose up against him, and moments later an endless shudder shook them as their passion became complete.

They remained entwined, staring into each other's eyes. Gradually their breathing became regular. Miranda stroked Christopher's face. "Oh, Paul, I do love you," she sighed. Her eyes brightened. "Whoever you are." She turned her head to kiss his hand, and noticed for the first time the webwork of white scar tissue otherwise concealed behind his watch. "What is this, Paul?" she asked as she looked up at him.

"That is who I am," said Christopher. He smiled at her.

"But what—"

Christopher shook his head. "Not yet," he said. "Another time."

"Yes, Paul," said Miranda. She touched his face. "We'll have many other times."

Christopher kissed her nose. Miranda snuggled against him, giggling to herself. "What is it?" he asked.

"I was thinking of all the time that we're going to have. And how we're going to spend it."

"And that makes you laugh?" asked Christopher. He tickled her ribs.

"Stop it!" Miranda bit him playfully on the arm. "No. Now that I've given up my book." Miranda stretched languorously. "I get filled with . . . desires when I'm between books."

"You've given it up, then?" Christopher asked.

"I told you I had," said Miranda. "*One* of us had to do something. Besides, I'm an honest reporter—I'd have had to report on *this*." Her laughter filled the steamy sauna as her fingers found him once more. "And I want to keep this all to myself."

Christopher laughed with her, but he also knew how hard her decision had been. "I love you, Miranda," he said.

"I gave up a hell of a book for you, Mr. Christopher," she said. "Now, how are you going to make it up to me?"

"Any number of ways," said Christopher with a grin.

"I do hope that's a promise," said Miranda.

"It is," said Christopher, beginning to prove it. "Besides," he said, mimicking her, "the book might have failed."

"The hell you say!" exclaimed Miranda, putting her hands hard against his chest. Her eyes laughed at Christopher.

He winked at her. "I was simply thinking that you might have had trouble doing me . . . justice," he said.

Miranda's mouth opened wide, but she did not speak. Christopher felt her arms tighten too late to catch himself, and when she shoved, he tumbled back into the pool. Miranda hooted with laughter.

Christopher floated at the center of the pool. Each time he moved through the water toward Miranda, she moved away from him. They stalked each other for a moment in the steam. "It's warm in here," Christopher said invitingly.

"It's warm out here," said Miranda in reply.

"But I'm in here," he said.

"That's true," said Miranda before she swung her legs over the lip of the pool and lowered herself into the hot water.

Christopher pulled Miranda immediately to him, and as her arms circled his back, their bodies melded once more. Pulses of hot water struck their bodies and Miranda locked her legs around the small of Christopher's broad back. They moved through water together, their own fevered rhythm in synch with the pool's jets. Miranda's cries echoed off the sauna's walls. She clung fiercely to Christopher as he lifted her up and out of the water, bracing her on the pool's lip as he kissed her own lips. Her knees rose nearly to his shoulders, passion making her frantic. Miranda wailed and then whimpered his name. She bucked against him almost convulsively before he exploded; then she collapsed, her arms draped limply around him.

Many minutes passed before either was able to move. Christopher at last forced himself to his feet and pulled Miranda up after him. She sagged into him, murmuring only, "Sleepy . . ."

"Too much steam, my love," Christopher whispered close to her ear.

"Too much *you*," Miranda said softly. "Not that such a thing could ever be." Christopher switched off the pool's controls, and the water settled. He took two long, heavy robes from a cabinet, and pulled his own on only after he had wrapped Miranda's around her and belted it snugly. Christopher kissed her once, then swung her up into his arms and carried her from the room.

Later that night, when they were curled close in his wide bed, Miranda's strength returned. Christopher lay beneath her, deliciously trapped, letting Miranda make love to him. Snow fell softly against the bedroom windows. In the room's gentle light Miranda's skin seemed to acquire a glow. She rocked from side to side above him, clenching him with her knees. At one point Miranda bent at the waist as though leaning to kiss Paul Christopher, but she did not. There was several inches between them, and Christopher could see clearly the wideness of Miranda's eyes as she was seized by sudden, unexpected ecstasy. She tightened herself around him, her gentle rocking became a more violent, almost desperate writhing. Christopher rose within her. They shuddered together, and within moments were both lost in a deep sleep that lasted until they were awakened by the morning's first light.

Christopher and Miranda shared a long, lazy shower that became nearly as steamy as yesterday's sauna. Afterward they dressed and busied themselves with the construction of an enormous breakfast. Christopher sliced and broiled tomatoes while Miranda scrambled half a dozen eggs. Only after they finished eating and faced each other over fresh mugs of hot black coffee did their conversation grow serious.

"So," said Miranda. "We are lovers."

"I think that's a safe conclusion," said Christopher.

"And I'm out a book."

"There are other books, you said," Christopher reminded her. He sipped his coffee.

"Yes," said Miranda. She seemed distracted.

"What is it?" he asked.

Miranda toyed with her mug for a moment before answering him. "I was thinking . . . when you discover how and from whom I obtained the solidus—what will happen?"

Christopher could not answer the question. "I'm sorry, Miranda," he said.

"No, please," she said almost shyly. "It's all right, Paul. I knew what I was doing. What we were doing, what we were getting ourselves into. Now we must simply see where it leads."

"I would cause you no pain," Christopher said solemnly.

"I know that." She averted her eyes for a moment, and drank some coffee. When she looked back at him it was with a broad smile illuminating her features. "Where do we go next?" she asked brightly.

Christopher took her hand. "Back to bed, I think."

Miranda rolled her eyes. "An excellent suggestion. But I meant after Oslo."

"We'll be here another day at least," Christopher said. "There are some things to see. The Edvard Munch Museum, the countryside around the city. After that: Paris."

"The Georges V, I hope," Miranda said, and Christopher pictured her in one of the great hotel's wonderful rooms.

"If that is your wish," he said.

"And after that?" Miranda asked eagerly.

"Perhaps Bonn, perhaps Madrid. And end up in Rome for the wedding of a dear girl whose name is Maria Conti."

"Maria," she said slowly, as though speaking the name for the first time. "Like your first love."

Christopher waved the observation away. "This Maria is the daughter of an old and close friend, Giancarlo Conti. But then, of course you know from your research—"

"A *wedding,"* said Miranda dreamily.

"Yes," said Paul Christopher, but before he could say more, he was summoned to the telephone for a priority access call and all of the tranquility he and Miranda had assembled was shattered.

Christopher excused himself from the kitchen to accept the call. When he returned to Miranda his face was grim, his voice flat and emotionless. He stared at Miranda as though she were a stranger. "My car will take you to your hotel," he told her. "I'm returning to Paris. Should you wish to accompany me, you must pack quickly. We'll be airborne within the hour."

Miranda half-rose from her chair. "Paul?"

"Last evening was more eventful than we knew," he said, his back half-turned to her. "While we . . . diverted ourselves, Rita Sue Cedric was kidnapped. Her bodyguards—*my* employees—were killed." Christopher held his voice even. "Obviously, her abductors possessed inside information. I've little doubt that it came from the same source as your coin."

"What do you—"

Christopher's eyes were as clear and hard as diamonds. "I will expect, Miranda, you to tell me who provided you with the coin."

16

MIRANDA STARED UP at Christopher. She had never seen a face so set in determination. He did not blink, and the look that Miranda found in his eyes hurt her. She took a moment to find her voice. "I can't do that, Paul," she said. "You know that."

Christopher was astonished. "Don't be ridiculous, Miranda," he snapped. "You've said yourself that you surrendered the story."

"It's not that—" she began.

"Then what?" Christopher shouted. "A woman's life is in danger. Good men have been killed. Who gave you the coin?"

Miranda shook her head. "No," she said firmly. "I will not reveal a source. Not even to you, my love."

"Rita Sue Cedric may die because of your false sense of ethics!"

"Paul, I am sorry, but I just *can't*," Miranda replied. "Don't you know me well enough to understand that?"

"Not even when a human life may be saved by your honesty?" Paul Christopher's words were clipped, his tone brutal.

"No, Paul. You are asking me to violate something . . . fundamental. I can't do that." She stared at him for a moment. "I am truly sorry," she said.

"Don't waste your breath," said Christopher. "Or any more time. The car is waiting downstairs. Are you coming to Paris?"

"Yes." Miranda said no more for fear her voice would falter.

"Then be at the airport in forty-five minutes. I'll meet you there. But I will not wait for you."

"I'll be there," said Miranda Glenn.

"Good-bye, Miranda," said Paul Christopher.

"Paul!" she called after him. But Christopher had left the room. Miranda returned to her hotel and began to pack.

Christopher seated himself behind his desk and turned his attention to his computer terminal. Angus Hill had fed him what few facts CSI had regarding the kidnapping of Lady Rita Sue Cedric. The abduction took place in the early morning as Rita Sue's Bentley motored toward Beauvais. She was taking a roundabout route to Paris, enjoying the French countryside that she cared for so deeply. The Bentley had broken down. When her guards stepped out to examine the engine, they were shot by high-powered rifle. *They didn't have a chance,* Christopher realized. Their bodies were found next to the Bentley. One of them— *or Rita Sue*—had managed to activate a transmitter that notified CSI/Paris of a problem. Thus far there had been no ransom note; nor any indication that the press knew of the abduction. Christopher picked up the telephone and was connected with Angus. During their brief initial conversation, Christopher had learned only that Rita Sue had been taken, that his men had been killed. He'd asked Angus to call immediately each of the members of his inner circle and summon them to the château Christopher maintained outside Beauvais. Then Christopher had left to confront Miranda. Back at his desk he was still stung by the pain he'd seen in her eyes before he left her.

There is no time for that now, he thought. "Angus," Christopher said. "Who have you spoken with?"

"I started with those farthest away, Paul," the Scot said. "Rahjit first; he's on his way." Desai in Delhi, as well as the CSI executives in Hong Kong, Tokyo, and Sydney had been contacted.

"All right," said Christopher. "Call the rest as soon as we're finished. I'll speak to Barbara myself." He drew breath. "Now. Is there anything else?"

"We're following everything we can, Paul," Angus said. "But they had some time, they could be anywhere."

"What about Hemmings?" The biologist's lengthy disappearance had become suspicious again.

"We've begun interrogation, Paul," said Angus. "He's denying everything, and our monitors are supporting him."

"All right," said Christopher. "Don't be too rough —Rita Sue will have more than enough to curse me for without our harming one of her employees."

"Yes, Paul."

"Start moving equipment to the château, Angus. I want to be able to arm a strike force of whatever strength we need, once we have Rita Sue located. Get yourself to France as soon as you've spoken with the others."

"Aye, Paul."

"And bring whomever of our people you think we'll need. I want our best, and I want them ready to move. Whether I've reached France or not. The moment you have a fix on them, Angus, go after them and get Rita Sue out. You're in charge of that end until I arrive."

"Yes, Paul," Angus said.

Christopher sighed. "Well, old friend, we may be giving *WISP* a field test sooner than we'd thought."

"I included half a dozen among the weapons sent ahead to the château," Angus said. "They'll be on their way within the hour."

"Good. And, Angus—" Christopher was interrupted by a chime that indicated an incoming message on his terminal. "Are you sending anything now?"

"No," said Angus Hill. "Our transmission's ended."

Christopher's fingers stabbed keys. The message was simple and appeared instantly. ALPHASOME FOR EVERYONE, it read, OR THE LADY DIES. The access code employed was a private one, known only to Paul Christopher—and his closest advisers.

Christopher swore bitterly even as he called over the intercom for Olaf Nyquist. "Activate a tracer program, *now!*" he barked. If they could trap the electronic interloper within their system, at least they would have something to work with. "It's one of us, Angus," Christopher said into the telephone. "And the betrayal is not only of me, of the company—now a client is endangered. Find Rita Sue Cedric!"

"Aye, lad, we will," said Angus.

Christopher broke the connection. Olaf Nyquist hustled CSI's top software team into action in pursuit of the electronic ransom. Paul Christopher dialed Buenos Aires. He wondered as he did so if his scrambling system and communications lines were still secure. *How much has been given away? And how much hope have we of saving Rita Sue?*

The call awoke Barbara Webster. Esteban stirred beside her, one of his muscular arms draped across her. Barbara extricated herself carefully from his embrace so as not to wake him. "Paul?" she asked in a hushed voice when she heard Christopher. "What is it?"

"Rita Sue Cedric has been kidnapped," Christopher said. "Two of our people are dead."

"My God." Barbara sat up straight in bed, holding the telephone receiver tight. "When?"

Christopher gave Barbara a quick synopsis of the situation as it was understood. "We've received a sort of ransom demand," he explained, and quoted the message that came over his terminal. "Olaf says there's little chance of our backtracking through the computer system—the fact that the kidnappers have the private code made it easy for them to get in and out."

"Damn," said Barbara.

"My sentiments exactly," Christopher said with a wry bitterness. "All codes, by the way, are being altered immediately; if they come back to us by way of computer, we should be able to track them without difficulty."

"But they won't," said Barbara.

"No," Christopher said. "They're too smart for that. I've summoned the entire circle to France, Barbara. I want them with me as we go into this."

"Shall I—"

"No. Stay in Buenos Aires. I'll need you there to take care of damage control if this breaks to the press."

"If this breaks to the press, Paul, there will be a fair amount of damage to control," Barbara said. She managed a brave laugh.

Paul Christopher did not laugh. "One member of the press is already aware of the kidnapping, Barbara. You should be aware of that."

"Miranda Glenn?"

"Yes," said Christopher. He did not allow himself to think of Miranda's face.

"And what do you think she'll do with this knowledge?"

"I really can't say." Christopher ran his fingertips over the surface of his desk. "I must admit, though, it's one hell of a story," he said.

"Paul—"

Christopher did not allow his old friend to interrupt. "She will be coming to France with me. I intend to keep her close, if only because by doing so we may keep her under surveillance." He was silent for a moment. "Damn her," he said at last in a low voice.

"Oh, Paul," said Barbara Webster. "Is she so—"

"She holds the answer! She could give us the information we need to free Rita Sue!" Christopher shouted. He made himself calm before speaking again. "Miranda Glenn knows who the traitor in CSI is. Were she to give me the name, we could resolve this quickly. I have no doubts. Damn her!" he said again.

"Well, Paul, we have our ways, as they say. Why not turn her over to Angus or Giancarlo for special interrogation?"

Christopher said nothing for a moment. "She says she is protecting a *source.*" He made the word ugly.

"I doubt her defenses could withstand a hard interrogation, Paul," Barbara said. She looked down at Esteban, and despite the seriousness of Christopher's words, a smile appeared on Barbara's lips. She stroked Esteban's forehead. He smiled in his sleep and after a moment opened one eye. Barbara pressed a finger to his lips to silence any questions he might have. She could answer Esteban's questions later. "Go ahead, Paul. Let out all the stops. Give her a shot of Serum Sixty—that should open her up. Or how about a little old-fashioned torture—"

"Enough, Barbara!" Christopher said angrily.

"Is it?" Barbara asked. "You curse her for not revealing a confidence—the same virtue you praise in your own employees."

"No," said Christopher. "Not when there is a life at stake."

"As you will, Paul," Barbara said.

"Now," said Christopher, "what about the Chemical request?"

"I intend to handle it as though nothing has changed. If the story breaks in the midst of negotiations, well—I don't think Chemical will be the only bank to have hesitations."

For a moment the line was silent. Then Christopher spoke once more. "The best of luck to you, Barbara," he said seriously. "And I do hope that you don't need it."

"Thanks, Paul," said Barbara Webster. "My first concern is for Rita Sue, of course."

"Yes," said Christopher. "And mine."

"Be careful, Paul."

"Do not be worried about me, Barbara. I will be fine." His sigh was heavy. "But when I find the traitor . . ." Christopher's voice trailed off.

"Good luck, Paul," Barbara Webster said before the connection was broken. She had no idea whether or not he heard her.

Esteban Rojas looked up at Barbara. "My darling, what—"

Barbara gave the Argentine banker a quick summary of Paul Christopher's conversation. Esteban's face grew grim as he heard of Rita Sue's kidnapping. "And right in the middle of all of it is Miranda Glenn," Barbara said as she finished.

"Who can make the biggest headlines in the world, should she so choose," Esteban said softly.

"And bring Christopher Security International tumbling down even as her own career climbs higher," Barbara said.

"Do you think she will?"

Barbara shrugged her bare shoulders, snuggled deeper into the bed and closer to Esteban. "I have no idea, my love. From some things that Angus said, I would have thought—" She shrugged again. "Our first worry, of course—the *company's* first worry—is Lady Cedric's well-being. You must understand that. Whatever it costs us personally. Whatever it costs all of those dependent upon this acquisition. Our first concern must be for our client."

Esteban's eyes were wide and dark, filled with concern and understanding. "Of course I understand that, my darling. That is the sort of integrity, of dedication that attracted me to Paul Christopher and his company in the first place." He reached to stroke her cheek. "I expected no less from the moment you began speaking."

Barbara nodded. "But until it *does* become public," she said with a grin that seemed almost savage, "until then, we proceed as though nothing has happened. When we speak with Chemical Bank in the morning—"

"We smile and are confident and show them not a care in the world!" said Esteban. "And if it all should fall around us—"

"We walk out with our heads held high and set to work immediately to rebuild our companies and our careers!" Barbara Webster finished for him.

Esteban Rojas nodded. His right hand strayed to Barbara's breasts, caressing them gently.

"In a few hours we could be ruined," Barbara said.

"No," said Esteban, his mouth close to her, his breath hot upon her. "Not so long as we share each other."

"Esteban," Barbara said. "If we are knocked from the pinnacle—"

"We climb back *together*, my darling." His mouth covered hers for a moment. "But we climb back."

"While we are here . . ." Barbara began.

Esteban moved over her. "Yes?"

"Make love to me one more time, Esteban, while we are here, at the top."

Their bodies moved as one.

Rahjit Desai paced back and forth on the long dhurrie rug. Soon he would go to the roof of the office building to board the helicopter for the airport. The din of Delhi's bustle reached him even at the high floor on which his office was located. Desai stepped to the window, but for once was unmoved by the panoramic view. He had other things to think about.

Angus Hill's call had him worried. It was routine for all of CSI's offices to be notified of a branch crisis. Delhi branch had just come off alert, in fact, following the resolution of Nigel Hemmings's disappearance. The kidnapping of a client, or for that matter a client's employee, would certainly result in a worldwide alert. But for all of Paul Christopher's advisers to be summoned to his side on no notice was unprecedented. Desai found himself picturing the fury of the flame that must be burning in Christopher's eyes. Desai was not looking forward to the gathering. *To summon all of us—* He did not complete the thought.

His palms were damp and he drew a silk handkerchief from the breast pocket of his linen jacket and dried them. The prospect of facing Paul Christopher suddenly frightened him. They had known each other for so long. Rahjit Desai knew that Paul Christopher's integrity was supported by an equal ruthlessness. Betrayed, Paul Christopher could be expected to show no mercy. The thought caused Desai some pain.

He paced until he received word that the helicopter had arrived, and then, attempting to leave his apprehension behind him, Desai ascended to the heliport and began the first leg of his journey to France.

James Helmers kept his voice flat during the conversation with Angus Hill. Helmers had no interest in revealing to Hill the hope that suddenly flared within him. *So Paul Christopher finally finds himself in difficulty,* he thought almost gleefully after the Scot had broken the connection. *That should not cause me as much pleasure as it does.* He buzzed his secretary and instructed her to arrange for him the fastest possible transportation to Europe. He cleared his desk.

Then, for just a moment, James Helmers paused. He thumbed the ProTech seal on his desk safe and when the drawer opened he stared for several long seconds at the ancient coins that rested within. A smile spread across his face. Then he closed the safe and left his office. He did not wish to miss a moment of Paul Christopher's discomfort.

Warm Mediterranean sunshine played across the broad tiled terrace that jutted out from Giancarlo Conti's villa. A gentle breeze toyed with the tall flowers that blossomed from squat planters scattered about the terrace. The song of soaring and perching birds was joined by soft gasps and cries of pleasure from the lips of the Italian starlet who moved fluidly above Giancarlo Conti. Both were nude in the hot sunlight.

Else—she was known on screen and in person only by her first name—was nineteen, but had already graced more than a dozen low-budget films. Conti encountered her at an engagement party for his daughter. It had required little effort for him to steer Else from the other revelers—this must have been Maria's *seventh* prenuptial party—and from there to his private villa and this terrace, where they'd spent hours at fevered coupling. Else proved herself as talented at the act of love as she was not at the art of acting. The starlet's wantonness, the completeness of her surrender to sexual sensuality, surprised even Giancarlo Conti, who was not unaccustomed to the company of young women. They were an indulgence in which Conti took continual and unapologetic pleasure. Tonight, though, for the first time after a long night of lovemaking, he had found himself feeling old. It was not that Conti had trouble keeping up with Else, but that there seemed something callous, something distracted, about her. Lovemaking was for her only another diversion, Conti perceived, another way of passing a few hours. She seemed only to be going through the motions, Expert, exciting, erotic motions to be sure, but some kernel of concentration in Else was kept separate from their actions. There was a reserve, an *ennui*, he could not break through. The pleasure she took was obvious: even now she shivered and cried as another climax began to sweep through her. But there remained that certain distance in her eyes. The distance annoyed Conti's sense of order, and he thrust up harder within her.

Else's eyes widened, but that served only to make more obvious to Conti the vapid boredom that resided there. Perhaps it was just her age. Else was a year younger than Maria. Conti wondered if any woman that age—still a girl!—could truly appreciate the erotic arts. Perhaps not. Not without tutelage at least, and he had provided such instruction to many young women. Else held herself back, though, unwilling to accept his instruction. She continued to buck and writhe over him, those vacant eyes now beginning to roll upward. "Giancarlo," she whispered, adding a few obscene endearments. "Giancarlo—" she moaned more energetically, and clenched him as though she would crush him in her attempt to spur his own climax.

After which, thought Giancarlo Conti, *she will wiggle once more and then roll off me, that slightly dissatisfied smile on her face that she has shown me more than once these past few hours.* Conti dug his fingers into the flesh of her buttocks and arched his back that he might move more deeply within her. Else cried out, and bent forward to offer her breasts to his lips.

They were interrupted by the unmistakable chime of a priority access call. Giancarlo immediately stiffened, and Else, convinced that she was the source of his sudden rigor, cried out exultantly, her gyrations achieving a new frenzy above Conti. When he roughly pushed her off him she began to curse loudly. Conti paid no attention, and padded nude across the warm tiles and into the study where he maintained an office. He grabbed the telephone.

"Conti." He stood beside the desk and stared out at Else. There was a measure of cold fury in her eyes as she stared back at him. Else moved slowly over the chaise, arranging herself as though for his inspection. Her full mouth pouted, she dragged her hands roughly across her breasts, lower. Conti looked away as the line came alive.

"Giancarlo, it's Angus," came the urgent voice from the other end of the connection.

"Si, Angus. What is—"

Angus Hill interrupted him with a quick recapitulation of Rita Sue's kidnapping. Conti felt himself grow cold at the thought of what such a plot meant.

"Paul is on his way back?"

"Aye," said Angus.

"I will depart immediately," Conti said. "Is there anything from Rome you need?"

"You might bring Franco," Angus said. "Assuming we find the kidnappers, we'll be going up against them. We'll want our very best, Giancarlo."

"He will be with me. Is there anything else?"

"Just yourself, Giancarlo."

"My friend, I am on my way," Conti said.

"It's a hell of a note, this, to spring on you before the wedding."

Conti shrugged as he answered. "The company must come first. We must not allow anything to happen to it."

"Aye, Giancarlo. But Maria—"

"Maria will be fine," said Conti. "Let us now concern ourselves with Rita Sue."

"Aye. You're right. We'll look for you this afternoon."

"And I will be there, Angus." The connection was severed.

For a moment Conti stood beside his desk motionless. His thoughts were mechanical and cold. He recalled the first time he'd met Paul Christopher, nearly fifteen years earlier. Christopher had been little more than a boy then, though only in years. His eyes revealed the hardness, the ruthlessness and determination that would guide him as he built his company. Conti had been a private investigator, supporting his family on what he could earn by following faithless spouses, or providing the occasional private security job. Maria had been five then, his beautiful daughter with her beautiful eyes and angelic smile. Conti looked at a photograph on a wall near his desk. Within the photo's frame was a candid picture of Paul Christopher bouncing Maria Conti upon his knee. Maria was six when the photograph was taken; Conti had taken the picture himself. That was the year that Christopher Security opened its Rome office with Giancarlo Conti at its helm. How proud he had been of the confidence Paul Christopher showed; and how quickly Conti had repaid that confidence by building CSI/Italy into one of the company's most profitable branches.

Where have all the years gone? Conti wondered suddenly. Now Maria was to be married, and to a count. His daughter would become royalty, and that made not only Giancarlo Conti but also Paul Christopher proud. Christopher and Maria had always been close, and in recent years, when Maria passed through typical adolescent problems, Christopher had never stopped caring for her, never stopped asking after her each time he spoke with her father. *My little girl is to be married,* Conti thought once more, and my dearest friend finds himself facing the largest crisis of his career. He swore aloud and rage began to boil within him. *To do such a thing—* Conti cut off the thought. He called his office and in clipped tones ordered Franco Vertucci to arm himself and meet him at the airport in an hour.

Conti walked back onto the terrace. Else stared up at him with something like defiance in her eyes, and Conti found a target for his rage. He approached the chaise and roughly opened Else's legs, then pierced her with a single thrust. He stared hard into her eyes as he moved violently above her, showing her nothing but the fierceness of his determination. He did not relax or vary his assault; he rode her until she cried out, her eyes wide, with nothing in their gaze but her surrender to him. He kept at her until she was spent and limp beneath him.

Then Giancarlo Conti left Else whimpering on the terrace. He dressed and departed for the airport, determined to come to Paul Christopher's assistance.

Angus Hill cradled the telephone. That was the last of them, he thought. Soon he would be leaving for the airport himself. The strike force would be assembled at the château by late afternoon; those among Christopher's advisers who had the farthest distances to travel would straggle in through tomorrow morning. Angus hoped that the situation would be resolved long before the morning.

He thought of Lady Cedric, and offered a silent wish that she was being well treated. Angus Hill was a realist, though, and understood that each hour's passing meant less chance that Lady Cedric could be rescued unharmed. Angus poured himself a glass of whiskey and tossed it off. The prospect of a client's abduction was bad enough—to think of that fine Texas woman whom he admired so deeply being held prisoner sent a river of rage through Angus.

But Angus Hill was a professional, and he knew that rage was in the long run counterproductive. What mattered now was absolute control of every detail possible, and that meant controlling their tempers while they waited for additional ransom information to arrive. Paul Christopher could understand that; Angus had heard no emotion whatsoever in Christopher's voice the last time they spoke. ALPHASOME FOR EVERYONE, the message had read. It was a damned shame that Olaf's people had been unable to trap the intruder within CSI's computer system.

And it was an even larger shame that the kidnappers had achieved access to the most guarded areas of that system. The traitor within CSI had given away more than an ancient coin—the secrets that were at the very heart of Christopher Security International had obviously been compromised. How many of their secrets had been sold? And at what price? Angus still found it hard to comprehend that there was someone among the advisers who could so callously betray Paul Christopher and the company that had been so painstakingly built over the past decade.

Angus rose from his desk and stepped to a cabinet recessed into the far wall. He thumbed the ProTech seal and the cabinet swung open. From a rack mounted inside, Angus withdrew a long-barreled Smith & Wesson revolver and slid it into the holster that nestled beneath his left shoulder. He would carry a *WISP* with him should they make an assault on the kidnappers, but Angus took comfort in the heaviness of the revolver. It had seen him through more than one dangerous situation, and he did not want to be without it now.

Miranda Glenn stared at Paul Christopher across the narrow aisle that separated the seats in his jet. Several seats ahead of them Olaf Nyquist was bent over a portable computer. Miranda could hear the click of keys as the Norwegian worked. Christopher's gaze was straight ahead, he would not look her way. Miranda thought that she might cry, but she had already cried enough. First James Howard Dennis had died. Now the love of her life had lasted only a single evening. Miranda could not think of the time that she and Paul Christopher had so recently passed without being flooded by an almost overpowering sense of sadness.

Christopher had spoken only curtly to her when they boarded the aircraft. He made it clear that he had no interest in hearing any explanations she might have to offer him. The one time she tried to draw a comparison between her protection of a source and his own commitment to his clients, Christopher's face had twisted contemptuously. Miranda could not stand it. She gazed out the window as the sleek jet soared from the Oslo airport. The snow-covered city disappeared quickly beneath the clouds and was gone.

Now they were approaching their destination. Miranda buckled her seat belt. At first, she did not hear Christopher when he began to speak to her.

"Miranda," he said again.

She looked up. "Yes?"

Christopher's eyes were hard and emotionless. Miranda found it difficult to endure their gaze, but she did not look away from him as he spoke. "We will be going to a château I maintain near Beauvais," Christopher said. "From there we will mount whatever operations are necessary." He gave her a grim smile. "I will expect you to maintain our confidentiality while any operation is under way. Afterward—" He raised his hand and brought it down in a swift chopping gesture.

"What do you mean?" she asked, her voice quivering slightly.

"I mean, Miranda, that you now truly have a story—a *breaking* story, as you call it. An *exclusive*. I ask simply that you not reveal the story until it is resolved. To do otherwise would be to further endanger Rita Sue's life."

"But, I—"

"Don't protest to *me*," Christopher said harshly. "Your choice is obvious by your refusal to give me the name of my traitor."

"But, Paul, I *can't!*" Miranda cried. "Why can't you see that? Why *won't* you?"

Christopher waited a moment before answering her. "I cannot accept your answer, Miranda," he said. "To do so would be to put myself on the same level as anyone who places *ideals* above human life. And what makes such attitudes different from those which drove *idealists* to murder your James Howard Dennis?"

Miranda's eyes filled with tears but she did not look away from Christopher. "You bastard," she said.

"Perhaps," said Christopher with an icy calm. "But I do understand the world, Miranda. And I understand that a fine woman who has done nothing but good for the world is now held captive, while her guards—*my* people, Miranda!—lie dead. Shall I tell their wives and children about your *ideals?*"

Miranda felt herself reeling, and could no longer face him. She shut her eyes tight, and did not open them until the jet had landed. Without speaking, she followed Christopher out of the aircraft and into the helicopter that would ferry them to his château.

17

THREE OF HIS advisers were still in transit when Paul Christopher summoned the others into the large conference room at the château. He was not willing to wait any longer; he could confront the others in private, individually, after they arrived in France. Afternoon shadows were beginning to gather around the château. It would be evening in a few hours. In the conference room a fire crackled cheerily, but there was no cheer in the mood of those gathered there. There had been no further word from Rita Sue Cedric's kidnappers.

Christopher drew a deep breath before rising in front of men and women he had trusted more completely than any others. For a moment he did not speak, but stared at them, his eyes moving slowly from face to familiar face. "We are faced, you and I," he began at last, "with a situation unprecedented in CSI's history. Each of you has received certain details pertaining to the situation. Two of our people are dead. A client has been successfully kidnapped. The automobile in which they traveled was tampered with by someone equipped with the information needed to bypass our security devices. The company's computer integrity has been compromised. New access codes and protective software are being put into place now." Christopher smiled grimly at his advisers. "One of your number is responsible," he said flatly.

Christopher watched as understanding sank in. He studied his advisers' expressions, in search of a reaction that would reveal to him his quarry. There was no such telling reaction, of course, nor had Paul Christopher expected one. His people were too highly skilled at their professions. The same talents and abilities that guided them to the top of the security industry now made it possible for them to mask their guilt and hide it from him. Christopher saw their shock, their concern, their indignation—but no guilt.

Of course it is possible that the traitor is one who has not yet reached France, Christopher thought. *But would unmasking Rahjit or either of the others be a simpler task?* Christopher stared at his people.

Before he could resume his speech he was interrupted by a soft knock at the conference-room door. Angus Hill rose from his seat at the long polished table and opened the door. He spoke in hushed tones with the secretary who stood there. After a moment Angus looked toward Christopher and beckoned to him. Christopher nodded, then returned his attention to the group.

"Each of you has been important to me," Christopher said. "And I have been proud to count many of you among my friends as well as my associates. But a client's life has been endangered, and that violation far outweighs any considerations based upon friendship, upon personal relationships."

He fixed them with his stare. Christopher stared hard at his closest advisers. "Understand this. I *will* find out who it was who betrayed me and my company. And when I do—" Christopher left the conference room.

Angus awaited him in the corridor outside the room. The Scot held two large manila envelopes. "Just in, Paul," he said. Angus handed Christopher the larger envelope.

Inside was a black-and-white photograph of Rita Sue Cedric, nude, bound by thick rope to a simple straight-backed chair. Her cheeks were bruised, her lips swollen, her hair matted. But Rita Sue's eyes were wide and even in the grainy photograph Christopher could see the spark of vitality and defiance that he so cherished in her. A single sheet of paper accompanied the photograph. The message read:

Alphasome for everyone, or the lady dies. OR: pay $20 million American tomorrow morning. Details to come. Signed: War Council of the People's Liberation.

"Who are they?" Christopher asked.

"Up until now, nobody, Paul," Angus said. They walked down the corridor together. "No more than eight soldiers in this 'army,' as nearly as we can tell. Responsible for some petty crimes around the Continent. Not taken particularly seriously as revolutionaries. Certainly they've never tried anything like this."

"But they succeeded," Christopher said.

"Aye. With inside help."

"Yes," said Christopher. "When did it come?"

"It arrived at the Paris office an hour and a half ago."

"Delivered by?"

"An eight-year-old boy who says he was hired off a street corner. We're interrogating him now. But his story seems to check out."

"Hired in Paris. The bagmen are still in the country anyway."

"Aye," said Angus.

"What's the other envelope?" Christopher asked.

"A surprise," said Angus Hill. He handed the envelope to Paul Christopher.

Christopher gave its contents a cursory examination. He whistled softly. "Who else knows?"

Angus shook his head. "Nobody except our operatives. And they reported directly to me."

"All right," said Christopher. He sealed the envelope. "Thanks, Angus. I'll attend to this." He began to walk away.

"Paul," Angus said. "What about the others?"

"Let them sweat for a bit," said Paul Christopher. "I'll make amends in the morning. To those who remain." Christopher pulled the corridor door shut behind him.

Moments later he found Miranda Glenn standing at the low wall which bordered the château's broad patio. The late afternoon was beginning to turn cold, and Miranda had drawn a bright yellow sweater about her shoulders. She looked up at his approach, and Christopher could see that Miranda had been crying. His fingers tightened on the envelopes he carried. He stopped a few paces from her. "Miranda," he said softly.

"Yes, Paul?" She held her head high and her shoulders steady as she faced him. "What is it?"

"I must speak with you," Christopher said.

"Go ahead, then," said Miranda emotionlessly. "What's stopping you?" She held her ground as he stepped forward.

Christopher waited a moment before he spoke. "I would not cause you—"

"What?" said Miranda with the fury of a curse. *"Pain?* You would not *hurt* me, Paul? Is that it?" Her eyes blazed. "Don't value yourself so highly, Paul

Christopher. You've already hurt me. But I can live with that. So go ahead. I'm getting used to your hurting me." She broke off, but did not look away from him.

Paul Christopher drew himself to his full height and squared his shoulders. He stripped all emotion from his voice as he spoke. "Miranda," he said, "we must reach an accommodation, you and I. Rita Sue is in great danger. I must know from whom you obtained the solidus."

"No," said Miranda. "I cannot do that. Not even for you."

"Please do not answer so quickly," said Christopher. "As I said, I seek . . . accommodation." He held up the envelopes Angus had given him. "There are circumstances of which you are not yet aware."

Miranda's eyes strayed to the envelopes, and then back to Christopher. "Go ahead," she said, although her caution was clear in her voice.

"You say you must protect your source."

"That's right," Miranda said. "As jealously as you protect your own clients. Or your past."

"I understand that," said Christopher.

"*Do* you?" asked Miranda with a sneer.

"As a matter of fact, Miranda, I do." Christopher carried the envelopes with him as he walked along the patio wall. He looked out over the château's grounds. Miranda waited where she stood, and after a moment Christopher turned to face her. "Did James Howard Dennis share your concerns?" Christopher asked.

"You know he did!"

"But suppose a source could provide you with the materials for James Howard's last story? The story of his killers. Would you—"

"*Bastard!*" Miranda spat the word.

"Not theory now, Miranda," Christopher said, and held the envelopes aloft. "The real world."

Comprehension broke over her face. Miranda took a sudden single step forward before catching herself. "Have you—"

"I have their names, I know where they are," Christopher said. "My people have them under surveillance. We have proof that they murdered James Howard Dennis." His voice was cold.

"The police—" Miranda began.

"Our proof would not be acceptable in today's courts," Christopher explained. "Besides, there are sources to be protected." Miranda showed him a look filled with hatred.

She turned from him. Her shoulders shook, but Christopher offered her no comfort. He felt cold inside. Miranda did not look at him when she spoke. "You know what you are doing to us?" she asked.

"I know," said Christopher, and wondered if Miranda could hear the pain in his voice. *It does not matter,* he told himself, but did not come close to believing it. "But I must answer to myself, as well."

"And still you—"

Christopher could take no more. "Enough!" he said sharply. Better to break cleanly with her now. "Enough, Miranda," he said in more even tones. "We cause each other nothing but pain. Enough of that." Paul Christopher flung the envelope to the bricks at Miranda's feet. "Take it! You'll find the names and locations of James Howard Dennis's killers. Use them as you will."

Miranda did not move.

"And here," Christopher said brutally. He tore the other envelope open and pulled out the photograph of Rita Sue. "By all rights this photograph should belong to you. Put it in your damned book!"

Christopher left the patio before Miranda bent to pick up the photograph. He did not look back.

Miranda Glenn stared at the photograph of Rita Sue Cedric for a long time. She held the other, still-unopened envelope close to her. Inside it waited information that would not bring James Howard Dennis back to her, but that would go a distance toward avenging him. Miranda thought of James Howard's wonderful smile, of his many kindnesses toward her. What would he do, were she the one dead? Miranda knew the answer without really thinking about it, and it disturbed her far less than she thought it would. James Howard would not have rested until her killers were found—and the story written and filed. It would have been his way of showing her memory his respect. *Can I do less for his?* Miranda wondered.

She looked again at the photograph of Rita Sue Cedric. It sickened her, but she would not look away. She recalled the photographs James Howard had once shown her, of children maimed and murdered in the name of ideals. This picture gave her the same feeling, and she shivered. A momentary bitterness took her. *I write so much about making the world better,* she thought. Her grip tightened on the photograph, wrinkling it.

When she stood up, Miranda Glenn felt light-headed for a moment, and leaned against the patio's low wall for support. Something within her had changed, she realized. *Many things. But not my feelings for Paul,* Miranda thought, and a wave of emotion broke through her. She did not cry, although the thought of losing Paul Christopher left her feeling desolate and empty. *He was right, and part of me will always be bitter about that,* Miranda thought. *But not a large part. Not a large part at all. The rest of me will spend my time missing him.* Miranda gathered the envelopes and went into the château, walking resolutely, her purpose clear.

She found Paul Christopher in his private office. He stood beside his desk and said nothing to her as she entered the room. Miranda closed the door behind her. "Oh, Paul," she said when she reached his desk. Her eyes brimmed with tears.

"No, Miranda," Christopher said. "This is no time for sentiment."

She nodded, and blinked back the tears. "You are right, of course. I can see that now."

Christopher stared wordlessly at her.

"I'm going to tell you, Paul," Miranda said. She spoke slowly and deliberately.

Paul Christopher stiffened slightly.

"It was Conti," Miranda said. She watched Christopher carefully, but he displayed no emotion. Miranda told him the story. "I'd been looking around the edges of CSI for a couple of months," she said. "He approached me. He offered to sell me something that would buy unlimited access to you. He said no more. My publishers advanced the money—"

"How much?" Christopher asked.

"One hundred thousand dollars."

"So little," said Christopher with a bitter smile.

Miranda did not reply.

"Why?" he asked.

"I don't know," said Miranda. She shook her head, then reached up to brush back auburn curls. "He—"

"No," said Christopher. "Why did you tell me?"

Miranda handed him the photograph of Rita Sue Cedric. "A picture's worth—" she began, but her voice faltered.

"No," said Christopher. "Miranda, tell me."

She drew a breath. "Because . . . we loved each other, Paul, James Howard and me." A sad laugh escaped her. "Not in any immortal way. Not anything like what you and I—" For a moment she could not find words. Miranda shrugged. "I loved him, he loved me. And the James Howard Dennis I loved would not have stood by while anyone was tied and beaten and—"

Christopher interrupted her. "I must go now, Miranda," he said.

"What will happen to Conti?"

"I won't answer that," said Christopher.

"And James Howard's killers?" Miranda stared at Christopher.

"What about them?"

"Your people are watching them?"

"Yes," said Christopher.

"His notes, the film—you can get them back?"

"We have a good chance," said Christopher. He said nothing more, and it was clear to Miranda that he would offer her no assistance. He would make her ask.

"Would you get them back for me, Paul?"

"Yes," said Christopher. "And the ones who stole it?"

"Paul—"

"No, Miranda," said Christopher. There was a terrible finality in his voice. "I must know." His gray eyes were insistent.

For a moment Miranda had difficulty finding her voice. But she knew what she must say. "Kill them, Paul," Miranda said. Then she turned and fled from his office.

Paul Christopher poured himself a brandy and drank it quickly against the chill which flowered within him. *Giancarlo,* he thought, and poured another finger of brandy. Christopher put the decanter away and carried the snifter to his desk. He seated himself and waited. A moment later Giancarlo Conti entered Paul Christopher's office.

"Have a seat," said Christopher.

Conti nodded and positioned himself opposite Christopher. The Italian did not speak.

"You are aware that I have had a traveling companion these last few days, Giancarlo?" Christopher asked.

"Si." Conti did not shy from Christopher's gaze. "Yes, Paul."

"You sold her a Byzantine solidus," said Christopher. Before Conti could reply, he added a warning: "Do not lie to me again, Giancarlo."

Conti moved forward in the leather chair until he was perched upon the edge of the seat. "I am sorry, Paul," Conti said in an empty voice.

"Why, Giancarlo?" Christopher asked quietly.

Conti shook his head, he shrugged. "I needed the money—"

"You could have asked me for the money," Christopher said.

"No, Paul, I could not," Conti said. "It was for Maria."

"Maria?"

"Si. Two years ago, when Maria was having her troubles—" Conti broke off.

Christopher recalled Maria's rebellious phase, the worries it had caused Conti. "Go ahead, Giancarlo," he said firmly.

After a moment Conti gathered his composure. "It was worse than you knew, Paul. Worse than you could know. There were drugs, there were . . . She became an *addict,* my beautiful little girl." For a moment

Conti buried his face in his hands. "Have you any idea what heroin can do to even an angel like my Maria?" he asked, weeping.

"Spare me, Giancarlo," Christopher said. "And *look* at me when you speak!"

Conti slowly raised his head. "They ruined her. They turned her into a . . . *whore* for them and their plans."

"Who did this?" Christopher demanded.

"The People's Liberation, they call themselves."

Paul Christopher nodded. "And with all the resources of CSI you felt you had to pay them off?" His voice held contempt.

"Oh, Paul. When we found her we put her into a rehabilitation program. My thoughts were of Maria, you can understand that, Paul?"

Christopher would not answer.

"She begged me to leave them alone. And she began to grow well, she blossomed once more, she came back to life." He spread his hands wide. "Paul, Maria became *happy* once more. She fell in love, the wedding became—"

Christopher slammed his hands onto his desk. "Why did you betray me, Giancarlo?" he shouted.

Conti reeled as though Christopher had struck him. "As the wedding began to attract publicity, I received some film from . . . *them*." He looked at Christopher, his eyes wide and filled with anguish. "Filthy things, Paul, bestial things. My Maria! They threatened to make them public, to spoil her future as they had spoiled her childhood."

"And you paid them?" Christopher said angrily.

"I had no choice. My Maria! How could I not?"

"You could have come to me, Giancarlo. We could have shut them down completely and no one would have—"

"How could I take that chance with Maria's future? If word had gotten out—"

"So you sold the solidus to Miranda Glenn."

"I knew that you would be able to handle her, Paul. I knew that you could turn her away without—"

"And then you sold Rita Sue Cedric's life!" Christopher said.

Conti trembled as though a frightened child. "No, no . . . Paul, you must understand. They came back to me. They demanded more . . . it was during the Hemmings disappearance. Rita Sue was simply in the wrong place. I gave them access to our system, that is all. I—"

"That is *all?*" Christopher rose to his feet. Muscles bunched across his shoulders and stood out on his neck. He narrowed his eyes and stared at Conti. It was all Christopher could do to keep from spitting at him, from stepping around his desk and beating Conti until no life was left within him.

"Paul, *please,* you must—"

"How dare you try to tell me what I must do?" Christopher said. "You who betrayed everything we've ever worked for."

"Paul, I must—"

"Giancarlo, I will tell you now what you *must* do." Christopher said. "You find out where Rita Sue is being held. You find out how many there are holding her. And you have the information to me within two hours."

"But, Paul, I can't—"

"But, Giancarlo," Christopher said, "you *must.*"

After a moment Giancarlo Conti rose from his seat. He moved slowly, all of his vitality gone, a bent and broken old man making his way from Paul Christopher's office.

Christopher waited until Conti had nearly reached

the door. "And, Giancarlo," he called after him. "Do not seek any coward's way out of this. If you do, *I* will ruin Maria's life."

Conti looked back at his employer. "You would do such a thing?"

"Yes," said Christopher. "Believe it."

"Oh, Paul," said Giancarlo Conti. He rested his hand for a moment upon the doorknob. "I will have your information for you," he said.

Christopher waited until Conti had left the office before he finished his brandy. Its heat still stinging his throat, he summoned Angus Hill, and began to develop a plan that might set Rita Sue Cedric free.

18

BARBARA WEBSTER AND Esteban Rojas sat silently in his office, awaiting a telephone call from New York. They did not look at each other. An hour had passed since Barbara presented her counteroffer to the Chemical Bank officer in charge of the CSI loan. The officer had agreed to consider the offer.

Barbara sighed and Esteban looked up. "I wish Angus would call," she said to the Argentine banker. "I wish we knew what was going on in France."

Esteban shook his head. "Ah, Barbara, there is nothing we can do," he said. "And we have done everything that we can. So perhaps it is better that we *not* know. At any rate, for now we should just relax and wait. The time will pass."

"Just relax?" Barbara asked with a quick grin.

"Of course. Do not allow the tensions to affect you." Esteban shrugged his broad shoulders.

Barbara laughed, the sound disconcerting in the large, quiet office. "You're so relaxed," she said mockingly. "Just look at you." Scattered across the glass top of the coffee table before Esteban were dozens of paper clips, twisted and bent into various shapes. He was twisting a fresh paper clip even as Barbara Webster spoke.

Esteban laughed. "A habit," he said, and held up

the clip. "You would have me start smoking again, as a way of making the moments pass?" Esteban deftly manipulated the thin metal, then tossed it onto the coffee table. He immediately took up another clip.

Barbara pressed her palms together. They felt damp, clammy. She dried her hands on a tissue. A moment later she took a sip of coffee, but it had grown cold and she put the cup down with more clatter than she'd intended. Barbara turned her attention to the telephone, staring at it and willing it to ring. It did not. Silently she offered her wishes that Christopher resolve Rita Sue's abduction swiftly and safely. She glanced at her watch, but only three minutes had passed since she last checked. She sighed again.

At last she looked back at Esteban. "I quit smoking a long time ago too," she said. The laugh she managed was horrid, and she cut it off abruptly. "Hand me some of those paper clips," she said. "If you can't beat them . . ."

The minutes passed slowly.

Angus Hill called the members of the strike force together in the large barn that Christopher had renovated when he purchased the château. Angus and the others worked swiftly, checking and rechecking their weapons, ensuring that their gear was combat-ready. Angus had little doubt that before the crisis was ended they would need these special tools. Their lives would depend upon them.

Paul Christopher was still at the main house, awaiting Giancarlo's report. As he worked, Angus shook his head and muttered to himself. He had known Giancarlo for nearly as long as he'd known Paul Christopher. Angus could not count the number of times he and Giancarlo had drunk and toasted the ladies until dawn. Like Christopher, Angus had watched Maria Conti as she flowered from adorable child into attractive, poised woman. Angus recalled the sympathy he'd felt for Giancarlo when Maria became rebellious, spiteful. The Italian and the Scot had shared more than one round of drinks over which Giancarlo had poured out his concern for his daughter. When Maria became engaged, Angus was the second person Giancarlo Conti called, after Paul Christopher. Angus hoped that he never saw Giancarlo again. His fingers tightened around the grip of the machine pistol he held.

If he saw Giancarlo he hoped he could restrain himself.

Angus swore beneath his breath and studied the weapon before him. *WISP,* he thought. Its sturdy body bore a family resemblance to an Uzi, but *WISP* was as light as a target pistol. Weightless Individual Silenced Pistol was the name the Argentines had given it, in order to derive the marketable acronym. But Angus Hill preferred to think that the weapon's name sprang from the silence with which the machine pistol worked. A *WISP* was capable of firing over eight hundred rounds per minute, as silently as any weapon Angus had ever handled. *WISP* was a perfect piece for commando and night operations, and Angus foresaw an immense market for the weapon. Along with *ASP,* Christopher's Argentine operation would have a corner on a billion-dollar global market. *Larger than that, lad,* Angus thought. The numbers would grow geometrically, and Angus again felt thrilled with anticipation. Since Christopher had told Angus he would be in charge of the new division, once it was acquired, Angus had felt a renewed vigor. To be at the helm of all that! Angus was ready—even anxious—for the task that lay ahead.

Assuming I get there, he thought.

He looked up at the good people who worked around him. Angus knew each of them well; he'd trained most of them. Any one of them would be an asset in a firefight or at close quarters. Together they made an assault team that could handle ten times its number. Counting Christopher, there would be seven of them going in. Before too many hours, some of them might be dead. *But that's the contract we've made,* Angus reminded himself somberly. *And if we die saving Lady Cedric, so be it.* Angus finished checking the first *WISP*, then set to work upon Christopher's. He worked carefully, but more than once caught himself thinking of the chaos that would follow a failed mission. Everything would tumble down, and with the Argentine deal on the line, the fall would come quickly. *Should Lady Cedric be killed,* Angus thought, *or Paul—*

Angus stood straight and clapped his hands together. The others looked up and Angus nodded at each of them. For a moment they did not speak, four men and two women who understood clearly the nature of the job that lay before them. Angus felt all of his other concerns fade as he looked at the members of his team. They were the best in the business, and a sudden pride surged through him. He folded his arms across his broad chest and showed them a ferocious grin. "All right, lads and lassies," Angus Hill said. "The sun's going down. Playtime is over and our work begins soon." He looked at his watch. "Five minutes to finish the equipment check, and then shall we dress for the evening?"

Miranda Glenn moved slowly through the château's large study. From time to time she took a volume from the shelves, or paused to admire one of the

Picasso prints that hung on the walls. Although she spent long moments motionless before each picture, Miranda saw nothing. Her mind's eye was filled with a single image. Wherever she looked, Miranda Glenn saw Paul Christopher.

They had not spoken since she revealed Giancarlo Conti's guilt. The last time she saw Christopher, the lines of his face were drawn tight, his features a mask of completely controlled fury. It was his control that frightened Miranda, as much as his anger.

I can understand his rage, she admitted to herself as she stood before a painting. She wondered if his fury would lead Christopher to kill Conti. She recalled how gleefully she had entered into her bargain with Giancarlo, how exultant she'd felt when the solidus had accomplished its purpose and she was first invited to Paul Christopher's office. It seemed to her that months rather than days had passed since that first meeting. *How could I ever not have loved him?* Miranda thought. She grew cold now when she thought of Giancarlo Conti.

His fate was not her concern. She understood that. Conti's fate was up to Paul. *Would Paul kill him?* Miranda wondered. *And would that make me an accomplice? Didn't I just order an execution?* Miranda drew a breath. *But I would not withdraw the order. I would not spare the vermin who killed James Howard. Let them die slowly.*

Miranda moved to stand before the fireplace, but it did not warm her. She looked into the flames, but was not certain what she hoped to see. *I am more like him than I would have guessed,* she thought, and was no longer surprised by that. Miranda thought of the photograph of Lady Cedric. Those were the sorts of acts Paul Christopher opposed. *So do I.* Miranda felt fear begin to gnaw at her: Paul Christopher would be facing those people before the night ended. She knew that he might be killed. *If that happened part of me would die.* The force of that realization left Miranda shaken and unsteady. *I love him.*

She was distracted by a low, steady sound from outside the château. Miranda stepped to a window and drew back the heavy drapery. It was dark outside, but she could make out the shapes of two helicopters settling like birds of prey upon the lawn. *I may never see him again.* She wanted to run from the study and find Paul. And when she had found him she would fling her arms around him and hold him close. None of the rest mattered—she loved Paul Christopher, and prayed that she be allowed to tell him so before he departed. For him to face death without knowing that she would accept his love without conditions or questions was unthinkable to her.

But she could not leave the study. As clearly as she knew that she loved Paul Christopher, she understood that there was a drama to be played out first. *And I will play my part,* she thought. *I will wait.*

Paul Christopher pulled the navy turtleneck over his shoulders and adjusted its fit. He went through a quick series of stretches, adjusting his clothing until his freedom of movement was fluid and unencumbered. He slipped his arms through the loops of an oiled dark shoulder holster, and then picked up the long-barreled Colt revolver that lay in the center of his desk. Christopher had purchased the pistol at a small shop in Paris, not long after he first arrived in France. *All those years ago,* he thought as he slipped the pistol into the holster.

The commando sweater was warm. Christopher stepped to the window and gazed outside. The helicopters had arrived while he dressed, and the sun had fallen. The night was moonless, which would prove to be an advantage. He hoped.

There was no moon the night my Maria died, Christopher thought. He gave a harsh laugh as he considered the story Giancarlo had told him about the other Maria. *So she became a whore in the name of ideals! People's Liberation. And Giancarlo betrayed me to such filth.*

Christopher slipped the Colt from its snug holster and snapped open the cylinder. The pistol was loaded, and Christopher spun the cylinder. The Colt was in perfect condition. Paul Christopher holstered it and awaited the return of Giancarlo Conti.

The corridor seemed endless to Giancarlo as he made his way to Christopher's office. Each step took an eternity, yet Giancarlo would not have hurried himself to his destination. He knew what awaited him in Paul Christopher's presence. The thought of his own death no longer terrified Conti. Instead, he found himself thinking of all the years he and Paul Christopher had been friends. Every pleasant memory was turned to ashes now, and Giancarlo knew that he alone was responsible. Paul Christopher had never shown him anything but kindness and trust. *If killing me will help repay this treason I've committed, then I will gladly die,* Conti thought. His only regret was that he would never again see his daughter.

Christopher was seated at his desk. He looked up when Conti entered the office. Neither spoke as Conti handed Christopher a single sheet of paper. Christopher did not look at it.

"She is being held in a farmhouse near Rambouillet," Conti said. "The precise information is there on the paper."

"How many?"

"They acquired a few extra hands for this, Paul. There are eleven of them there."

"You obtained the information without compromising our plans?" Christopher's voice was flat.

"*Si*. Yes, Paul. No one knows."

"And you've got the names of anyone else involved?"

Conti nodded. "There are only three more. They're still in Paris. Waiting for the ransom. You'll get the details by midnight."

"By midnight they will be dead," Christopher said.

"They are armed to the teeth at that farmhouse, Paul. You will want to—"

"I will want to handle this myself, Giancarlo," Christopher said.

"Of course." Giancarlo Conti stood facing Paul Christopher. "Be careful."

Christopher said nothing for a moment. He glanced at the paper.

Conti forced himself to speak. "Paul, I—"

"What is it, Giancarlo?"

"Your plans for me. Before you leave, I would know—"

Christopher let the paper flutter to the desk. "You'll know what I choose to tell you, Giancarlo."

Conti drew himself up. His heart pounded furiously. "Go ahead, then, Paul."

"What is it you expect, Giancarlo?"

"I expect to pay for what I have done to you. I expect, Paul, to die."

Christopher's smile was cruel and he let Conti study it for a long time before he answered him. Conti shifted from foot to foot. "Why, I have no intention of killing you, Giancarlo."

Conti did not feel relief at the words. "Then—"

"Be silent. You wish to know my plans?"

Conti nodded.

"You will remain at the château until word arrives that Rita Sue has been freed in good health. We will return here after the operation is completed. I do not want you here when I return."

Conti's shoulders quivered against his will.

"Giancarlo, you will never communicate with me again. You will never have dealings with my firm, with any of our clients. Professionally or socially—you will decline their invitations, you will remain in your home. You will depart our industry as absolutely and as completely as if you were dead. But you will not be dead, Giancarlo. I will not allow you to die. It is my intention, in fact, to see that you live a very long life."

Conti would not allow himself to blink. Paul Christopher displayed no emotion, and Conti sought to match him.

"To that end, Giancarlo, I will extend certain protections to you." Christopher smiled again. "You will be watched, Giancarlo. You will be kept under surveillance as closely as, *more* closely than any surveillance you've ever mounted.

"Your telephone lines. Your computer terminal. Your automobile and your credit cards. Your conversations, Giancarlo, and when the technology permits, your very *thoughts*." Christopher drew a breath and Conti thought that he might wither in his gaze. "For the rest of your life, Giancarlo. From this moment forward."

"I understand, Paul," Conti said in a voice that he did not recognize.

"*Do* you, Giancarlo? I don't think so." Christopher seemed to take pleasure in the words. He spoke slowly. "I don't believe that you *can* understand yet. I think that it will take you a year, perhaps longer, fully to comprehend what I am talking about. For the monitoring is not all. Each time your actions or conversations offend me, you will be notified. And you will correct your actions. Do you understand?"

Conti stared at Christopher.

"And I will look forward to reading the reports of your behavior. Of how you . . . come to terms with our arrangement." Christopher's gaze grew distant for a moment. "To be watched forever . . . I do not envy you, Giancarlo."

"Purgatory," said Conti softly.

Christopher shook his head. "Not at all, my old *friend.*" He made the word into something savage. "Purgatory offers hope of redemption. I do not. I'm damning you, Giancarlo, to a hell of my own making." He narrowed his eyes. "And it gives me great pleasure."

Conti lowered his eyes, turned and began to shuffle slowly from Christopher's office. "Giancarlo!" Christopher called after him. Conti stopped, but did not turn around. "I would remind you again that you will not find your way out of this by taking your own life. Do you understand that, Giancarlo?"

Conti kept his head bowed, his eyes averted. "Have you found some way to punish me even after my death, Paul?"

Christopher laughed at him, and it stung Giancarlo as though flicked with a whip. "Not you, Giancarlo. Your daughter."

Conti spun and stared at Christopher. "Paul—"

"Giancarlo, if you kill yourself, I will publish those photographs of Maria myself."

"You couldn't—" Conti said, even as he realized that Paul Christopher certainly could. "You—"

"That's enough, Giancarlo. I hope never to see you

again." Paul Christopher turned his back, and after a moment Giancarlo Conti quietly left the office and closed the door behind him.

Christopher punched the intercom code and waited for Angus to answer. "We've got it," he said when the Scot picked up.

"All *right,* lad," said Angus. "The choppers are fueled and ready to go."

Christopher read him the coordinates of the kidnappers' farm. "Bring the maps up and begin planning our approach," he said.

"Aye. And Giancarlo?"

"He's been dealt with, Angus. It was not easy."

"No, lad. Nor will this evening be."

"Are our people ready?"

Angus gave a bark of laughter. "These are *our* people, Paul. Do you have to ask?"

"Of course not, Angus," Christopher said. He felt his tensions begin to lift, and in their place flowered a growing excitement. "Get the maps ready. We're going up against eleven of them—"

"They've acquired more talent," said Angus.

"Aye," said Christopher in a burr, and they laughed. "We'll be airborne within the hour."

"We'll be ready, Paul."

Christopher replaced the telephone in its cradle. He took the sheet of paper Giancarlo had given him and folded it neatly. Tucking the paper into a pocket, he switched off the office lights. Christopher walked outside and across the patio toward the stone barn. He stopped when he saw Miranda Glenn standing to one side of the patio, shrouded in shadow. Christopher walked to her.

She said his name.

"I have only a moment, Miranda," he said. "I must go."

She nodded. "I understand that." She reached up to brush back wings of hair that fluttered in the evening breeze.

"You'll grow chill out here," Christopher said.

For a long moment neither spoke. At last a smile creased Christopher's face. "I never have told you my story."

"It's not important," said Miranda softly. A tear glinted on her cheek.

"But it is to me, Miranda. That you know everything."

"I look forward to knowing," said Miranda. She sniffled, then laughed and brushed away her tear. "You can tell me in Oslo. There are museums we haven't seen."

She came into his arms, but their kiss was fleeting and wistful. Christopher stroked her hair. "Miranda," he said before he drew back and turned away from her.

"Oh, Paul, come back to me," Miranda said. But she did not cry, and when Christopher looked at her she was standing tall, her eyes bright and proud.

Christopher touched her face. "Miranda, I do love you so," he said. A moment later he left her and hurried across the lawn until he was enveloped by the night.

19

Two HELICOPTERS CUT through the night, flying low over the French countryside. Christopher sat beside Angus Hill but they did not talk. Their preparations were as complete as they could be. The team had spent fifteen minutes going over terrain maps, rehearsing their roles. When they landed at the staging point—a nearby farm whose owner had agreed to silence—there would be recent photographs of the kidnappers' farm. Other than that, they were on their own.

From time to time Christopher glanced down at the land over which they passed. In the darkness the countryside seemed almost featureless. Christopher recalled a similar night, during whose endless hours he had lost his first love and fled his homeland. *As well as accomplished my first killing,* he thought. Christopher looked at the others in the helicopter. Their faces were blackened with cork. Their hands were steady. They were professionals, ready for anything the night assault might bring. *As am I,* Christopher thought. *A far cry from the night I escaped the Soviets.*

A smile crossed his lips when he thought of his homeland. He still loved the country to which he could never return. Not so long as it was occupied by the men who killed Maria.

The soldiers had swirled around him, wielding their rifles like clubs, and Paul had been torn from Maria's body. He never saw her again, but was swept along by the crowd and the chaos, until he darted down a side street in search of escape. He had to get out of Prague, he knew that. Christopher could still smell the acrid gasoline fumes, could still hear the terrifying rumble of the Soviet tanks and personnel carriers, the screams of his countrymen as they were run down. He recalled running through the madness of the streets, skittering around corners in flight from uniformed pursuit. Night was falling as he finally left the city.

He was limping from some forgotten blow. He could not forget that look of anguish and fear on Maria's face as she was clubbed to death. When Paul saw her die he felt as though his own life were being extinguished. He thought of Father Josef as he hobbled along the road. More than once he had to fling himself into the bushes at the approach of a convoy bearing more invaders. The sight of each soldier served only to fuel Paul's rage, and he made his way toward his village steadily, ignoring his pain, walking with a grim, inflexible determination. Father Josef's advice to his parish rang in Paul's ears as he walked, and it, too, fed the flames within him.

Father Josef, he thought, his hero, his mentor. The man who had taught him so many things. And who had so disappointed Paul as the crisis built. After all the talk of freedom, all the fine words about the flowering of liberty, the importance of debate and discourse—after all of the *words*, Father Josef had betrayed him when the time came for action. As the Soviets had massed on the borders, as the political crisis had escalated, the priest had counseled his people not to resist an invasion. He had advocated patience and tolerance. Paul had been bitterly hurt, and had argued with the priest, and defied him by going with Maria to Prague to stand up to the tanks.

And now Maria lay dead.

It was near midnight when Paul finally reached his village. He made his way carefully around its perimeter, on the lookout for sentries. He was determined to confront Father Josef while his rage was still new. Paul wanted to show the priest what he had learned from his *new* mentors.

An unfamiliar car was parked outside the church, and Paul slipped into the shadows, working his way along the side of the priest's quarters. He lay on his belly and inched to a window, rising slowly until he could see into Father Josef's study. It was the room where Paul had felt himself come alive under the priest's tutelage. He knew every inch of the room from long childhood hours spent there; he'd handled every item on the room's crowded shelves many times. There were models of fine sailing ships that Paul and the priest had built together. There were books, Stevenson, Kipling, Wells, that they had read and studied. There was the coin collection whose acquisition had allowed young Paul to feel that he was truly touching history. It was a room Paul loved.

Paul squinted until he could see clearly the group gathered there now. Father Josef had the coin collection out, its carefully carved display cases open on his broad desk. Two men in heavy topcoats faced Father Josef, laughing as they talked, pointing at various items in the collection. The priest did not laugh with them, but stared at them expectantly. At last the taller of the two nodded vigorously, dug into his coat and withdrew a small cloth bag, tied at the top. He loosened the knot and spilled the contents of the bag on the desk before the priest.

Coins, dozens of gold and silver coins. Paul

watched as the priest's eyes widened with delight, as he clutched one coin after another and examined them joyously. After a moment Paul could watch no more, and he tore himself from the window and stumbled to the door. He caught his breath before entering the building, and took a moment to look around for a weapon. He found only a stack of firewood, but felt around it until he clutched the handle of Father Josef's ax. Paul crept into the building through a side door and made his way to the priest's study.

He held the ax to his chest as he waited outside the study. Paul feared his heart might explode, and he felt a constriction in his chest as though he were drowning in air. He tightened his grip and waited until he once more heard laughter coming from the study. In an instant he tightened his muscles and sprang into the room, taking only a second to find his first target and swing the ax with all the strength he could muster.

The amount of blood surprised Paul, and his hands flew from the ax as the tall Russian fell dead from the blow. Naked horror flowed across Father Josef's face. The other Russian gave an oddly high-pitched scream, fumbled a gun from inside his coat and snapped off a single shot. His aim was wild. The bullet passed through Paul's left wrist, but he felt no pain. A wave of adrenaline carried him as he fell upon the Russian. The gun skittered across the floor and they fumbled for it. Christopher would always remember the coldness of the metal when his fingers found the pistol. The report was muffled by the Russian's body; the slug pierced his heart and he gave a single great shiver before dying. Paul lay beside him for a moment, breathing heavily before he rose to face Father Josef.

The priest's clothing was splattered with bright blood. The blood seemed to Paul much brighter, much more vivid than had been Maria's. He shook his head, clearing his eyes. His wrist began to ache, and he looked at it numbly.

"You're hurt, Paul," said Father Josef, oddly solicitous.

Christopher waved away his concern. "You sold our trust," he said, shaking. He bent and picked up the Russian's pistol.

"You must bandage yourself, Paul. You've quite a nasty wound."

Paul stared at the priest in disbelief. "Maria is dead," he said tonelessly. "They killed her. And you sold us to them for . . . what?"

The priest's eyes were vacant. It was obvious that he could not comprehend the evening's events. He spoke of Maria as though she would be coming through the door any moment. "And, Paul, we must not neglect your lessons. There are things to learn." His face became as cheerful as a delighted child's. "And we have new coins to catalog! New pieces of history to touch and feel! See all of them, Paul, see all the coins!" Father Josef gave a giggle and his fingers reached toward the coins which had bought his betrayal.

Paul stared at him and thought of Maria. He looked at the coins scattered across the desk. He watched as though from a distance as he raised the pistol to Father Josef's temple and pulled the trigger once. The recoil snapped his arm back, and the priest tumbled from his chair and onto the floor. Paul stared at the body for several minutes; then he gathered the coins and fled into the night.

By dawn he was miles from the village. His wrist ached but he had cleansed the wound and bandaged it as carefully as he could. He'd found a money belt on one of the Russians and had filled its pouches with

Father Josef's coin collection. The coins would fetch a fine price in the West, enough money for Paul to live on while he established himself. He hid by day, and during the night made his way through darkness across the border to freedom.

Within a month he had a new name and was enrolled at the Sorbonne, entranced by the fervor and freedom with which the radicals there expressed their ideals. But as he came to know them he saw that they were as bankrupt as Father Josef, as rigid and mechanical as the invaders who'd destroyed his country and killed the girl he loved. Paul Christopher left Paris with his coins, and over two years he sold them carefully, getting good prices, setting the money aside, planning his career.

And when I came out of hiding it was to launch my first office and shortly thereafter buy Giancarlo Conti's agency, Christopher thought. The steady thrum of the helicopter's engine filled his ears. He glanced at the time, the dark Rolex he wore completely covering the scars of his first battle. Christopher knew he had scars from that battle that no one had ever seen. They were too personal, too close to his heart. He thought then of Miranda, and nudged Angus Hill. The Scot leaned close.

"We'll be landing soon, Paul," Angus said.

Christopher nodded. "Our job will be done soon."

"Always the optimist," Angus said with a grin.

"No," said Christopher. "If anything happens—"

"Paul—"

"A precaution, Angus, nothing more," Christopher said.

Angus was not reassured, but went along with him. "Yes?"

"Tell her who I am. Tell her as much of my story as you know, and give the word to the others as well.

Among you there is scattered a pretty good piece of my history. She deserves that much."

"She deserves more than that, lad."

"I know that well, Angus," Christopher said. His spirit and his grin returned. "That's why I plan to return to her." The helicopters descended through the night. "Shall we go to work, Angus?"

"We shall indeed, Paul," Angus said.

20

ON THE GROUND they spent a few moments crouched over the photographs Christopher's operatives had taken. The farm had been under surveillance, but the watchers were hesitant to move too close for fear of alarming Rita Sue's captors.

"Moving close is our work," said Angus. He rose from the photographs. "And I suppose we'd best get to it." Christopher had put Angus in charge of the operation, and the Scot now snapped his final instructions. "And good luck to us every one," he said, and moved off silently in the night.

Paul Christopher turned and faced his partner for the evening. Together they had the trickiest part of the assault. They would hit the farmhouse through a main door or window and seek to take out the room's occupants before Rita Sue was harmed. "Let's hope they've posted a heavy picket," Christopher said.

"Yes, sir."

"I meant to thank you for the job you did the other day. It was first-rate."

"Thank you, sir," Edmund Patterson said to Paul Christopher. "But, God help me, this is more my line of work."

Christopher nodded. "Let's go." They set out at an

easy jog across the field. When they reached the forest their going would be more difficult. Angus's schedule called for them to be in position in forty minutes— through darkness and without alerting any of the guards posted outside. Surveillance had revealed four pickets already; that left seven kidnappers unaccounted for. Christopher offered again the hope that most of them were outside. He and Patterson moved into the forest.

They joined Angus precisely as scheduled. Christopher and Patterson huddled close to him in the bower of a tall tree. "We've found four more," said Angus. "Each has a *WISP* trained on him."

"And the house?"

"At least four, Paul," Angus whispered gravely. "And one wild card."

"Can you work a sniper?"

"We'll do what we can, but the angles are tricky and it's going to be close quarters."

Christopher nodded. "How about our approach?"

Angus's grin could be seen in the gloom. "That's the good news. We've got a bit more cover than we thought. Enough for another man."

"All right," said Christopher. "I assume you want the door?"

"It's one of my specialties, after all!" said Angus. He looked at his watch. "Time, gentlemen!" They crawled to the edge of the forest. The stone farmhouse stood forty yards from them, and Christopher took a moment to study the terrain as closely as the night allowed. He steadied his breathing and relaxed his muscles. As he watched the farmhouse he saw the lights in the front rooms extinguished. The house went dark, its windows lighted only by the glow from a fireplace. Christopher swore under his breath. Was the darkening of the farmhouse a precautionary measure? Did they know Christopher's people were approaching?

"Let's hope they're just going to sleep," whispered Angus, then he tapped Christopher's shoulder and nodded. Christopher crawled as slowly as he could from the cover of the forest. He kept himself pressed upon the earth, his face down as he moved. He could neither hear nor see Angus Hill or Edmund Patterson, but he knew they were nearby, making their way carefully to their targets. Christopher paused halfway across the yard. He kept himself low, hidden in the shadows cast by a woodpile. Above him he could see outlined against the night the long handle of an ax whose blade was embedded in a stout piece of wood. Christopher smiled grimly. He looked toward the house, at the window that was his goal.

The window was latched midway up its right edge, hinged on the left. Christopher placed his *WISP* gingerly on the ground near the woodpile. This close in, the silenced weapon would be of little benefit to him; his revolver's loud report would add to the confusion he hoped the surprise attack would create. Christopher ran his eyes once more across the front of the house, then drew a breath and moved across the gap between the woodpile and the house. Once he'd touched the wall, Christopher paused for a moment, every sense alert. He inched through shrubbery until he was positioned beneath the window. He could hear low male voices and guttural laughter, but could not make out the words. Christopher heard a bray of laughter that was unmistakably Rita Sue, and heard the laughter cut off with sickening abruptness. Rising so slowly that it seemed to take hours, Christopher brought his head up until he could peep through the window.

He saw Rita Sue in profile. Her hands were bound

behind her back, and she was outlined in the firelight. Two of the kidnappers were seated on a low couch, facing her as though they were an audience and she a performer. Each of the men held studdy machine pistols at the ready. Behind Rita Sue stood a tall blond man who seemed to be stroking Rita Sue's hair with the barrel of his pistol. He said something and the others laughed. Christopher's fingers found the window latch and pressed against it. He worked slowly, hoping the latch was not rusted, or the window permanently sealed, hoping the kidnappers' laughter would cover any noise he made. The latch snicked open with the barest of clicks, and Christopher touched the window lightly to keep it from springing open. He pressed himself against the wall and melded with the shadows, waiting for Angus to get into position and kick the door.

The seconds passed slowly. Christopher watched the events in the room with a mounting horror as it became obvious why the lights had been extinguished. One of the seated riflemen rose and his fingers fumbled at his belt. *Keep quiet, Rita Sue,* Christopher prayed, but he knew Rita Sue too well. She laughed contemptuously at the kidnapper and lewdly mocked his inadequacy. Christopher drew his pistol and let the window slip open a bit. He tried to figure his trajectory—he wanted to get the window open and Rita Sue down as swiftly as possible. He wished she would shut up, but her mockery became more defiant. Christopher watched as the rifleman drew back the butt of his weapon and twisted himself in preparation for striking Rita Sue. Christopher's heart stopped beating at that moment. He knew the scene too well. *Angus!* he thought. *Now!*

The Scot was as good as his word. The front door burst open and Angus gave a great shout that filled the night. Christopher tugged the window open and brought his pistol up, putting a single heavy slug through the skull of the man who would crush Rita Sue's. Christopher's knees tautened and he shoved himself over the sill and into the room, rolling across the floor to stay beneath Angus's line of fire, rolling twice until his fingers caught hold of the chair legs and he pulled Rita Sue to the ground. Angus fired once and the blond kidnapper fell. The dying man convulsively squeezed the trigger of his machine pistol, and a bullet struck Christopher, spinning him. Christopher brought up his own pistol and fired twice. The seated kidnapper had not moved, and died with an expression of amazement still fresh on his face.

"Two of them still missing!" Angus shouted, and ran into the narrow hallway that led from the room. Edmund Patterson knelt, covering the front door with his *WISP*. Christopher turned to Rita Sue and with his one good hand began untying her. His left shoulder ached and his sweater was soaked with blood. Christopher ignored the pain. He reached across and dragged a blanket from the couch, wrapped it around Rita Sue Cedric. Her shoulders quivered, and Christopher steadied her as best he could.

"It took you long enough," she said to him when she was able to speak. "And they were talking about Alphasome! What the *hell* is going on?" Her eyes blazed and color began to return to her cheeks. She tried to stand, but Christopher held her down. Rita Sue's hand strayed to his chest, as though to push him away. But she pulled her fingers back bloody and cried out, "Paul!"

"Be quiet, Rita Sue, and *stay* down!" Christopher ordered. "We don't know—"

Angus Hill, grinning broadly, walked back into the room. "All done," he said. "The lassies caught them coming out the back door. Ann got one, Betsy the other." His chest swelled. "Eleven down, Paul, it's all over."

Christopher nodded wearily. Rita Sue looked at Angus. "There was an army of them—I didn't hear anything—"

"Aye," said Angus, and his grin grew ferocious. "Isn't it wonderful!" The Scot stepped close and helped Rita Sue to her feet. Christopher stood up and leaned against the mantel. Angus stretched out a broad hand to help him. "Ah, Paul," he said as he looked at the wound. "Do you see what happens when you bring top management along on a job?" Christopher tried to shrug Angus's attentions away, but the Scot forced him to a chair and began cutting away his sweater. Other members of the assault team arrived. Fresh clothing was brought out for Rita Sue, and her cuts and bruises were examined. She had not been seriously harmed.

Nor had Paul Christopher. The bullet passed cleanly through the meat of his left shoulder. "You'll be fine in no time, lad," said Angus. He helped Christopher pull on a loose jacket. "And you'll have a new scar to show the ladies."

"Just what I need," said Christopher. He found the strength to rise to his feet, and then stepped close to Rita Sue Cedric.

She looked up at him and he could not read her expression. "What the hell happened, Paul? Did they kill my bodyguards?"

Paul Christopher nodded. "It's a long story, Rita Sue," he said.

"Well, I expect you'd better make time to tell it to me in the next day or so."

"Yes."

"Am I going to like it?" she asked. Rita Sue

swatted away Patterson, who was trying to tape a cut on her cheek.

"Probably not," said Christopher. "I don't."

Rita Sue nodded, and her eyes widened. "How mad am I likely to get?" she asked. Christopher could see the edges of a smile forming on her features.

"As mad as a Texas tiger," he said, and laughed.

"Honey, there's no such creature," said Rita Sue. She stood up by herself. "The papers had pictures of me?" she said. "My kidnapping been on the news?"

Christopher stood tall. "No. We kept it quiet."

Rita Sue Cedric stared hard at Paul Christopher for a moment. "To save your hides—or Alphasome?"

"I thought it best, Rita Sue," Paul Christopher said.

"I see," she said. "Sounds to me like I might have the goods on you, Paul?" Again he could see a hint of a smile lurking on her face.

"You just might," he said.

"Well, we'll have to talk and see what kind of arrangement we can reach, won't we?"

Christopher nodded to her. She winked back.

"Paul, you just may have bought yourself one whale of a lot of donated services for my new project. You'll have to show me how well you can defend something like my greenhouses."

"Yes, Rita Sue," Paul Christopher said. He held out his hand to her.

Her gaze became serious. "Thank you, Paul," she said softly. "And Angus and the rest. You gave those bastards what they deserved." Her grip tightened around his hand. "As always." Rita Sue Cedric turned and followed Edmund Patterson from the farmhouse. "You reckon you can get me to Paris before anyone sees me dressed this way?" she asked.

Christopher turned to Angus. "Well done," he said.

Angus Hill shrugged. "*WISP* worked wonders out there, Paul. It's going to be very big."

Christopher nodded.

"You'll want to get your shoulder attended to," Angus said.

"I'll be all right," said Christopher. "I want to get back to the château. They can stitch me up there. We've still got things to deal with."

"Aye," said Angus Hill.

"And I suppose," Paul Christopher said, "one of us should call Buenos Aires and let Barbara know that everything's all right."

In New York a decision was reached to proceed with the loan—at Christopher Security International's interest level. Barbara Webster's counteroffer was accepted. Relays clicked, electrons moved, a signal bounced from earth to satellite, and back to earth again. In Buenos Aires Barbara Webster and Esteban Rojas stared at the terminal as the transfer of funds was made complete.

"Congratulations, Barbara," Esteban said.

"And so it ends in success," she said, and sipped champagne.

"And in success *we* begin," said Esteban.

"Begin what, my love?" asked Barbara.

"Why, the next stage of our climb," Esteban said. He came close to her.

"Higher?" she said.

"Yes," said Esteban. "Always higher."

Barbara took him into her arms and they came together to celebrate their climb.

It was nearly dawn when Paul Christopher finally returned to his bedroom at the château. In the hour since landing he had taken stitches in his shoulder, and transmitted his pride and well-wishes to Barbara and Esteban. Christopher and Angus shared a toast to Angus's new position—and to the safety of Rita Sue Cedric. Now Christopher stripped off his shirt and stepped toward the bed.

She stood before wide windows and in the early light the lines of her body were revealed through the sheer silk negligee she wore. She turned to face him. "You came back to me," Miranda Glenn said.

"How could I not?" asked Christopher hoarsely. He did not move as she approached him, but when she was close he reached roughly to draw her to him. He felt filled with a terrible need for Miranda, for her warmth, for the affirmation he found in her body.

She saw his bandages and cried out, concern filling her face.

"It's all right, Miranda," Christopher said soothingly. "I'm fine."

Miranda stared at him for a moment before speaking. "And Rita Sue?" She quivered against him and her fingers pressed tenderly against the tight muscles in his back.

"She's safe. It's over."

"Oh, Paul," Miranda said, and before she could say more, Christopher covered her lips with his own. There had been too much talk already. They could talk later. When the kiss finally broke, Christopher slipped the negligee from Miranda's shoulders. It fell silently to the carpet. Her body gleamed before him and Christopher ran his hands down her back, cupped her buttocks and pulled her close. He buried his face in the hollow of her neck and kissed the pulse that beat strongly there. Miranda shuddered and then drew back a bit. Her fingers found their way to his waist. She loosened his belt and stripped him bare. She clutched at his hardness and Christopher felt himself swell at her touch. He pushed her to the bed and she lay before him.

All that had passed between them became prelude to the love they now made. Miranda opened herself to Christopher's entry more fully than ever before, crying out his name as he pressed himself against her warmth. Then she surrounded him and Christopher, deep inside her, moved over her until their union was complete. Held within her, he said her name softly, lovingly. For a moment they held themselves motionless, reveling in the heat that flooded them. Miranda's eyes were wide as she stared up at Christopher, and he saw her trust in those eyes. He drew back with an almost teasing slowness, then filled her once more. Miranda's hips rose to meet his thrusts, and their pace increased until it became frenzied, building to an eruption that overwhelmed both of them.

Afterward she said his name softly. "My love." She huddled close to him and Christopher held her, Miranda's body seeming suddenly small and almost fragile. He wanted to protect her. "I was afraid they would kill you," she said.

"No," said Paul Christopher. "Not with you to come back to. Not with you to share my life." He caressed her face, stroked her back until she slept. For a time he lay beside her, listening to the soft sounds she made as she slept. Christopher could not sleep yet. He thought of the coins in the safe of his New York office, of the few coins he had not yet located. He had spent so much of his life in their pursuit, gathering them back into his possession as though with them he could buy back a past that he knew was long dead. The coins no longer interested him. With Miranda beside him the past seemed more distant than ever, the future more promising. It was time to let the coins go. He would save the solidus alone, and have it hung from a golden chain for Miranda. As for the rest of Father Josef's collection—Christopher resolved to send the coins to Giancarlo Conti—who could do with them what he would.

He drew a deep breath. His shoulder ached, and his eyes felt heavy. He would sleep for a while. And when he awoke he would gaze once more into Miranda Glenn's eyes. Paul Christopher had a story to tell her.

Harold Robbins

The World's Best Storyteller

When you enter the world of Harold Robbins, you enter a world of passion and struggle, of poverty and power, of wealth and glamour . . .

A world that spans the six continents and the inner secrets, desires and fantasies of the human mind and heart.

Every Harold Robbins bestseller is available to you from Pocket Books.

____**THE ADVENTURERS** 53151/$4.95
____**THE BETSY** 55861/$4.50
____**THE CARPETBAGGERS** 47984/$4.50
____**DESCENT FROM XANADU** 41635/$4.50
____**THE DREAM MERCHANTS** 82307/$4.50
____**DREAMS DIE FIRST** 53152/$4.50
____**GOODBYE JANETTE** 55742/$4.50
____**THE INHERITORS** 44590/$3.95
____**THE LONELY LADY** 46475/$3.95
____**MEMORIES OF ANOTHER DAY** 55743/$4.95
____**NEVER LOVE A STRANGER** 55863/$4.50
____**THE PIRATE** 55864/$4.50
____**79 PARK AVE** 55865/$4.50
____**SPELLBINDER** 55859/$4.50
____**A STONE FOR DANNY FISHER** 54763/$4.50
____**WHERE LOVE HAS GONE** 55866/$4.50